Jane Morell was born in England but has spent most of her adult life abroad. An educator and poet, her work has taken her from the Peruvian Cordillera to the jungles of New Guinea, and for more than ten years to various parts of the Middle and Far East. She and her husband have a home in Mid-Wales, to which they return as often as they can.

STINGRAY

A vile act of betrayal by his twin brother, Sean, leaves James Mallory amnesic — all memory of his terrorist past erased ... Terrorist operation Stingray nears its climax and Trader of MI5, investigating the Mallory brothers' history, discovers a grim secret; this information could help him gain access to the mission's detailed plans. However, he needs the co-operation of Steven Court, aka James Mallory ... Forty-eight hours before Stingray's climax, Trader contacts Court — will he assist? Or if, as a former terrorist, he refuses — four British cities will suffer the death and destruction wrought by gunmen and suicide bombers.

JANE MORELL

STINGRAY

Complete and Unabridged

ULVERSCROFT
Leicester

First published in Great Britain in 2008 by
Robert Hale Limited
London

First Large Print Edition
published 2009
by arrangement with
Robert Hale Limited
London

British Library CIP Data

Morell, Jane.
   Stingray
   1. Twins- -Fiction 2. Terrorists- -Fiction. 3. Amnesiacs- -
Fiction. 4. Intelligence service- -Great Britain- -Fiction.
5. Suspense fiction. 6. Large type books
I. Title
823.9'14–dc22

   ISBN 978–1–84782–782–1

Published by
F. A. Thorpe (Publishing)
Anstey, Leicestershire
Set by Words & Graphics Ltd.
Anstey, Leicestershire
Printed and bound in Great Britain by
T. J. International Ltd., Padstow, Cornwall

This book is printed on acid-free paper

Say this to the terrorist:

'If you ask, 'What is your aim?' I can answer with one word: 'Victory'. For without victory there is no survival.'

Churchill, House of Commons,
May 1940

1

Ballymena, Ulster, March 1994. Cristin Daley's cottage on the outskirts of a hamlet five miles from the town. 22.15.

'This is the last time I'm asking you, Cristin. Say no again now, and I'm out of your life for ever!' Swinging furiously round to face her, James Mallory saw her sitting at the table in the middle of her big kitchen, hands clasped tightly on its oak surface, white-knuckled with tension as she sought to control the anger and despair seething inside her. Her head was down; she had been refusing to look at him since the argument — the old, old argument between them — had started again ten minutes ago. '*Will you marry me?*'

'Not while you're an activist in that murderous organization. You know that; you've known it ever since we first made love together.' She looked up at him as she spoke and the slight lilt in her low voice stirred his heart the way it always had. Her hair was honey-blonde, thick and silky; urchin-cut and rebelliously tousled, it framed her face sweetly.

'For God's sake! You and I — we're twenty-eight years old, we've been lovers since we were seventeen and we have a daughter who's just had her eleventh birthday!' Strong black brows drawn together, he threw the words at her roughly. 'I'll not go on the way we are, living separately. I want you for my wife, want us to make a home together and have more kids. I *need* that, Cristin. Need a wife, a home, a family — '

'I'll have no place in the life you lead.' On her feet, face white with anger, she challenged him. 'I'll never be wife to an IRA activist — *never!*'

'Hasn't stopped you loving me, though, has it?' He took a step closer to her, a violence rising in him.

'No, it hasn't. I don't think anything ever will — '

'Then marry me, for God's sake!'

'I tell you, Jamie, that's no way for a man to live his life! To be *wife* to you, our lives woven together like that, I'd have to believe in the things you seem to believe in — and I don't, *I never will*! I'd have to lie and deceive to support the double life you lead — and Jamie, know this: it makes me *ashamed* to see you doing it. Ashamed to myself, I mean, outsiders can go hang. It hurts me, *inside*, to see you so. Can't you understand that?' Her

2

full mouth twisted — then she could no longer hold back the hatred roiling inside her, and it flooded out. 'Your brother Sean and men like him, they've forgotten — never knew, more like — what it's all about. He's no true *conviction* terrorist — all the killing and maiming — he does it because he *enjoys doing it*! Jamie, *stop being like him*. It's evil — '

'Lay off Sean!' Slate-grey eyes narrowed, the gypsy-dark skin of his face tautened to lean, hard menace. 'Keep your tongue off Sean or I swear to God I'll — ' But he broke off, suddenly aware of the brutality of what he had been about to say and despising himself for it. 'It's over between us, isn't' it?' he went on, quietly now. 'I'll be going to England for good tomorrow like I told you an hour or two back.'

'Yes. Just after we'd made love.' Cold out of the comprehensive aloneness of irretrievable loss.

'As you say: just after we'd made love . . . Strange, how life works out. I've loved you, Cristin, but it's gone now. You've killed it; and — you know what? — I think maybe that's worse than if it had never been. From now on, for me, you and Melissa belong only in the past: there'll be no part for either of you in my life.'

She turned away to hide her face from him. 'Where will you be? I'd just . . . like to know.'

'That's no concern of yours. From when I walk out of here tonight, *nothing* about me concerns you. *Nothing*. Remember that, live with it. I'll send money for the two of you — '

'*Don't!*' She turned on him, sea-green eyes burning in a face drained of vitality. 'I don't need — '

'I'll send you money, I said! There's Melissa — '

'And there's something the girl you and I made together will need more than money.'

Deep in his throat, James Mallory laughed: a small sound, loaded with a kind of bitter grief. 'Love, I suppose you mean,' he said. 'Give her all yours, then; give her all you've got it in you to give, I don't bloody need it!' And turning on his heel he stormed out of Cristin Daley's cottage into the moonlight-and-shadows night.

She heard the door slam behind him. When he had laughed just then she had started to reach out her hands towards him, but at the words which followed had swiftly drawn them back, folding them loosely together in her lap. Looking down at them now she thought of his hands, Jamie's hands: the long loving caresses smoothing all over her body as they

4

lay together, his hands knowing every part of her, loving every part of her.

She shivered, but after a moment squared her shoulders, lifted her chin. I'll stay true to Jamie, she vowed inside her head, true to 'Jamie-remembered': the Jamie who had been beginning to break free of the IRA, of Sean. The Jamie who had been turning to that British MI5 officer he called Trader with whom — *but for Sean* — he would surely already have allied himself, to serve with those who worked *to defeat* terrorism. Sean would be pleased she had lost out, that was certain: pleased that Jamie had left her. Sean took all the real love Jamie had in him to give. Looking back now, she thought, I see I should have realized years ago how it would be in the end, I should have seen this would happen eventually. The Mallory twins: identical in all but the soul . . . And Sean always the leader: ever since we were all children together Sean was leader, Jamie his shadow, his disciple. Always, if Sean calls Jamie goes running to him, ready to do whatever he asks. Always in the end, Jamie falls in with *Sean's* plans. Sometimes with his way of thinking, too. Like just recently: during these last eighteen months Jamie began to doubt his commitment to the IRA, seeing it — despite all its protestations to the contrary — building itself a venal power-base

5

through drug-running, intimidation, money-laundering — but Sean talked him out of it, led him back into the fold. I suppose — finally I understand — that Jamie loves Sean with *all* of his heart. Me, he only ever loved with one part of it, the man-woman thing. Which wouldn't matter so much, wouldn't hurt so much, if Sean was actually *worth* Jamie's to-the-death devotion. But he's not. He never has been: he's gifted with charisma, with the silver tongue, with the quick, clever brain and the flashing physical prowess and courage, but he's a *taker*, is Sean Mallory. He never *gives* wholeheartedly: it simply isn't in him to do so.

One day, Jamie might find that out. Or maybe he knows it already? Knows and doesn't care? Accepts it because that's the way Sean *is*, and he loves him? Oh Jamie, my dear love, watch out against that brother-twin of yours! For should that really be the way of things between you, Sean will take from you everything he wants and, as he does so, there'll be that glint of laughter behind his eyes. He'll be mocking you, Jamie, he'll be laughing at you because he's always known he can take you any time he likes . . .

★ ★ ★

Outside, the night was lit by fitful moonlight, with broken cloud running inland on a strong wind blowing in from the sea some fifteen miles to the east. Slamming Cristin's front door behind him, James Mallory thrust his hands into the pockets of his black chinos and turned his face to the sky. 'Oh Christ,' he whispered to the darkness up there. '*Oh Christ.*'

But the thing was done now. Cristin had made her choice; the long destructive argument between them was over at last, and so was the loving, on his part at least. True, he had not told her about the latest development between himself and the man he knew as Trader; that was a situation too fraught with dangerous possibilities to be confided in her unless the trust between them was absolute — and recently it had not been; Cristin had been putting too much pressure on him, trying ever more desperately to turn him against his brother.

So James Mallory went on his way. Going quickly along the grassed path leading to the side road he got into his black Renault, which he had parked there five hours earlier, and set off for Ballymena, intending to drive on through to Belfast and take the first available flight to London; he had packed earlier, his luggage was in the back of the car.

But then suddenly, as he pulled clear of a roundabout, a new and entirely different idea sprang clear of the maelstrom of thoughts swirling around inside his head and stood proudly alone, sure of its absolute rightness for him at that moment: *it would be good to see Sean once more before leaving for England.*

And at once and without debate with himself James drove to his twin brother's house three miles away.

★   ★   ★

'It's on the cards I'll be moving over to London myself in a day or two.' Sean Mallory grinned at his brother who was sitting opposite him across the kitchen table.

'Something in the wind, then?' James asked. Over an hour had passed since he had knocked on Sean's door and been welcomed inside, and the level of whiskey in the bottle standing between them had gone down considerably. Straight off, he had told his brother about his clean and permanent break from Cristin. Sean had laughed, proposed and drunk a toast to 'Goodbye Cristin' — then turned the talk to the one subject which really interested him, the plans of the IRA and its separate-but-linked splinter groups, and those of other terrorist organizations with clout and a hunger for direct action.

'Potentially big things are afoot in London, Jay.' Sean sat forward, elbows on the table, slate-grey eyes brilliant, restless. 'There's an Islamist terror network looking for support from our people. It's one of those scenarios which, if you're lucky enough to get in on it at the start, has the potential to put you in working contact with movers and shakers throughout international terrorism — '

'I get the point. Give me the plot.'

'Our people are willing to co-operate with them — '

'At the sharp end, you mean? I'd have thought they'd got enough of their own.'

'It wouldn't be the sharp end to begin with. Logistics only.'

'But that's not your style, Sean! *Logistics?* Never thought I'd live to see the day — '

'It's *a start*. I'm thinking long-term, Jay. There's a big world out there, and native English speakers already experienced in terrorist action will surely find takers for their expertise among the Islamist set-ups. *Big* stuff: money behind it on a scale to dream on.'

'Sounds great.' James spoke with the requisite enthusiasm, but inside his head a small voice whispered, this is top-grade intelligence. I'll have something of real importance to give Trader if I decide to go with him for good as I've been thinking of doing. 'Tell me more about this fundamentalist group; how they're operating, their imtermediaries among our people.'

But, suddenly, Sean sat back, his eyes probing his brother's. Mirror image to each other in every facet and nuance of face and body, for a few tense seconds the two men held eye contact, the strip-lighting on the ceiling throwing the cut planes of their faces into strong relief as each sought to discover the truth of the mindset of the other in regard to the present strategies and tactics of the IRA. For during the last year Sean had grown just a little suspicious that his twin might be losing faith in that organization; while James feared it had lost its honour, that it had sunk deeper into being violently criminal in order to boost and then retain its power, and that this all-embracingly loved brother of his approved of those policies, and still aspired to rise within its hierarchy.

'I think you've lost it, Jay.' Abruptly, Sean pushed himself to his feet, chairlegs screeching across the floor. 'I'll not tell you more.' He started to turn away, but then a new thought struck him and he swung round to face his brother again. 'Are you still in contact with that bastard from MI5?' he demanded.

'With Trader? Yes, sure I am. So were you — '

'Briefly, for a one-off that suited my purpose at the time; you and I agreed on that, worked on it together. You haven't *committed* yourself to him, though, have you?'

'No! All I've passed him is stuff on the Cullybackey murder, like we said.'

'Sure, Jay; those bastards were after my blood so best dealt with.' The handsome face lit with a flashing grin and he sat down again, reached for the bottle and topped up both drinks. 'I'm bloody glad you came round tonight,' he went on, 'I'm in a bit of trouble, something that could go seriously wrong for me. I shot a bloke dead.'

Nothing new in that for you, James thought sombrely. 'Tell me about it,' he said.

Sean sipped his whiskey, wiped a hand across his mouth then banged his glass down on the table and stood up again.

'Not much to tell,' he said. 'There was this publican — Donovan, you knew him — who was causing my girlfriend a lot of grief: blackmail, with menaces. So I called on him, to set him straight. But he wouldn't listen to reason so . . . well, in the end it came down to the fact that I was quicker with my gun than he was with his. End of story.'

11

'The police are after you, then?'

'Hell, no; I could deal with that. Worse, much worse: at the time, Donovan was paying protection money to the IRA.'

'*Jesus!*' For a moment James stared up at him, appalled; then he asked the obvious question, 'Do they know it was you?'

'As far as I'm aware, they don't have any clues to the identity of the killer. I did a good job on that side of things, called in some heavy debts to work up a solid alibi. At least, I'm hoping it's solid.'

'When was this killing?' James's face was riven with anguish, he feared for the life of this twin brother of his whom he loved above all things known to him in his world.

Which fact Sean was fully aware of. He had realized it first when they were small fry growing up together; then over the years, as he came to perceive the possibilities inherent in his twin's unconditional devotion to him, he had often used it to secure advantage for himself. Mostly he had done so for small benefits; but deep inside him lived the certain knowledge that he would always be able to count on Jay's love for him, that it was embedded in his brother's psyche, there to be plundered at will should he, Sean, ever be in need of it. Resuming his seat, he picked up his glass and — as he quite often did when

Jay was involved — answered with a lie in order to establish a situation which might prove useful to him later.

'It happened long enough ago for me to be fairly sure by now that I'm in the clear,' he said, dismissively. 'Sorry I brought it up. Forget it.' Then he drained his glass, looked across at his twin and got his easy charm working, brother-love smooth in his face and alight in his eyes. 'Look, Jay, it's bloody late, why don't you kip down here for the night?' he suggested. 'Then maybe we can take off for England together tomorrow.'

At once pleased by the idea, James pushed back his chair and stood up. 'Nothing I'd like better,' he said, then tossed off his drink, took the two glasses to the sink, rinsed them and put them back in the cupboard. 'Arrangements as usual?'

'Sure. The sleeping bag's where it always is, and the sofa in the front room hasn't gone walkabout, I imagine. Hope you'll be comfortable.'

'It's always done me proud in the past. The whiskey helps, mind you.'

★ ★ ★

But that night James Mallory found the whiskey no help at all. When Sean had gone

13

up to his bedroom at the top of the stairs in the hall he fetched the sleeping-bag and pillows, laid them ready on the sofa in the sitting-room; but then he turned away, knowing he would not be able to sleep yet, harrowed as he was by an inchoate anger underpinned by an unnerving sense of lack of purpose such as he had never experienced before. Restlessly pacing the carpet, he let his mind skim back over times past but discovered there only cause for bitterness and disillusion. Brought up to honour and embrace the IRA, during his mid-twenties he had come to perceive its ethos increasingly tainted yet — with Sean, its committed sharp-end activist, always at hand to sing its praises — had been unwilling to break away from it and now, earlier that evening, *because* he refused to make that break he had lost Cristin and Melissa.

Therefore, he reasoned, as he stood head-down by the piano in Sean's sitting-room with the sleeves of his dark-red sweatshirt pushed above the elbow and arms akimbo, the one person he could rely on to give him unconditional love, give it any time and without question, was Sean. Sean: brother and twin whom he would trust with *his life*. And then inside his head, James Mallory relived the day when Sean had quite literally saved his life. Ten years old they'd been, and the two of them visiting their aunt Roisin over the border during the spring holiday from school. Hilly, wooded country she lived in, and that afternoon they were playing I'm-better-than-you-are boys' games down by the river which was in spate, yellow-brown with topsoil gouged out of the hillsides, raging along between steep, rocky banks, looking for trouble. The twins' game evolved into a chase, catch-me-if-you-can: down through the woods they went, James on the run, Sean in hot pursuit. Reaching the river-bank James turned and fought his way along it, scrambling over granite boulders slippery with wet moss, squelching through patches of reed and sedge. Tired now, the boy James, hands scratched and bloody, feet slip-sliding across spray-drenched rock but Sean's gaining on him so he must keep going, must give it his best shot —

Suddenly his feet slid away from under him and he was *in the river*! The rush of it swept him along — then hurled him in amongst the branches of a half-submerged uprooted tree that had hooked itself into the bank — *and he was stuck there*! The branches held him down under the water and when he tried to breathe, water came in instead of air — but then suddenly *Sean* was beside him so it was

15

all right! Sean grabbed him around the waist and hoisted him up. *Sean was with him so he was safe —*

Thump-thump! Heavy knocking on Sean's front door annihilated memories and the present claimed James Mallory for its own. For a moment he tensed because it was a strange time of night for anyone to come calling, but then he relaxed — with Sean anything went, and all his friends knew it. So, thinking his brother fast asleep by now, James went out into the hall to answer the knock, switching on the light as he went, then cast a glance up the stairs and saw nothing but darkness there; no sign of Sean being awake.

Opening up, he was confronted by two men dressed in dark battle blouses and jeans and on the instant the taller one pushed inside and stood with his back against the door; the other had a revolver in his hand and it was trained on James's heart.

'Sean Mallory, the captain wants you for questioning,' said the man with the gun, staring James in the eye.

'Won't it wait till morning?' At once James played for time, knowing the man facing him for an IRA enforcement officer by the name of Seamus Murphy so fearing the worst because of the Donovan murder Sean had committed, and determined to protect his

16

brother at all costs.

'It will not. You've an unauthorized killing to answer for.'

'*Walk!*' The man shouldered back against the door — O'Donaghue, Murphy's senior and unknown to James — jabbed the gun he'd drawn into James's side. 'The car's down the road. Get going.'

And immediately James stepped out into the night because to do so seemed to him the only way to give Sean time to get away. He heard the door slammed shut behind him and, quickly, by torchlight, the two men frisked him. Then with Murphy beside him and O'Donaghue at his back, he walked on along the road, the three of them wrapped up together in the moonlit night. As he did so the words he and Sean had said to each other when, safe from the water but soaked to the skin and bitter cold, they had stood shivering on the bank of the river at their aunt Roisin's farm said themselves over again in his mind. 'I owe you my life,' he'd said to Sean then, and his brother had made a joke of it. 'You'd better remember that, Jay,' he'd answered with a grin, 'maybe you can pay me back some time'.

So perhaps this was his chance to 'pay back', James Mallory thought now. That door slamming would awaken Sean. He'd go downstairs to see what was up, find no one there, then realize something of what must have happened so *make a run for it*. Himself, he'd keep up his act for long enough to allow Sean time to get well away, then tell Murphy and his mate who he really was. Likely they'd give him the beating of a lifetime for the deception, but, by Christ, he'd bloody well make a fight of it, same as Sean would have done.

★ ★ ★

Half asleep in his bedroom, Sean Mallory came wide awake at the double knock on his front door and at once slipped one hand under his pillow, took out the pistol there then pushed back the covers and padded across to the door. Easing it open slightly he pressed his side against it and, loaded weapon now held alongside his thigh, stood very still and listened. If, as was only too likely, they had come for him about Donovan, he was ready to shoot his way clear and make a run for it. But it might not be that, might be some friend or other, so it would be best if he let Jay answer the door. From his place at the top of the stairs he'd be able to hear what his caller had come about, then take charge of the situation . . . Seconds later, brilliance flared through the crack between bedroom door and its jamb as, below him in the hall, the light came on.

Sean Mallory could not hear all that was said between his brother and the men at the door that night, but he heard enough. 'Sean Mallory, the captain wants you for questioning' . . . 'You've an unauthorized killing to answer for'. The words came up to him clearly and knowing the two men who had come for him to be IRA enforcers he straightened up and made as though to go down — but immediately other imperatives kicked in and *he froze*. It sounded as if Jay had realized what was up and had decided to help him out; had reckoned it was odds-on that Sean was listening to what was going on down in the hall and was deliberately giving him a chance to get away. Safe at the top of the stairs, Sean Mallory smiled. Good for you, Jay, he thought, I'll be happy to go along with that. Of course, when you're in front of the captain and try to convince him that you're *not* me you'll doubtless get more than you bargained for, brother mine, but the choice was yours —

'*Walk!*' The order peremptory from below, and Sean knew there would be guns backing it up. 'The car's down the road. Get going.'

Giving silent thanks that his brother had

left his Renault at the rear of the house, Sean heard his front door slam and a minute or two later heard a car start up along the main road and speed away.

Then, came only silence. Going swiftly downstairs he stood in the now unlit hall staring at his closed front door, listening to the silence. And he admitted to himself the finality of what he had allowed to happen. For if Jay was indeed planning to declare his true identity later, he surely was a dead man: such a declaration, in such a situation, would have no chance of being believed. Inevitably his inquisitor — the captain referred to by the abduction detail — would sweep aside any such assertion, would dismiss it as a ludicrous and contemptible attempt to avoid just punishment.

In the secret darkness, Sean Mallory stood motionless, considering his next move. Someone must have grassed on him, he reasoned, must have named him as Donovan's killer; so the captain would be wanting to find out the names of his accomplices in that crime. But Jay wouldn't be able to give him that — he *could* not. So, as Sean Mallory, he would be executed on two counts: one, by killing Donovan he had contravened an IRA diktat; two, when questioned on that matter he had refused to

20

co-operate. Two offences of such magnitude, Jay, and you're condemned, he thought. I know it, you know it, everyone in this land of ours knows it.

And turning away Sean — never a man to look a gift horse in the mouth — went into his sitting-room, poured himself a whiskey, sat down with the bottle to hand and swiftly, coolly, summed up the situation, then worked out how he might use his brother's expected death to his own advantage.

Some twenty minutes later, he had decided on a course of action which, provided he could carry it out successfully, would enable him to run clear for ever of Donovan's murder and the IRA's punishment of it. Jay had told him everything about his break with Cristin Daley, so he could keep that side of life going in accordance with what had been said between those two earlier that night. Also, it had come out in the course of their conversation that Jay's clothes, passport and so on were all in his Renault parked at the back of the house, and his wallet and card-case were on the mantelpiece in the sitting-room, Sean had seen them there earlier on, with his mobile beside them. And if anyone came forward to say that Jay had told them he was going to see his brother that night then he, Sean, would simply say — hell, whatever, Jay didn't show up at my place. And as for living as Jay, the way he was minded to do, he could make that work OK, could carry through the impersonation; the two of them were dead ringers one for the other — and he knew everything there was to know about his twin, *everything*, every single bloody thing.

Sure, it would be a bit of a gamble. Should anything go wrong for him, he was dead, but the cards seemed stacked in his favour — and winner takes all. In this case, *he gets to stay alive*.

★ ★ ★

In the small hours of the morning, Sean Mallory drove away from his house in his brother's black Renault, leaving his own car in his garage and his front door unlocked as had the IRA detail when they took James away. Inside the house no trace of James's presence there remained: his mobile, wallet, card-case and so on were in Sean's keeping, sleeping-bag and pillows were back in their rightful place in the cupboard under the stairs. In the Renault, the light trenchcoat James had left in the car — he had been wearing a dark sweatshirt and chinos when Sean opened his door to him — still lay

22

across the back of the front passenger seat.

Sean was heading for Belfast, as James had been doing, and in keeping with his brother's plans, from there he was going to fly to London. Once there, however, he had decided he would proceed more discreetly at first. He intended to call in a longstanding debt owed him by a man known for the last five years as Richard Haines, a seemingly irrefutably upright citizen with a good job. It was an identity which Sean, at considerable risk and cost to himself, had organized and paid for on his behalf to enable him to escape state prosecution for two sectarian murders in Belfast. All Sean wanted from him now was to be given bed-and-breakfast in his home for a few days: a secret hideout in which he could bide his time until he was sure Jay was out of the picture — permanently.

★　★　★

His plans went smoothly, Haines had never met James, and had always addressed or referred to Sean simply as Mallory. When Sean knocked at the door of the detached house in Ealing at half past eleven the next morning, he was made welcome, given a meal and one of the two spare rooms was placed at his disposal.

'My house is yours,' he said to Sean quietly as they sat over a coffee. 'My life, too, any time.'

'I'd do the same again if you asked it of me.' Haines made no reply to that, but looking into his eyes Sean perceived that the fool believed it. 'Are you still in the same job?' he went on, not caring in the least but reckoning it only common sense to keep the man on side. 'It seemed to me — ' He broke off as, still in his pocket and switched on, James's mobile rang. Instantly on edge, he pushed himself to his feet, strode across to the far side of the room and took the call with his back to Haines.

'Yes?' he said.

Came a split second pause, then 'Who's that speaking?'

He did not recognize the voice. 'Who's calling?' he asked.

There was no hesitation this time. 'Trader. What's up, Sailor? Is something wrong? You sound — '

But Sean had heard enough. 'It's over, Trader,' he said. 'Over. Finished. You'll get no more from me.'

'Why's that?' The MI5 man's voice sharpened. 'Something's happened, hasn't it? Tell me. Maybe we can sort it out — '

'There's nothing to be sorted. I'm done

with you. The break's final. Don't call me again, Sailor out.' Sean switched off and slid the mobile back into his pocket.

'Everything OK?' Haines asked casually, glancing up at his self-invited guest as he came back to the table, but quickly looking away again, finding the anger in Mallory's eyes too hot to handle. 'Sorry, no business of mine,' he muttered, and reached for the stainless-steel percolator in front of him. 'More coffee? I'm not in a hurry if you're not.'

'Sure, I'd be glad of it.' Resuming his seat Sean stared unseeingly at the steaming mug Haines pushed towards him, slowly mastering the fury consuming him. Now, he knew for sure: Jay had lied to him, Jay had *not* terminated all contact with the MI5 man Trader as soon as they'd got all they wanted from him, which was what they'd agreed to do. Jay had broken his word — his word to *him*, Sean. Jay *was* still in touch with Trader, he *was* still feeding him info . . . *Jesus!* Sean thought, so help me God, my brother *deserved* to die last night; there's a sort of rough justice in what happened then, that he got the bullet in the back of the head instead of me, in my place —

He looked up at Haines, asking, 'Do you recall what I said during that call I just took?'

His voice was quiet on the question; yet to Haines its very lack of overt menace suggested the omnipresence of lethal threat and, again, he looked away.

'Can't say I do,' he answered, his eyes on his coffee. 'Wasn't really listening.'

2

Place: a small circular clearing on a thickly wooded hillside ten miles east of Ballymena, towards the sea.
Time: 02.30 on the night of the abduction of 'Sean Mallory'

Out in the wooded countryside the night was alive with ever-changing light-and-shadow patterns as wind-chased clouds fragmented across stars and near-full moon.

In the clearing, the only light came from a hurricane lamp on the ground near its centre. Within that circle of brilliance stood four men, all darkly clad; beyond it, trees and undergrowth loomed close, a shadowed leafy world secret to itself.

Standing alone with the lamp behind him: the captain appointed Sean Mallory's inquisitor, a tall, thin man, his head in its dark mask bulked blackly characterless, only his eyes visible, cold and without any trace of mercy through the vision-slits, riveted on the traitor facing him, a mere three yards between them. The prisoner's head was down, his arms hung loose at his sides; there was mud all over his ripped and bloodstained sweatshirt and chinos and his face was bruised, smeared with his own blood. Twice O'Donaghue and Murphy had laid into him for 'refusing the captain the co-operation he requested'. The two of them were standing behind him, at ease now; they had beaten the shit out of him, but he had not given in so they knew it would be the gun for him soon; the captain would give the order.

'For the last time, Sean Mallory.' The captain stepped close up to him, stared him in the eye as he raised his head. 'Name your accomplices in the murder of Michael Donovan.'

'No comment.' But James Mallory knew he hadn't much time left. His interrogation had been extremely violent but he had not given — he *could not* give — the captain the information he had been ordered to extort from Sean Mallory, though none of his tormentors was aware of that fact. And during his second beating he had realized the truth of his situation: his trial was no more than a sham, the IRA already knew Sean had killed Donovan and the death sentence was on him *whether or not* these men won from him the names of the accomplices he'd had in perpetrating that crime. Swiftly then, with the fear of death on him, James had roughed out a plan of escape. There was no finesse to it, but now he sensed the captain's angry frustration mounting and knew the time had come —

Risking a quick glance behind him, he glimpsed his two minders at ease, guns held alongside their thighs; swung round to his front again, saw the captain looking down — so jumped him on the instant. Raising his right arm as he sprang he slammed it across the masked face to send him reeling sideways, then sprinted for the trees. Half crouched and jinking, he ran for his life towards the woods behind the captain where darkness and leafy hiding places might be his friend, his saviour. The first bullet hit earth ahead of him; the second was off to one side; the third zipped through his sleeve, nicked flesh — then he made it, smashed his way blindly into the undergrowth at the side of the wood and kept going.

Night and the trees closed in around him. Fitful moonlight his guardian angel, the only thought in him to escape the men hunting him, he made hard-fought passage through the wood, then, in the hope of deceiving his pursuers swerved sharp left, pushed deep into massy undergrowth that at once swung back into place to disguise the trace of his new course, flung himself down on the soft ground and listened. His heart pounded, chest heaved as he gulped in air; *listened . . . ?*

Heard sounds of pursuit off to his left. One man only, behind him but coming closer . . . drawing level with him now. Turning his head, he glimpsed torchlight flickering through the darkness shrouding his hiding-place . . . then it was past him and he knew himself safe — *for the moment.* Since he'd heard/seen only one man go past, the other minder might still be behind him so he must get going again at once. Brushing his hand across his face he bit down hard on pain, scrambled to his feet and stumbled on . . . no moonlight now and the going rough . . . fewer trees and the terrain more rocky, the undergrowth less tall but denser. Wounded arm throbbing, he spat out blood, licked his lips and fought his way forward, half blinded by sweat, blood and dirt, forcing his bruised and aching body to keep going. He had no idea where he was, but reasoned hazily from the length of the car journey to the woods that he couldn't be more than ten miles from Ballymena. *Push on*, he ordered himself, somewhere ahead of you there must be a farm, a house, a road — there must be *something* to do with humankind so just keep going and —

Suddenly, he found himself fighting for breath. Stopped dead and bent double, gulping in air, but heard behind him a shout of surprise followed by the sounds of someone falling and in a second he set off again. The breath tearing at his throat he blundered on through the moondark night, clawed at by brambles snaking round his ankles, whipped across face and thrusting hands by branches blocking his way. Scrambling up the slanting face of a ridge of pale rock rearing out of the undergrowth, he prayed that from its highest point he might be able to spy out the land ahead and discover therein some sort of hope, a house — but as he reached the top of the ridge its edge, sharply undercut by erosion, gave way beneath his weight. His feet slipped away from under him; his fingers clawed for a hold that wasn't there — and his beaten exhausted body slithered down the scree slope below him, gathering speed as it went. As he fell he put his arms out to fend himself off a protruding boulder — but there was no strength left in him and he crashed headlong into it, the left side of his skull striking riven granite. He lost consciousness at once, but his own weight carried him on down to the bottom of the slope and into the thicket of green growth and hazel bushes growing there.

Sprawled amongst the lush tangle of wild flowers, ferns and creepers flourishing around him he lay senseless, limbs outflung, blood oozing thickly from the abraded contusion on his head. The foliage of the hazels and the leaves and blossoms of the plants crowded in over his body: he lay on leaf-mould within a small, green-roofed pavilion of his own, secret to the night . . .

★ ★ ★

In the clearing, O'Donaghue and Murphy had hastily agreed on a pincer-movement strategy of pursuit in the hope of trapping Mallory between them. And ten minutes into their hunt Murphy, skirting the overhung ridge with its concave incline of scree and boulders sweeping down into a hazel thicket, passed within some eight yards of the place where his quarry lay hidden. At that moment the sky had cleared and moonlight cast the shadows stark and black. Murphy glanced across at the stand of hazel bushes and the darkness pooled beneath them without giving it a second thought then pressed on towards the nearby road, on which he and O'Donaghue had driven an hour or more before with Mallory. They had parked their vehicle at the designated spot and hustled him through the woods to the captain, who had come in his own car and was now driving back to base leaving the two executioners to carry out their job.

But, as he went on through the trees, Murphy was beginning to panic because it was looking increasingly likely that Mallory had made it to the road and if he had, it was possible they would lose him altogether. Soon now, he and O'Donaghue would, as they'd planned, meet by the car. And since neither of them had caught and executed Mallory — they'd agreed to shoot him dead on capture, but he'd heard no shots — it was obvious that they would have to concoct some sort of story and come up with a way to avoid being blamed for the self-threatening disaster into which their night's duty was developing.

Coming out of the woods, Murphy saw O'Donaghue standing by their car at the roadside thirty yards away, and joined him.

'So you had no luck either, then?' he asked, eyeing him bleakly.

Grim-faced, thin as a rake in body and weasel-cunning of mind, O'Donaghue spat to one side then wiped a hand across his mouth,

'Not a bloody sign of the bastard,' he said, scowling.

'So what the hell do we do now?'

'I've been thinking.' Pale-blue eyes nar-rowed, he searched Murphy's face — a younger, less hard-bitten face than his own.

'So? What've you got in mind?'

'You want to go back and report we lost him?'

'Bloody hell, of course not. Do that, and — ' But seeing O'Donaghue's eyes mocking him, sneering at his youth and inexperience, he broke off. After a second, he said miserably, 'What else is there to do? We *have* lost him — '

O'Donaghue smacked him open-handed across the face, hard.

'Grow up!' He gritted it out, shoulders hunched, bony face tight with rage because he too feared the consequences of their failure — and to know himself afraid roused in him a vicious gut-hatred of the man causing his fear. 'We simply go ahead; carry on, the two of us, as was planned . . . *up to a point.*'

'What?' Bemused, Murphy stared up at him. 'Lie about it, you mean?'

'Why not?'

'But . . . we don't have a body.'

'And who's to know we didn't have one? We say we caught Mallory in the woods and shot him dead. The only blokes who'll know any different are you, me, and the body-disposal unit — our friends over the border

34

who, if you agree to my idea and fork out half the cash we give them, will say there *was* a body but no longer *is* one. They're farmers, remember: pig farmers. So we pay them — well over the odds, of course — to report that they disposed of the body this time not by burying it but by having it totally consumed. And once that's done, my friend, you and me will be in the clear — *for ever.*'

'Christ.' Murphy turned away, his head down. He knew what the original plan had been for the disposal of Mallory's body — a routine affair, a burial at some undivulged location over the border — and he had no problem with that. But what O'Donaghue was suggesting was different: it was another ball-game altogether. Murphy had heard the stories and, until that night he had considered the method of body-disposal they referred to as disgusting and a shame upon all who practised or condoned it. But that perception altered there and then as he stood on the moonlit road with O'Donaghue. Although sickened by the idea, he saw O'Donaghue's plan as the only way for the two of them to avoid personal — and drastic in the extreme — punishment. Therefore in the interests of personal survival he decided to ditch his moral scruples and accept it. Seconds later, however, he saw a possible difficulty ahead if he went along with it.

'But what if, later on, Sean Mallory turns up alive and free?' he asked, looking up into the hard blue eyes. 'If that happens you and me will — '

'You fool! Think, man; think it through. Sean Mallory may indeed survive tonight, it looks quite possible he will. But from this night on he can never in all his life allow that fact to become known. Think on it, Murphy! The man murdered Donovan, who was under IRA protection; then he refused to co-operate when under questioning; finally, he escaped IRA custody *by the use of force.*'

'So? I still don't see — '

The saturnine face was thrust close to his. 'Sean Mallory was under the death sentence at the time of his escape,' O'Donaghue said, eyes alight with malice and triumph. 'From this night on, as I said, should he turn up alive and lay claim to that identity, the IRA would have him killed.'

'And of course he'll know that.' Murphy stepped back, a great weight lifting from his mind as the truth of O'Donaghue's words came home to him and he saw there was indeed a way out for them.

'That's brilliant!' he cried, his face loose with relief. 'Christ, that'll get us off the hook *for keeps*!' But then he frowned and asked,

'Are you sure you'll be able to square it, though? With the blokes across the border?'

O'Donaghue had already turned away. 'Sure I'm sure. Like I said, you and me pay them extra and they report they've done the job, body disposed of,' he said over his shoulder as he slid his key into the door of the car and got in behind the wheel. 'We're all on the same side, and for them it's more cash in the hand for a lie here and there and a tight mouth thereafter. Besides,' he added with a grin, a snide amusement in his voice, 'knowing them I reckon they'll get a kick out of it, see it as a sort of taking the mickey out of central authority, showing their own independence.'

But Murphy did not smile. In the dark of the night, he shivered, and deep inside him a tiny worm of guilt stirred, came to life.

★ ★ ★

What a fucking rotten night this has turned out to be! thought Joe Anderson. At the wheel of his white Passat he blinked his tired eyes then refocused them on the road unreeling steadily in front of him as his headlights tunnelled the darkness ahead. A forty-year old ambulance driver based in Ballymena, he had driven north to Balleymoney early that evening to attend a lecture-and-discussion event. That had run on rather late. Then on his way home, when only a few miles out of Balleymoney, he had found his way blocked by the busy, ordered aftermath of a recent traffic accident, had stopped to help with first aid and then ferried a couple of uninjured but deeply shocked teenagers back to their homes in Balleymoney.

Now, dead beat and lusting for a stiff whiskey and his bed, he was heading for his bungalow on the outskirts of Moorhill, a hamlet five miles east of Ballymena. As he drove clear of Balleymoney for the second time that night, the road had been quiet. At the accident scene he found one half of the carriageway open, and drove on carefully and not too fast, the road empty before him, a two-car wide strip of asphalt now corridored between the trees crowding down to the grassed verges either side. Not far now, he was thinking, his eyes on the left-hand verge and the road in front of him as his headlights lit his way, soon he'd be mixing himself that whiskey —

Suddenly he saw a man on the verge ahead! A hunched-up figure shambling along with his back to him — stopping now, turning to face him and stretching both arms out towards the approaching vehicle in the age-old gesture beseeching succour. Anderson pulled the Passat up a yard or two from him — and the man fell to his knees then keeled over and lay sprawled on his back, his face turned up to the stars somewhere out there far beyond the sphere of humankind light now cocooning him.

Out of the car and to his side fast, Anderson stood looking down at him, professional eye noting the bruised and blood-streaked face, the filthy bleeding gash to the left side of the head, the torn, dark sweatshirt, the ripped chinos. Then he was down on his knees beside him. After a swift examination of the man's injuries, and taking into account his overall condition, he came to the conclusion that there were only two possible reasons for the state he was in: either he was the victim of an at-speed hit-and-run road accident, or he had been savagely beaten up by men experienced in that black art.

Scrambling to his feet Anderson stood tense, nerves on edge, mind racing as he sought to identify and then assess the implications of this fraught situation he had been pitched into. He realized that, given the tensions of the political state of the country at that time, he might at the moment be in danger himself: the nature of the man's injuries and the practised skill with which most of them had been inflicted, together with the hour of the night and the loneliness of the place of the assault on him, all indicated a sectarian group at work, and were that the case the man's attackers might still be in pursuit of him, might arrive on the scene *any moment*. Might, or might not. Whatever, this man who had come into his life out of the darkness of the night was probably in great danger and certainly was in urgent need of medical attention. Left lying where he was and unattended, he would likely be dead by morning.

The man on the ground groaned, his hands jerked then clawed into the earth and at once Anderson was down on his knees beside him again. Slipping one arm beneath his shoulders, he cradled the bloodied head against his chest. 'Come on, mate,' he said to him. 'We're going to get you out of here, but you've got to help me.'

The stranger's eyes opened, stared up into his: they were slate-grey and in them he saw a wild, lost look, but then suddenly there was only fear in them and 'Run, must run, must keep going,' he mumbled, his feet scrabbling at the ground for purchase but achieving nothing and his whole body twitching with frantic but unco-ordinated attempts to force himself upright.

Anderson was not so tall as the stranger but he was strong, and experienced in handling the weak and physically wounded. His decision made, he got on with the job as quickly as possible because clearly the man had rough enemies and they might still be around. Hoisting the slack body upright he drew the left arm around his own neck and shoulder, held it in place there with one hand, then gripped the man around the waist with the other and pulled him firmly in against his side.

'Right, mate?' he asked, setting himself to take the strain of the new weight and move forward.

The dark-haired, blood-caked head lolling against him moved as though the man was trying to look at him but he couldn't make it, hadn't the strength left in him. 'Right,' he whispered.

'Then we'll get in the car now — '

'*Car?*' The lax body tensed, feebly struggled to break free. 'No-no-no! Won't go in car. Let me go — '

'Easy now, easy.' Anderson tightened his grip and the struggling ceased. 'I'm your friend, you'll be with me in the car. The blokes that did this to you, they won't show now. They lost you, mate, they lost you and they aren't here any more. So the thing you and I have to do now is get you into *my* car. Then I'll drive you out of here, right away to my own house. You'll be safe there.'

'But where'll I go? I've . . . I've nowhere to go.' His words were an anguished whisper. 'Nowhere they can't get at me.'

'Yes you have; you're coming home with me. I'll take you home with me, clean you up a bit then let you get some sleep. We'll think about what comes next later; it doesn't matter for the time being. So come on, let's get going. OK?'

After a moment, 'Thanks,' he murmured. To Anderson the one word seemed to be dredged up out of a well of pain and despair and exhaustion, clearly it cost him dear to utter it.

That — considering the state he was in and the fear of pursuit bedevilling him — he should make such effort to express his gratitude touched a chord in Anderson, but for the moment he simply got on with what had to be done. Taking most of the man's weight himself he half-dragged, half-carried him across the verge to the Passat, then manoeuvred him into its passenger seat. Sweating and muscle-tired by the time it was done, he found himself already drawn to the stranger, this fellow-creature so completely at his mercy and so greatly in need of care; and out of the respect he felt for the fortitude with which the man had borne the intense pain he had suffered during all that manoeuvring, there was coming alive in Anderson a sense of an affinity with him, an incipient rapport.

★ ★ ★

Three-quarters of an hour later, the Passat was locked in the garage at the side of Anderson's bungalow at Moorhill, and the wounded stranger was in the study-cum-workroom, splayed rag-doll loosely in the cretonne-covered armchair, his head resting on the bathsheet Anderson had thrown across it, his befouled bruised face tilted to the ceiling. The towel was smeared with dirt and the blood still oozing from the long gash on the side of his head; he was breathing heavily through half-open lips, and his eyes were closed.

They opened as Anderson came back in through the door pushing a trolley before him and, turning his head, he watched the man who had rescued him roll it into place alongside the armchair. It was loaded, he saw, with a large bowl of water, a pile of surgical dressings and an array of medicaments. Then he looked up into the face of the man who had brought him into this warm friendly-feeling place where he now was, and for a moment a blissful sense of contentment, of beautiful *safeness* possessed him, but then, horribly, the savage fear boiled up again inside him and engulfed him.

'Keep them out!' he shouted, straining forward in his chair, glaring past Anderson to the empty doorway behind him. 'Don't let them come in here, they're after me they'll kill me, *don't let them come in here!*'

'Sure, I'll keep them out.' Quickly at his side, Anderson forced him back into the chair, but at the same time he gentled him, was careful of his abused body and talked to him with soft-spoken friendliness, letting his hands speak of solicitude and comradeship even as they coerced him. Joe was a quiet man of great inner self-belief, and he had dealt with hurt and frightened people for many years; in doing so he had always — no, *almost* always — found that the sound of a friendly voice can ease the spirit of a person in pain, not necessarily because of what is actually said but simply because of the common humanity it establishes.

When the man lay relaxed once more with his head resting against the towel and his eyes half-closed, his hands clasped loosely in his lap, Anderson picked up a wad of lint from the trolley.

'I'll clean that head wound first,' he said,

'be able to assess the damage better after that.' And laying a hand on his arm he asked quietly, 'What's your name, friend? I always like to know who it is I'm doctoring.'

There was no answer. Looking down at the still figure in the chair, he saw the slack fingers begin to tighten — then suddenly grip hard together into a two-handed, white-knuckled fist. Doesn't want to tell me, does he? he thought. Could be I've made a mistake here, maybe I ought to call the police —

'*What's your name?*' he demanded roughly, the sudden anger of consummate weariness flaring in him. 'If you won't tell me who you are maybe the best thing is I take you to hospital! These days I'd be a fool to help a bloke I found in your state in the dead of night if he won't even tell me who he is. So come on, what's your bloody name?'

For a count of twenty Anderson waited, willing him to answer but seeing him lying in the chair unmoving, the only violence in him imprisoned in that white-knuckled fist. Then, slowly, the blood-streaked face turned and the man stared up at him, slate-grey eyes anguished.

'I can't remember it,' he whispered, the words soul-wrenchingly desolate out of his bruised and swollen mouth, a lost look in his bloodshot eyes which then suddenly widened with shock as the implications of what he had just said struck home inside his head and he fully comprehended the dreadful thing that had come upon him. 'I don't know who I am,' he said slowly and quite clearly. Then he sat bolt upright, eyes tight shut as he fought to control the sense of utter aloneness, of total disorientation that now assailed and possessed him.

'*I don't know who I am.*' At once the mind-blowing horror encapsulated in that bald statement of fact annihilated Anderson's anger. To him it seemed a fearful thing to fall on a man and strike him down: it must surely be destructive beyond the imagining, a denial of . . . selfhood? Whatever, whether the man was a hit-and-run casualty, criminal, or punishment victim of one of the vicious political groups became of no importance when set against such bitter-cold darkness as was ravaging this stranger. Without further questioning, Anderson set about cleansing and dressing the man's wounds. He doctored him as if he were his own son, so great was the care and tenderness he gave him that night.

3

Four days later

Joe Anderson was something of a loner. Liked and respected by local people, he gave most of himself to his job; for the rest he liked his own company and that of his books, which were mostly historical biographies and military histories — with detective novels on the side, in which genre he himself had recently had modest success, his third such was to be published in four months' time. The bungalow he had lived in for the last eight years was set in its own acre of land; surrounded by farmland, it was reached along a single-track unmetalled byway branching off a minor road into Moorhill.

Anderson was no soft touch, neither was he a fool. He knew there was danger to himself in his harbouring of the wounded stranger: clearly, those who had beaten him up, be they politicos or be they simply common criminals, were hardcore blokes and should they discover the present whereabouts of their victim . . . Well, if they did so they might come around to that place one dark night in which case it certainly wouldn't be to say 'Thanks for looking after our friend', would it? But on the whole he considered that scenario fairly unlikely: he had encountered no one else on the way home that night, and his cover story that a relative of his had fallen ill and had come to stay with him for a while had been accepted with expressions of sympathy and well-wishing by such of his workmates and neighbours as he had thought it necessary to tell. Also — and oddly, as he admitted to himself, since he had never been one to give either friendship or trust easily — he had a gut feeling that the man still holed up in his bungalow and now in reasonably good nick was, essentially, a good guy. In all probability he was no pillar of society — he hadn't been beaten up so severely for no reason, surely! — but Anderson liked him. The rapport between them had grown strong: both men knew it, and recognized it for something to be valued. Also — and this above all, perhaps — Joe felt for him. 'I don't know who I am!' — words welling up out of the depths of the soul-destroying despair, fear and dreadful loneliness ravaging the stranger's face as he'd said them.

At first it had been as if the man were dying inside himself, Anderson thought as, arriving home at 8 a.m. after a night shift at the hospital in Ballymena, he let himself in through his front door. But together they had fought through that and now he, Anderson, wanted quite desperately to give him back — not his actual already lived life, that was beyond his power or anyone else's — at least a life, together with the wherewithal and opportunity to live it.

'Hi, Joe! I'm in here!' The call came from the kitchen so, leaving his briefcase in the hall, Anderson went on through. 'Heard your key in the lock,' went on the man leaning back against the windowsill on the far side of the room, slanting a grin at him. 'Coffee's ready.'

Sitting down at the table Anderson looked across at this tall, well-built stranger, saw the cut planes of his face accentuated by the rigours of the tough few days he had just endured, noted the dressing along his head wound.

'How d'you fancy the name Steven?' he asked him.

'Steve.' He tried the feel of it on his tongue, then went across to the table, picked up the percolator standing on it and poured coffee into the two mugs beside it; slid one over to Anderson and sat down opposite him. For a moment or two neither of them spoke; it was a companionable silence, they had already become close enough for that. Then he asked, 'Do you have a surname to go with it?'

'Court.' Anderson was watching him closely. He had tried, and failed utterly and miserably, to imagine to the full what it would be like to lose one's memory as completely as this man had. Not to know even your own name; to have everything that had made you what you were suddenly snuffed out — gone as if it had never been, leaving you unbelonging anywhere, without foundation, a ghost adrift in a void. However, the trying and the failing had given rise to a great determination within him to do everything he could to as it were integrate this lost man into society: to help him to do that in every way he could because his need was great.

'Steven Court . . . Yeah, I could live with that.' He gave a faint smile. 'It's better than nothing, isn't it?' But then the smile vanished and, leaning across the table towards Anderson he stared him in the eye, strong-featured face ugly with the pent-up but at present directionless anger running deep inside him. 'Sure, it sounds good, doesn't it?' he said, his voice tight, jeering. 'Only question is, how do I actually get to be him? Are you God Almighty, Joe Anderson, to create this bloke Steven Court out of nothing? For one thing he'll need a string of documents — '

'Shut up and listen.' Anderson's voice was unruffled, an assumed and faint amusement in it. 'I don't claim divine attributes, but I do have a couple of contacts who possess useful if wrong-side-of-the-law talents and abilities.'

A moment longer 'Steven Court' held Joe's steady blue eyes, black anger bedevilling him; then he sat back, a wry smile twisting his mouth.

'Sorry, Joe. Wasn't thinking straight. You've got something important to say to me, I believe. Go ahead, I'd like to hear it.'

Anderson drank the last of his coffee, then went on as asked. 'You and I have talked a lot, and you know a great deal about me by now,' he said. 'Also, although I don't know who you are, I do know certain things about you. I know you've got enemies who are men of violence and were probably intending to kill you that night. I know you have reasons to be afraid of the police — though not what those reasons are, any more than you do — because the day after I brought you here to my house, when I suggested I'd better take you in to A&E in Ballymena you blew your top, saying that would inevitably lead to police enquiries to establish your identity. And lastly, I know you're a dab hand at

51

advanced IT stuff because when I showed you my workroom with its database, website and so on, those things rang a bell for you, and since then you've shown you're a class act in that field, with a stack of experience — '

'No big deal, though, is it?' His head was down. 'It's the other things I need; things that tell me who I am, where I belong in this rotten world — '

'Quit with the self-pity,' Anderson snapped. 'Those talents you have could turn out to be a *big deal* — they could get you a life.'

'*That*, I'd give anything for.' The dark head lifted and his soul was in his eyes as he looked across at the man who had saved him.

His raw lust for an identity-giving new life was plain to see, and Anderson knew he had got what he had hoped for, what he had needled him for. 'Then listen to what I have in mind,' he said, sure now of the way ahead for both of them, and he proceeded to lay on the line his idea — his vision for this man. 'As you already know,' he went on, 'I write detective fiction and am, therefore, interested in criminals and criminal practices. And as you also know, being a paramedic occasionally brings me into contact, sometimes life-or-death contact, with both the perpetrators of violent crime and their victims. Well, six years ago I was called out on a small-hours-of-the-night 999 to collect a male casualty in an alley in north Belfast. When I got there I found this bloke was in a bad way. Among other things, he'd taken a bullet in the gut; but he was fully conscious and in pain, poor bastard, and I had to stay with him quite a while in that bloody alley because it became one of the hot spots in the police op in progress around it. Anyway, he and I . . . well, in circumstances like that you want the bloke to get really involved with you so he won't think about how he's hurting, and the two of us — '

'I get the picture.'

'Yes, I suppose you would.' Anderson smiled at him. 'Do you see where it's leading yet?' he asked.

'No idea. Sounds interesting, though. I'm still listening.'

'Glad to hear it. Well, as I was saying, this bloke and I hit it off, there in that alley.' Leaning back in his chair, Anderson gave a wry smile. 'Then later on it turned out he was one of the bad men, not a passing victim like I'd thought. Whatever, I visited him in hospital, then in gaol. He was a right character, was George Tomlin.'

'He could tell you his name. That makes him a lucky man — '

'George had to have his right leg amputated above the knee,' Anderson cut in hard. 'You've still got all four limbs and they're all in full working order. OK?'

'I suppose. Not sure I wouldn't trade, though.'

'Just let me finish — '

'Sure. You're visiting George in hospital, or in gaol.'

'He's out now, for which you may have cause to be thankful. If things work out the way I hope they will, I'll take you to meet him.'

'Has he gone straight? Reformed character?'

Anderson burst out laughing, regular-featured face creasing with mirth. 'George Tomlin, gone straight? That'd be the day! Lord, no! He came out of prison last year, and to my certain knowledge went right back into business. Doing even better than before, too, thanks to useful friendships built up inside. Anyway, the point is there are two important things in all that for us — for you. The first is that George and I are still buddies.' A smile flickered in his clear blue eyes. 'When he was locked up I used to visit him regularly. I'd buy him comics and take them in to him — it was all he ever read and, as he pointed out, they didn't have any in the prison library.'

'And the second thing? What's that?' There was an impatience in 'Steven Court', he craved something — *anything!* — that might give him hope for the future.

Anderson laid his forearms on the table, held the slate-grey eyes. 'The day before he was let out, George said something to me that I'd totally forgotten about until yesterday morning. Way back when he said it, it didn't seem to have any relevance for me, but it does now.'

'Why? How?'

'Because it could be the means to give you a new life — rather, could make it possible for you to live a life out in the real world — '

'*Tell me.*'

'George said to me, very privately, mark you, 'Any time you're on the run, cobber, and want a new ID, just you come to me. I'll get it set up for you, no sweat.' You see, one of his lines is trading in false documents of many kinds.'

'Oh Christ.' For a moment his mind blanked out, to him the possibilities inherent in this bombshell revelation seemed too wide-ranging and diverse to be fully compre-hended, let alone given instant credence, but then he was on his feet and leaning halfway across the table, hands planted palm-down on its bare wood and a terrible urgency in him as

55

he searched Anderson's face.

'Is that God's truth?' he demanded, quiet-hard. 'What you just said, *is it God's truth?*'

'It's God's own truth.'

'If later I find out you've lied to me, I'll kill you.'

Anderson read the certainty behind the threat in his eyes and smiled into them. 'So your name is Steven Court,' he said evenly. 'And Court is a man who will undoubtedly be able to develop his obivious talent in the field of electronics and get an interesting job therefore.'

Taking the words in, the man who did not know he was James Mallory straightened up and stood back. Then, slowly, he too smiled.

'A life, and a good job.' He said it with a kind of reverence, his hunger for those commonplace things a brilliance in his face.

★   ★   ★

However, later that day he said to Joe Anderson, 'I'll go on trying to find out who I really am, you know.'

'But you told me only yesterday that you have a feeling it might be better for you if you don't ever find out. And when I asked you why, you wouldn't say.'

'Yes, I remember.' Steven Court nodded, frowning. 'But I'll tell you now I can see a proper life ahead of me. It's because deep down I know there's something in my past that I'm deadly afraid of. I don't have any idea what it is, but *it's there* waiting to strike me down should anyone back in my other life find out or guess what happened to me that night you rescued me — and decide to put the boot in.'

'So if we go ahead with getting you a new ID that's something you'll just have to live with, isn't it?' Anderson was challenging him. 'In which case, are you still up for it?'

He smiled at his friend Joe. 'What do you think?'

Anderson read the answer in his eyes. 'I'll go see George tomorrow,' he said.

★ ★ ★

Saturday. Two weeks after both Sean and James Mallory have dropped out of life in Ballymena and its environs.

★ ★ ★

Early afternoon on a sunshine-and-showers sort of day, Cristin Daley was on her way home from the local shop ten minutes' walk

57

away. As she sped along the grassy, hedge-lined lane leading off the road to her outlying house, she worked out the time Melissa would get home from tennis practice at school, decided she had plenty of time yet and slowed down, strolled on enjoying the sunshine and the spring-coming-soon freshness of the air drifting to her from the surrounding fields. But then where the hedgerow ended and her house came into view, sudden panic rose inside her and she quickened her pace because the gate into her property was open and, just inside it, a man was standing on the path leading up to her front door. He was fair-haired and of medium height. She had never seen him before, and since Jamie had left her she had become afraid of strangers, especially male ones. To her, strangers could only mean trouble, and by the time she reached the gate she was almost running.

Hearing her coming the man turned and stood watching her, realizing who she must be. He saw a tallish slender woman wearing black jeans and a sky-blue top hurrying towards him; her blonde hair shone in the sunlight and she moved, he thought, with an enchanting grace. She stopped in front of him and stood searching his face.

'Who are you?' she demanded.

He read the fear in her eyes, in her whole self, and in that moment realized that from then on he wanted to stay in this woman's life: knew he was 'hers' from then on, the die was cast.

'You're Cristin, I think?' he said. 'Cristin Daley? I'm a friend of James Mallory's, and I've come to talk with you about him if you will.'

'There's a lot of Jamie's friends I don't know, and quite a few I don't like.'

He decided to take the risk. 'I left my car on the road, I've just come over from London, got a hire car in Ballymena. To James I'm known as Trader,' he said, and saw her lips part in a fragile gasp of hope. But her sea-green eyes remained hostile and he felt she was trying to search out his soul.

'*Prove* to me you're Trader,' she said.

Suddenly then, Trader laughed, breaking the spell which, to him, seemed to have woven itself around Cristin Daley and himself as they stood together in the sunshine on her garden path.

'What the hell are you laughing at?' she demanded furiously.

'At the memory of the time James gave me the sort of proof you've just asked me for.' He offered it contritely. 'You see, he and I were — '

'Leave that. Just prove that Jamie would call you friend.'

Trader studied her face, then nodded. 'He thought there might come a time when I'd need to prove to someone who mattered to him that he trusted me,' he said quietly, 'so he told me a physical fact about himself which, he stressed, only two other people of all those who knew him were aware of. He said my knowing it would be proof to either of those two that he trusted me; that he counted me his friend beyond all doubt.'

'And what was this physical fact?'

But he saw that the hostility had gone out of her and in its place he sensed a tentative gentleness and a sort of longing ... A longing — surely? — to talk about anything which might bring James Mallory-remembered back into her life however briefly, however only in the mind. And at that realization he felt a stab of anger against Mallory that he should be so careless of hurting her. Swiftly dismissing it, he gave her what she had asked him for.

'At the base of the little finger on his left hand, James has a small scar,' he said. 'It's from a dog bite he got when he was seven so it's very faint now, but it's still there. He and some friends were playing on a beach, he told me; he had his dog Ben with him and an

60

Alsatian running free there went for Ben, the two dogs were fighting and James tried to stop it — '

'And he got bitten!' Cristin interrupted. She was reliving the memory. 'I was with them, me and the twins were with my uncle and he took us all straight off to the doctor. I remember the doctor saying — joking to a hurting small boy — 'Scarred for life, you'll be, young man, scarred for life' — ' She broke off and, forcing herself back to present realities, fished in her pocket and brought out her house key. 'Jamie only told me a little about the man he called Trader,' she said, favouring him with a narrow smile. 'I've always wanted to know more; you'd better come in.'

'I'd like that very much,' he said, but she had already turned away and was walking on down the path.

Trader followed, and the two of them went into her house. She shut the door, faced him, and for the first time took proper stock of him. Saw him to be well built and athletic-looking, the short blond hair thick growing, his features well defined but ordinary — except for the eyes. His were the golden translucent brown of amber, she thought, and they gave the impression of a keen, perceptive mind behind them while at the same time having a guarded and uncompromising look. I like the feel of this man, she thought and, as she turned away and walked past him saying, 'Come through into the living-room', she was glad for Jamie that this man was his friend, was as it were on his side. Because he needed someone, did Jamie — he wasn't a self-serving lone wolf like his twin brother Sean, thank God.

'Sorry it's so untidy in here,' she said, as they went into the living-room and suddenly the general mayhem in there, which she was in the habit of dismissing as no more than the unavoidable untidiness of a mother and daughter who lived active, busy lives, struck her forcefully as being in truth an unholy and blameworthy mess.

It did not bother Trader. 'Melissa's at school?' he asked, gathering up the scarlet sweatshirt asprawl across an armchair, laying it across the back of the chair then sitting down.

'Sports afternoon. Tennis.' She stood looking at him. 'Have you got any children?' Why the hell did I ask him that? she wondered. Tired I am. And drained by loneliness.

'Have you heard from him?' Trader asked quietly.

Swinging away she went across to the long

window facing out over her garden and stood gazing out at the deep purple flowers of the lilac near the house.

'No. I shan't ever hear from him again. He told me so face-to-face and, unlike Sean, Jamie always means exactly what he says; you can count on it being the truth. So if you've come here hoping to leave a message for him you might as well go right now.'

'I came to see you.'

'Why?'

'Because you and he lived together for — '

'Lived and loved together.'

'Lived and loved together for, how long? Ten years and more. You must know him better than anyone.'

'Not necessarily.'

'Who, to know him better?'

'Sean.' She swung round, looked him in the eye and, as she went on, her voice was harsh with anger and bitterness. 'Twin brothers. One a bastard, a vicious unprincipled bastard. The other . . . Well, Jamie may be, and may have been, many things, but he's neither vicious nor unprincipled. As for knowing Jamie, Sean's the one for that. Sean knows Jamie from inside. Knows how he thinks, and therefore how he'll act and react; knows his loves and his hates, his hang-ups and — this most dangerously of all, I suspect

— knows his absolute devotion to his blood-brother twin.' She went close to Trader, stared down at him. 'Sean knows everything there is to know about Jamie,' she said to him, 'and he uses any or all of that knowledge in any way that may bring advantage to himself. He has always done that.'

'You're afraid of him.'

It came at her not as a question but as a statement of fact and her eyes widened as, suddenly, Trader came fully alive for her as more than simply Jamie's friend. She saw and accepted him as a man of perception and deep understanding. And from that moment on she trusted him.

'Yes, I'm afraid of Sean Mallory,' she said. 'A great many people are. With good reason.'

'But you with more reason than most, I suspect. You're afraid of him on Jamie's behalf, aren't you? Afraid for Jamie because he — '

'Jamie would trust Sean with his life, and given the kind of man Sean is, that could be a very dangerous thing for Jamie to do, to go on doing.' But then, fearing she had revealed too much of herself to this MI5 man whose code-name was Trader she broke clear of the rapport which suddenly and briefly had flared between them. Turning away she went on briskly, 'So, you want to know more about Jamie. Tell me why you do, then I'll decide how much to tell you. Or, of course, whether to tell you anything at all.' Pulling up a chair she sat down opposite him, not too close, not too far away.

But Trader had made it his business to glean as much information as he could about Cristin Daley. And among other things he had discovered her reported to be fiercely opposed to the use of militant violence in pursuit of political aims. Now, in the hope that doing so would make it easier for him to get from her what he wanted, he made use of that knowledge: explained to her how helpful the information James Mallory had passed to MI5 had been to British Intelligence in a recent undercover operation against a terror- ist cell based in London. He watched her carefully as he spoke, evaluating her reactions for he had gone to her that day with a nascent suspicion — a very tenuous, bizarre, but nevertheless troubling doubt regarding the James Mallory rumoured to have recently arrived in London who had made contact with known IRA sleepers there. He was hoping to leave with that vague suspicion either killed off completely or given sufficient credence to warrant further investigation.

When he fell silent, she said, 'Thank you.

It's good to know Jamie has helped. But I still don't understand, really, why you're here. Please, just tell me that. I need to know.'

Trader accepted that he would have to tell her more. 'James — no, hell, that doesn't sit right for me, to me he's always been Sailor so I'll stick with that,' he said. 'I have to tell you that Sailor has broken contact with me. He said the break was permanent.'

'Oh God, *no*!' Cristin stared at him, her face anguished. She looked *destroyed*, he thought; and felt for her. 'I was beginning to believe he — ' But she broke off, suddenly very still. 'So you must know where he is, how else — ?'

'No, I don't know that. Truly I don't.' It wasn't quite a lie, Trader reasoned; given his nagging suspicion it was surely no more than an evasion, a small mental dishonesty. Nevertheless, he quickly changed the subject. 'Can you tell me where Sean is at the moment?' he asked. 'We've lost track of him.'

'*Sean*?' Angered by his abrupt shift of interest, she was frowning, her voice hostile. 'You said you'd come to find out more about Jamie.'

'But he and Sean are closely bonded, aren't they, you said so yourself. Therefore, don't you see, to know James I have to know Sean.' Getting to his feet Trader went to her, put his hand on her arm. 'Cristin, bear with me. I want further information about how James and Sean were together, how — '

'*Were?*' She seized on the word, a new terror in her. 'Why the past tense?'

Trader took his hand away from her arm, stood back. 'Sean has disappeared. Didn't you know?'

She shook her head. 'No . . . People round here, they don't talk to me much about either of them; they gave up on that long ago. They think it's a kindness to me — most of them do, not all. *Disappeared.* In this place that's a deeply suggestive word nowadays; it's got many connotations, all of them grim.'

'As far as I know in this case it means simply what it says, no more but no less.'

'For Sean I wish it meant *dead.*' The words were ugly in her mouth.

Trader set about putting her obvious and vicious loathing of Sean Mallory to good use. 'I'd be happy to see him dead too,' he said to her, saw a narrow-lipped smile lighten her face and went on at once, 'so you see, you and I *should* talk about Sean. From your point of view, for your Jamie's sake; from mine, for my Sailor's sake, you and I should talk about his brother.'

For a moment she was silent. Then, 'I'm glad you're Jamie's friend,' she said quietly.

'We'll do that now.'

Trader sat down again, and for a while she made living pictures for him of Sean and James Mallory, identical-twin sons to an Irish farmer. Told him how she and the twins — their parents dead when they were eleven, killed in sectarian violence — had grown up together. Sean the born leader, charisma in him right from childhood. As a boy exciting to be with, danger-loving and fearless, not a nerve in his agile body; then as a man those same qualities winning him an honoured place, as had his father before him, among IRA activists. But from that time on, as Cristin saw it, the way of life of that terrorist organization *subsumed* him.

'He became blind to all else,' she told Trader, an angry intensity in her. 'He's cunning as a wolf, savage as a tiger, is Sean Mallory. He'll kill to order, and glory in the doing of it for The Cause, he says, but with him now that's only incidental: fundamentally, he's in the IRA for the violent action it gives him.'

'How can you know that?' Trader asked, as she fell silent.

'From growing up with the two of them. And then later, from Jamie.' She leaned a little towards him. 'He saw the violence corrupting Sean; Jamie *saw it happening*,' she

68

said. 'That's what made him change, Trader. It's the reason he contacted you at MI5.'

'*Corrupted* Sean? How d'you mean?'

She looked away, out into her garden: saw two chaffinches out there duelling for seed on the bird-table on the lawn. 'I suppose,' she said slowly, giving form at last to the truths she had realized over the years but never before dared speak about to anyone else, even Jamie — no, *especially* Jamie. 'I suppose it began soon after the two of them as it were graduated into the IRA active cadres. Sean took to the brutality they used like a duck to water, he revelled in it. But Jamie . . . As time went by Jamie began to question it because many of the things done seemed to him plain criminal. He said so to Sean and they had the most almighty quarrel about it. But they still stuck together — you know, the Mallory Twins; nothing will ever break that bond, I think. And Jamie stayed what he's always been, Sean's . . . Sean's *liegeman*, you might say.' Then softly she added, 'Always it's been the same: Sean takes everything Jamie has to give, but gives nothing in return . . . Nothing of value.'

'Liegeman.' Thoughtfully, Trader picked up on her word. 'That's a bit over the top, isn't it?'

'I don't think so. A loyal liegeman would

69

lay down his life to save that of the leader he has committed himself to: Jamie would do no less, for Sean.'

It seemed to Trader that at that moment there was a fey quality about Cristin: it was almost as though somehow, mentally and emotionally, she was with James Mallory, the long-time lover of whom she spoke with such certainty.

'Do you truly believe that?' he asked.

'*I know him.*' But then she came back to Trader. 'Of course I don't know Sean as well as I know Jamie,' she said.

'They're extraordinarily alike to look at, aren't they?' he said quickly, seeking to anchor her back down in common reality. 'I've studied mug shots of them, and visually I couldn't tell them one from the other.'

'Mirror-image.' She was still looking out into the garden: all was peaceful on the bird-table now, seed had been won and lost and all the chaffinches had flown away. 'And not only visually: speech, body language and all that — Jamie and Sean are dead ringers in every respect. But, come to think of it, I know one little difference. Just a small thing, but I've noticed it over the years and, somehow, it seems to show Sean for what he is, what he is inside.'

'Tell me, Cristin.' Carefully, he invaded the

silence she had retreated into.

She turned to him. 'It's their eyes. Sean, he never smiles at you with his eyes. Even when he's smiling with his mouth his eyes . . . they sort of stay separate — watchful of you, calculating. And, he doesn't laugh much; *really* laugh, I mean, that wonderful outburst that happens when your heart's in it.'

'And James, he's different?'

'Oh yes — ' But she broke off as across the room the door was flung open and a young girl came in and towards them, blonde hair all over the place and her tanned face eager, happy.

'Hi, Mum,' she cried, but then seeing the visitor she stopped dead, eyeing him curiously. 'Sorry, Mum, I didn't know — '

'Neither did I, so forget it.'

'I'll go and make tea, then, shall I? I'll bring the tray in here when everything's ready, and we can all have it together.' She grinned at Trader. 'We hardly ever have visitors so it'll be nice if you stay.'

'This is Melissa, my daughter,' Cristin said. Then she too smiled at Trader, having already decided she would keep in touch with him because Jamie had acknowledged him his friend and, therefore, it was possible that as time went on she might, through him, have news of Jamie. 'Do please stay for tea. We'd both like you to, if you're not in a hurry to get back to London.'

'I'd be glad to.' She had turned away from him, but Trader had seen her face as she looked at her daughter — child to her by James Mallory — and although he could not find words to describe the glow he had seen come in her then it told him that — now Jamie was gone — her life revolved around the girl.

That afternoon Trader came to know a great deal about Cristin Daley and her daughter Melissa. Among other things Cristin told him she had made up her mind to move to England at once: planned to buy a house near Hereford because an aunt of hers whom she was close to and frequently visited lived there. The travel firm she worked for, she'd said, had offices in the city and had arranged her transfer as soon as she'd asked.

Also, although he already knew a considerable amount about James and Sean Mallory, he had acquired invaluable knowledge regarding their personalities in both their private lives *and* their cover lives as consultants with a London-based IT company. And before he took his leave of her, Cristin had agreed to inform him of anything she might learn about the ongoing actions/plans/places of residence and so on of both the Mallory twins.

Of course, it was likely no information regarding either of them would come her way, Trader thought, as he drove off heading for Belfast. And then he admitted to himself that he had asked her to do it mostly because he wanted to keep in touch with her, to go on knowing her; the info-garnering reason had been something of a blind, protective colouring as it were . . .

He considered the facts known to him at present about the Mallory twins. He had lied to Cristin: he knew where James was — or, rather, where he was reported to be. Intelligence listed him presently resident in Soho, central London, at a safe house and in close contact with three known IRA agents there, all hard core activists.

But, wondered Trader as he approached Belfast, why had Sailor changed — and changed so suddenly? A couple of weeks or so earlier the Irishman had contacted him, passed him useful info. But then when he, Trader, had next telephoned him seeking clarification on something given him on the Saudi link, Sailor had hung up on him! Had cut him off, permanently: 'I'm done with you, Trader', he'd said. 'The break's final. Sailor out.' And just the previous day had come confirmation that James's mobile had been destroyed — also, MI5 agents had already reported that Sean Mallory had 'disappeared'. Of course, if it had been *Sean* newly arrived in London, MI5 would have had no reason to be surprised at the company he was keeping there. But it wasn't: it was James, who, as Sailor, had been his, Trader's, informant.

Thinking about it again now, James Mallory's volte-face seemed to him inexplicable. How could the man he knew as Sailor change so fast, and with such mind-boggling rejection of the ethos that had seemed to be driving him? The U-turn appeared to be beyond belief. Carefully then, Trader considered that last observation he had just made inside his head. And after a moment he carried it a step further: it was indeed beyond belief and therefore was not to be believed without more definite proof.

As he drove on, that concept, given credence by all he had learned from Cristin Daley about the Mallory twins, stayed with him. And, as his brain dug deeper into the possibilities inherent in the situation as he knew it, the vague doubts he had had regarding it crystallized into a disquieting supposition.

It was a way-out, totally unverified idea; Trader was aware of that. But he had always been fascinated by the strangeness and the occasionally sheer hair-raising wonder of fate and happenstance. And later that day he decided that even though he lacked factual proof he would take his supposition as a working hypothesis and keep it at the forefront of his mind; future developments would prove it either ridiculous or plain fact. Appalling, threatful *fact*.

★ ★ ★

'James Mallory.' In the safe house in Soho, Sean said his brother's name quietly to his own reflection in the mirror above the washbasin in his en-suite bathroom. He had just finished towelling himself dry after shaving and now, still holding the towel, he studied his face for a moment as he gave it the name it now lived with and — hopefully — would go on living with for the rest of his life. He was reasonably satisfied with the way things had gone for him so far. His impersonation of James was proceeding smoothly, undisputed from any quarter; and he had heard from a reliable source that Cristin had accepted that her long-time lover had cut himself free from her. However, his status within the London-based IRA cadre he had been posted to as James infuriated him, for he was finding himself treated as little more than an unquestionably loyal, obedient, and useful henchman.

And such a classification was abhorrent to Sean; it was not in his nature to sit doing admin work while others made the decisions and enforced the consequent action. Therefore, he had taken steps to rectify the situation, and that morning he hoped to make a start on achieving his aim, having secured for himself a one-to-one interview with the man code-named Liam, a mover and shaker within the London-based hierarchy who had the power to grant him what he craved.

Congratulating himself on that success, Sean grinned at his reflection. 'Thanks for giving me a life, Jay,' he murmured to it, but then slammed the flat of his hand over the mirror-image, obliterating it. 'It's good to know you're dead, you double-dealing shit!' he muttered, then turned away and went down into the street, strode along to the nearby pub where he was to present himself to Liam. He was well aware that he had to watch his step in putting his request to his superior: Liam had learned his trade in a hard school; among other things he had seen his father shot dead beside him during an IRA ambush which had been betrayed to the enemy. Nowadays Liam never gave anyone the benefit of the doubt; while to be discovered in a lie to him was to invite a swift death. And Sean knew he might have to lie to him, might need to. Whether he did or not would depend on the questions Liam put to him, but also on his own skill and quick-wittedness in circumventing any awkward ones which came his way.

It was two minutes before ten o'clock when he walked in off the street and there was only one man at the bar, a hard-faced bloke he knew for one of Liam's bodyguards.

'Up the stairs, first on the right, go straight in.' Leaning on the bar counter the heavy jerked a thumb towards the stairs on his left.

The room had no comfort in it and little furniture. As he entered, Sean had an impression of filing cabinets and electronic equipment against the walls and a table with chairs around it to his right, but his eyes went at once to the man facing him across an expanse of brown carpeting who was sitting at a desk studying the file open before him. Knowing him for Liam, Sean strode across and halted in front of him then stood at ease, waiting to be acknowledged.

A minute and a half passed; eventually the grey-haired head lifted and the pale eyes examined him in silence. And inside himself Sean felt a rush of exultation as he looked into the hollow-cheeked, sharp-boned face of this man who had the power to grant or deny him the kind of future he lusted after, because what he read in it gave promise that the interview would go his way. He perceived that Liam was a man of violence, so even though he was top brass they were brothers. He'll give me what I'm going to ask for, Sean thought, because were he in my position he'd be craving exactly the same thing. And on the instant he stiffened to full attention.

Liam knew men well — certain kinds of men, that is, and both the Mallory twins fell into those categories although reports had them down as very different one from the other. Noting the change in the body language of the man presented to him as James Mallory, he recognized it as one man's acceptance of another as both his compeer and his superior, and, at once, his interest in the man not only increased but also became more personal.

'James Mallory.' He said the name quietly, holding the slate-grey eyes. 'According to your application for an interview with me you have two requests to make. You refused the choice of submitting them in writing, citing privacy as your reason for doing so. State them to me now. I shall give you my decision on them at the end of the interview, and it will be binding and final.'

'Thank you, sir. Both are tied in with the disappearance of my brother Sean — '

'He is dead.'

'*How?*' Having a part to play he thought fast and spat the one word out hard, lacing it with anger. But his brain and heart rejoiced to hear the rumours confirmed from such an impeccable source.

'Execution for taking direct action in outright and knowing disobedience of our diktat.'

'Sir, I had begun to suspect him of allowing his personal affairs to subvert his loyalty to the Cause but I didn't realise . . . Is his death certain?'

'The two men detailed to implement the punishment reported the sentence carried out.' Liam gestured a certain impatience. 'Return to the matter in hand, state your first request.'

'Sir.' Still at attention, Sean dropped his eyes. 'I wish to ask for a posting to active service, to take effect at once.'

'Be more specific.'

'Certain of our cadres established here in London and elsewhere in Britain directly collaborate with Islamic Fundamentalist groups in the prosecution of terrorist strikes. I ask for a posting to such a cadre.'

Liam's face was carved in granite, his eyes

hostile. 'How do you know that the situation you have just outlined is a factual truth?' he demanded, 'Name your source for it.'

'My brother, Sean Mallory.' Dead men can't give one the lie.

'Then he was doubly deserving of his fate.'

Suddenly Sean perceived that there was advantage to be had here. 'It was because I suspected my brother of disloyalty that I requested active service,' he said swiftly. 'I considered some of his actions had brought shame on my family, and I saw it as a way to restore our honour.'

'You offer the possibility of an honourable death to atone for your brother's dishonourable one.' Quietly, Liam put the ideality into its present context, leaning back in his chair, dropping his chin on his chest. For a full two minutes he sat deep in thought. Then suddenly his head came up and he looked 'James Mallory' in the eye.

'First request granted,' he said curtly. 'Present the second.'

'It ties in with the first, sir.' Sean had done some fast thinking. 'My family's name stands shamed. I no longer wish to operate under it, and request that I be provided with a new ID.'

Liam searched the strong-browed, handsome face. Asked after a moment, 'Are you afraid, then, Mallory?'

'Why the hell should I be afraid?' Caught off balance, he responded fiercely, but then quickly crammed down the anger because he was *James* and should react in that character, not his own.

Liam stared him down, then said dispassionately, 'You yourself are the only man who can answer that question, James Mallory. Request refused.'

'But, sir — '

'My decision is final. In regard to your first request, you will be posted to a London-based cadre dedicated to undercover work in support of offensive missions and operating nationwide,' he went on, coldly impersonal. 'You will report for duty tomorrow, and will be advised of place and time by telephone this afternoon.'

★ ★ ★

Late in the afternoon of that same day Steven Court and Joe Anderson were sitting either side of a wooden table on the lawn in Joe's back garden, downing a lager apiece. The paramedic, enjoying a rest day, had been planting a young, just-bought apple tree, helped by the man he had succoured in the dark of the night not so long ago. Steve was recovering fast, but his new identity was not fully documented yet, Anderson's criminal friend George was relatively small fry in the underworld, at his operational level such things took time.

'It looks good,' Steve remarked into a silence.

'What does?'

'Your new tree.'

'Oh. Sure. Ought to, the price I paid for it.'

For the next few minutes neither spoke; then Steve sat forward, rested his forearms on the sun-warmed beechwood.

'I had a dream last night,' he said, frowning, 'Well, early morning it was really, around dawn. And it wasn't properly a dream.'

'So what was it?'

'Sort of . . . more like a memory, I suppose; words and mind-pictures. And it wasn't something that was actually happening, like it is in a dream; it was like something that had already happened, and I was remembering it. Half remembering, only, everything was hazy and disjointed.'

'Can you recall any of the words you heard?' All attention now, Joe put his question sharply.

'They were all faint . . . Someone — a man's voice, just, no faces with it, said, 'The car's down the road', but then that voice faded out and a different one said 'It's Sailor, isn't it? Sailor, who wants' — ' Breaking off, Steve flung himself back in his chair, covering his face with his hands. '*Hell!* Damn it to hell, the words are all gone. I can't *remember* — '

'Relax. Calm down, listen to me,' Joe was at his side, close. 'Look at me, Steve. Come on, look at me.'

Slowly, the tense arms relaxed; Steve sat forward again and clasped his hands on the table. Looked up at Joe Anderson then, tortured eyes focusing on the face of the man he knew to be his friend.

'Joe, I'm shit scared,' he whispered. 'Back in the half-dream there was more to it than just words. After them it went dead quiet, no words, no presences — there was only *fear*. I could feel it all around me and it was clawing at me, trying to get inside me. What have I done, back there in the past? *What*, to make me wake in the night sweating with fear? Joe, *what did I do? Something terrible* — '

Joe laid a hand on his arm. 'Leave it, Steve!' he said, with conviction. 'Whatever it is, that stuff belongs with a man neither you nor I know. Let it stay that way. Steve Court's got a life of his own to live. So drink up, then I'll get us another couple of cans and we'll drink to his future.'

Nevertheless, as he strolled thoughtfully across the lawn to fetch more drinks, Joe tucked away in his mind one particular word Steve had heard in his dream and remembered. 'Sailor': he said it over to himself. Then, as he trod sunlit grass, it occurred to him that quite possibly it had not been used in its straight meaning of 'mariner', 'seaman' and so on.

Rather, it might have been used as a nickname — or even, he thought suddenly, as a *nom-de-guerre*? Given the current political situation in Ulster, and the strange circumstances in which he had first encountered Steve, that last might be a possibility?

Sailor: Joe Anderson committed the word to memory, stored it away there ready to be recalled at will.

4

25 September 2005, Bahrain

Operation SeaSnake: four separate strikes at English cities — Torquay, Bournemouth, Bristol, Hereford. In the secrecy of his mind, lovingly as a miser his hoard of gold behind locked doors, Shakiri conned over the mission, his hooded dark eyes fixed on Majed Ansari, the young man (he was in his early thirties, which Shakiri counted as young) sitting opposite him across the low rosewood table between them and, at the moment, being served coffee by a tall, slim retainer in white dishdasha sashed in scarlet. Ansari had already proved himself clever, courageous, ruthless, brilliantly devious when required — and also dedicated beyond all doubt to furthering the aims of the Islamic fundamentalist terrorist organization he had been inducted into at fourteen years of age, Shakiri at that time newly acclaimed its leader.

And in addition to those admirable qualities, Shakiri thought, with a wry twist to his thin-lipped mouth, Ansari was very good-looking — auburn hair cut short, brown eyes steady and intelligent, good strong features and his complexion fair like that of many of his Palestinian brothers. He was gifted with considerable charisma and, when it suited his purpose, found it easy to assume a virile charm. All of which made him extremely attractive to women and, given his excellent English and his familiarity with western culture, to *English* women, which fact had marked him out as ideal for operation SeaSnake. What better tool could he have to his hand, Shakiri thought, now that the mission had advanced so successfully to its final phase?

Then, as the servant departed, soft-footed across the beautiful carpet from Isfahan, 'This is the first time you and I have met in person,' Shakiri said to Ansari. 'For the moment we will converse in English. I understand you speak and write the language fluently; tell me where you studied.'

He knows all that, of course, thought Ansari, it is available to him in my records. But if he asks, I answer; that is how things work.

'At school here in Bahrain I did well,' he said, 'and throughout my secondary education I attended evening classes at the British Council here. Then from 1990 I studied in Leeds, England, taking a two-year English

86

Language course. Following that I studied IT, gaining my degree in the UK in 1996.' He was sitting very straight in his richly upholstered armchair. Shakiri owned the entire second floor of the five-star hotel they were in and this room, which he sometimes used for interviews, was opulently furnished.

'Four years you had, then, in England. Did you make many friends there?'

Surprised by this line of questioning — his orders had specified simply a briefing on SeaSnake, the mission he had been on standby to undertake and was fully prepared for — Ansari hesitated for a moment, casting his mind back to those years he had spent in Britain, as a student, yes, but supplying low-level information to Shakiri's organization.

'Sir, I made many acquaintances whose company I enjoyed,' he said finally, choosing his words. 'Some of them, two or three, invited me into their homes. I stayed with them, met their families.' Briefly then, the serious cast to his face lightened, a smile hovered on his lips. 'I learned to play cricket,' he said, remembering, but then recollected where he was — and why — and the smile vanished. 'But amongst all those people there was not one whom I would call friend,' he stated; the smile might never have been, so cold were his eyes.

'And did *they* think of *you* as a friend?' The dark eyes were piercing in their regard of him.

Ansari met them with confidence, even arrogance. 'Yes, undoubtedly some of them did,' he answered, 'but it was only in the camaraderie of students, of student life. I dismissed them from my mind the day I returned to Bahrain. They have no call on me; they never will have.'

'That is assumed,' Shakiri observed frostily; then he sat forward, resting one manicured hand on the gold-and-blue brocaded arm of his chair. 'We will return to SeaSnake, and from now on we will use Arabic. As you know, the operation was initiated two years ago and consists of four simultaneous strikes on the English mainland, scheduled to climax in August 2006. It is time therefore to take steps to establish and safeguard your position over there, from early next year, as overall on-site commander of SeaSnake. The English girl — presently resident here — whom we will use to give solid credence to your presence in England has long since been selected, and our agents and sleepers there have carried out in-depth investigations into the lives of all the individuals involved with her, family, friends, and workmates. And, of course, since she arrived here three months ago she has been under our close covert surveillance. All that remains to be done is for you to entrap her.'

'I have successfully closed similar traps before.' Softly spoken, the words, but there was a steely confidence in his voice, also a callousness to chill the heart.

But not Shakiri's heart. 'One Iranian woman, one Lebanese: yes, you have those to your credit. But never, so far, a Caucasian girl to marry, to live with as husband and wife in her country.'

Majed Ansari smiled. 'That is true,' he murmured.

Watching him, Shakiri was satisfied. There was no suggestion of swagger in that smile, no overt vanity; only a strong, objective self-belief which promised well.

'Sir, may I ask, do we have a fall-back programme?' Ansari said.

'In the event of your failure with the girl at some stage?'

Ansari did not like the word 'failure' correlated with his own abilities. 'Sir, I have not yet met the girl,' he observed stiffly.

'We have a fall-back plan, naturally, but I don't anticipate having to use it. Its details remain classified; you will be informed at your final briefing of your own course of action in the event of it having to be implemented.' Shakiri answered sharply, then at once returned to the matter of the girl they planned to use to provide real-life cover for Ansari's presence in England and his travels over its southern counties. 'The girl is young and . . . she is not totally ignorant of the world you and I live in, the world of terrorism. To her it's known as one to be hated, feared, and at all costs shunned.'

Ansari was at once intrigued. 'Sir, how can you be so sure of that? So definite?'

Shakiri smiled his thin-lipped, mirthless smile. 'She was brought up that way.'

'Deliberately so?'

'Deliberately, indeed. First, however, to the girl herself. Her name is Melissa Daley. She is in her early twenties and presently in the employ of the Interact company here. You know it?'

'Of course. It is British-owned and active throughout the Gulf, working closely with the British Council, arranging educational and recreational courses and fixed-term visits to the UK by students from — '

'Enough.' Shakiri held up one elegant hand. 'Surveillance on the Daley girl reports her to be interested in her job and well thought of by both her employers and their clients.'

'And her social life?'

'Like most English girls of her age working here she enjoys a full social life. She does not lack escorts, but according to the reports none of them is what I believe is termed her 'boy-friend'. When you leave here one of my aides will escort you to safe house Talata in the city. There you will be briefed in detail on her, and her background.'

Ansari nodded, but then out of natural curiosity — the girl was to be his wife, after all! — returned to what Shakiri had told him a moment or two earlier.

'Sir, you said Melissa Daley was brought up to hate the world of terrorism — '

'There is a story behind that which, now we have reached the present stage in SeaSnake, you should be aware of. Melissa Daley's father was — and still is — an IRA activist, and the mother of the girl refused to marry him unless he renounced terrorism. He, of course, would not do that: he refused, walked out on the two of them when the girl was eleven and since that day has had no contact with either — '

'None at all?'

'There was deep anger and bitterness on both sides. According to our reports, no contact at all; each cut the other out of their life, and the girl was brought up solely by her mother.' Shakiri sat forward, hooded eyes piercing. 'This story is one which you will — you *must* — never discuss with either the girl or her mother. For them and for all the English people you will meet over there, your profile must be that of a man who, because of certain dreadful events in his own life, keeps well clear of discussions in which politics play any part.'

Mystified, frowning, 'But how does this story affect my part in SeaSnake?' Ansari asked.

'The IRA activist concerned, Melissa Daley's father, is James Mallory, your logistics liaison officer in the operation.'

For a moment it threw Ansari. Then he realized that if Shakiri was satisfied with the state of affairs he had outlined, he himself surely had no reason for doubt.

'A strange situation,' he remarked blandly.

'It is indeed. But discount any threat to us from it. The circumstances you will be operating under carry risks, certainly. But think further, Ansari; think deeper and you will perceive that should adverse circumstances arise, the background to the lives of Melissa Daley and her mother might prove to be useful to us in the prosecution of SeaSnake.'

'In what way and in what circumstances, sir? I don't — '

'Our reports emphasize an extremely strong love-tie between mother and daughter. Bearing that in mind, consider two points in conjunction. One: at the beginning of next year, with SeaSnake only a few months from climax, you will arrive in England — bringing your English bride with you — to take charge of its final phase. From then on we shall be vulnerable on many fronts; it will be possible for even a minor error on our part, or some event outside our control, to wreck our entire mission. Two: there is always the chance that the girl, being your wife and therefore to a certain extent cognisant of your movements, might chance to come upon something which causes her to suspect you of intrigue against her country and consider taking her discoveries to the police. In which case — '

'In which case we use the *mother*.' Ansari smiled. 'Force the girl to stay silent by threat of direct violence against her mother.'

The smile annoyed Shakiri, and at once he went back to the conduct of Operation SeaSnake. 'Being base commander of our operation you will, as you know, have four site captains, one in charge at each of the designated target areas,' he said coldly. 'Name them for me.'

Although surprised at such a surely unnecessary command, Ansari complied with it at once.

Eyeing him moodily, Shakiri heard him through, then asked him if he had familiarized himself with the layout of each of the sites.

'Of course, sir. I have a staff section at Operational Research — '

'I am aware of that. Yes . . . One more matter: once in England you may need to update your knowledge of the very latest developments in IT; for although the aim of the job you will have with my cousin's import/export business in London is to provide you with the deep cover required, it has to be carried out with proper diligence and authority.'

'Its nature suits my true purpose.' Ansari's face was alight at the prospect of action as, in his imagination, he lived the life of a 'visiting inspector of performance' for the long-established company Shakiri had referred to. 'It will take me on regular visits to six towns in the south of England — our four target towns among them. In the course of those visits I will talk the talk of the job and, being the boss at each, will be free to arrange my work schedule so that it gives me plenty of time to myself. During that, I will advise on and supervise local preparations for SeaSnake's strikes.'

'Indeed,' Regarding the fanaticism of others as an indispensible, if sometimes regrettably volatile, tool to be used to further one's acquisition of power within the hierarchy of one's organization, Shakiri welcomed it and made full use of it in the field, but he had little use for its verbal expression and now, swiftly but with due politeness, made it clear that the interview was at an end.

28 September 2005

Melissa noticed him — *noticed*, not simply saw — as her host Bill West, his hand at her elbow, escorted her through the hallway of his house and into the lounge. Facing her across the room was a tall broad-shouldered man she had not met before, his dark-red hair was cut short and he was standing loose-easy in a group of four, talking to a bosomy blonde in a tan-coloured dress, but now suddenly he wasn't looking at the blonde he was looking at *her*.

'I'd like you to meet Alastair Drummond, the new bloke at the Council,' Bill said at her side and, as it was his cocktail party, she turned to him, smiling.

'I'd love to,' she said. 'Tall, dark and handsome, I hope?'

But Alastair met only the first two of those criteria, and the only thing he showed any desire to talk about were shopping facilities for his wife and possible kindergarten places for his two young children, all of whom were shortly to join him at post.

'I've got a couple of friends with children who attend pre-school groups,' Melissa offered after a few minutes. 'Look, I'll introduce you to Heather, she teaches at the British School, primary. She's the dark girl sitting on the sofa over there, let's go across.'

Introductions completed, social duty discharged, she turned away.

'You're Melissa Daley, aren't you?' He was close in front of her, and for her the evening began in that moment, as he first spoke to her.

She nodded, smiling up at him. In her was a feeling she had never experienced before, a sense of having arrived somewhere new and uncharted, and being at once and marvellously enchanted by it, wanting to stay there for ever, for it to welcome her in and invite her to stay. His eyes were golden brown and full of life.

'My name is Majed Ansari,' he went on

across her silence, pleased that, clearly, she liked the look of him. Experience had taught him that first impressions were of great importance in the kind of job he was about to embark on.

'I've heard Bill West speak of you.' Her words said themselves out of social practice, her mind not on Bill. 'You were one of the Council's star pupils.'

'That was many years ago. When did you arrive in Bahrain, Miss Daley?'

'Oh, I haven't been here long. I only arrived in June, early June.' He's a *man*, not a boy like most of the young unmarried guys I've been squired around by since I got here. 'My degree's in Business Studies; I'm working with Interact now — '

'I know it. It's a very good company, and doing a valuable job. May I ask where you live in England? I've spent quite a lot of time there, maybe it's somewhere I know.'

'My mother and I live just outside Hereford; she works in the city.'

'And your father?'

She took it well, he observed, but saw she flushed a little.

'He's left us,' she said. 'There's just Cristin and me. Has been, since I was a child.' Why am I telling him all this about myself? she wondered. Answered herself: because behind our first time of meeting, socially acceptable interchanges, golden-brown eyes are speaking of other things and I like what they're saying. If he asked me what I'd had for lunch today I'd reel it all off just so we could go on standing here talking together. 'Cristin works for a travel agency. She's great. She plays good tennis, used to coach me. There's a man in her life who wants for them to marry, but she won't.'

Intuiting the reason behind the girl's rush of talk, Ansari was faintly amused and, being so, he made a mistake. He failed to perceive and seize an opportunity open to him as she spoke: he went on finding out more about Cristin Daley, leaving aside the life and personality of the man who loved her.

'Shall we go out on to the terrace?' he suggested. 'It's quieter out there, not so many people.'

Melissa smiled and went with him; gathered her rose-coloured silk skirt about her and sat down at one of the white-painted tables at one end of the long terrace where brilliant-flowered bougainvillea encroached.

'Where exactly does your mother live?' Ansari asked, as he sat down facing her, his rum-and-coke to hand. 'When I was studying in Leeds I had a good friend whose family had a farm fairly near to Hereford. I used to stay with them during Christmas and the long summer break, so I got to know the area quite well.'

'We're at Holme Lacey, a few miles south of the city. D'you know it? It's . . . oh, it's just glorious, I love it. It will be so beautiful there now, lazy end-of-summer time, flowers everywhere, cows knee-deep in butter-cups . . . '

He saw her seagreen eyes dreaming on Holme Lacey — and at once hi-jacked her dream, put himself in there with her. 'Tell me about it, Melissa,' he said, leaning across the table towards her. 'About Holme Lacey, and you and Cristin living there.'

She came back to him gladly. Said, smiling, 'But you're . . . you're a stranger. Why should you be interested?'

'A fascinating word, *stranger*.' He looked away. 'One that's open to subjective defini-tions, perhaps?' He said it quietly, but then his eyes came back to hers and she read a certain challenge in them. 'How would *you* define it?' he asked.

'In general, you mean?' Playing for time, and knowing she was.

'No, I don't mean in general. I mean in relation to me.'

Playing for time? How stupid, when she was so happy being with him. 'You're no stranger to me,' she said, coolly and straight into his eyes. 'Am I one, to you?'

'Only in the literal sense of us just having met for the first time.' He raised his glass to her. 'Well met, Melissa Daley,' he said to her, his eyes asking and telling her things beyond his small casual-seeming words.

'To two strangers who don't want to stay that way.' Oh God, I can't believe I said that, can't believe this is happening to me. I feel as if for the first time ever I've come alive, truly alive in every part of me. A man by the name of Majed Ansari. Please stay with me, Majed. Love . . . ? Love me . . . ?

That evening she told Ansari a great deal about herself and Cristin, and their home in Holme Lacey. He already knew many of the facts she gave him: Shakiri's agents in England had done their work well, had put him in the picture. But he learned more about the girl than any reports could ever have given him; also, he began to discover ways in which he might hope, when the right time came, to beguile her into believing his declaration of his love for her.

Other guests drifted across the terrace and talked to them from time to time. And finally their hostess — glamorous but observant in her cream-coloured cocktail dress — politely but very firmly collected Melissa, took her indoors and — '*Please*, darling!' — persuaded her to circulate, particularly among the half-dozen or so male, not-so-young, business-orientated guests who had arrived alone, were grouping together to talk shop and, therefore, with charm and diplomacy of course, should be encouraged to mix with their fellow-guests.

However, Ansari was a skilled operator. At 7.50 he attached himself to the animated group Melissa was with, joined in the talk. And when soon after eight o'clock the party began to break up, he was quickly at her side.

'May I see you home?' he asked, laying a hand on her bare arm, feeling her skin warm beneath his own.

Recognizing voice and touch, she turned to him at once. 'I'd like that,' she said. 'But I came with my flatmate in her car, so I'll have to go tell her. Won't take a minute.'

Recreational sports: riding, tennis, badminton. Outside interests: has a liking for adventurous outdoor activities.
(e.g. Last holiday trip was to Canada, white-water canoeing etc.)
See attached list for others . . .

Recalling these and other points from the reports of Shakiri's agents while he waited for her to rejoin him, Ansari was well satisfied:

taking account of these likes of hers, he had surely planned his next move well, he thought. Then, as he watched her walk back towards him — a tallish girl in a rose-coloured party dress, lovely figure, long blonde hair caught up at the back of her head then falling free — he counted himself fortunate indeed that she was so attractive. It would surely be no hardship to be — for a short while! — a loving husband to her. Going to meet her, he took her hand in his.

'Will you come out with me tomorrow?' he asked, as he drove his white Mercedes through Rashidiya.

'Where to, and what for?' She answered lightly, laughter in her voice and she thinking, how lucky, tomorrow's Friday, no work.

'A trip by dhow.'

She frowned. 'Tourist stuff. Thanks, but no thanks.'

Ansari stiffened. 'Ahmed Mansoor is not a man to do tourist stuff. I have known him since I was a child and consider him a friend. Coastal trading is his livelihood, and it is a way of life he loves. He learned the sea and this Gulf coast with his father; now, he in his turn trades along the Gulf, calling in at small places with a load of household goods, taking on board local produce for resale further on. His dhow is crafted for the shallow water it lives upon and the work he does, and it is beautiful to sail on her.' He stated these truths with a quiet but steely passion, his eyes intent on the road. Then he relaxed, gave her a quick grin. 'On Fridays he doesn't go far and I often sail with him,' he said. 'Come with me, Melissa. Ahmed is very pro-Brit, I have taken English friends down the Gulf with him before.'

'Women among them?'

'No.' He sensed she was tempted; the lure of the dhow excursion had been a good idea, he had *caught* her.

'Won't he . . . mind? Not want a woman on his boat?'

'You wear jeans and a loose, long-sleeved dark top, pin your hair up and put on a hat — well, you'll need one anyway, you know that. Then it will be all right, since you are with me.'

'Will a bush-hat do?'

'Perfect.'

So that Friday, Ahmed Mansoor sailed his dhow south along the Gulf coast with two passengers aboard her; and by the time the trip was over, Ansari was sure in his mind that Shakiri's plan in regard to himself and Melissa Daley would achieve its first aim. Care would have to be taken, work would have to be done, but given both, he opined, the girl would be his for the asking.

Harrow, south-west of London.
Mid-morning

'So what time do Deborah and the boys get back from swimming?' Joe Anderson asked. Having three days off work he had come to stay with Steve and his wife Deborah — together with their two boys, Josh the older at nine, Dan eight — at their home in a pleasant cul-de-sac off Greenhill Way. Still a workaholic bachelor, Joe lived six miles away in the bungalow he had inherited from his mother who had died eight months after he had succoured the man who could not remember even his own name. By then the two men had become firm friends, so when Joe moved to Harrow, Steven Court went with him. Physically recovered from his 'accident', and with his IT expertise updated by an advanced course in Belfast, Steve had soon found a job in Harrow and had quickly taken advantage of the opportunites for promotion it offered.

Now, having completed the installation of Deborah's new lean-to mini-greenhouse against the south-facing wall of the house, he and Steve, seated one either side of the dining-room table, were enjoying a well-earned lager.

'They should be back by midday, but with visits to the swimming pool you never can tell, it's absolute hell getting the two of them out of the water. Josh, he's open to reason. But Dan — Dan's trouble from the moment he's told to come out and go dress.' Steve ran a hand through his hair — from habit, tracing the narrow white streak that had grown back in along the scar from his head wound, a half-smile lighting his grey eyes.

Eyes which, Joe thought, watching him, still sometimes had the old, haunted look to them. 'He'll grow out of it,' he said. 'Eight's an awkward age, Deb tells me.' He had known the woman who had become Steve's wife longer than he had, she was daughter to his mother's next-door neighbour in Harrow and he himself had introduced her to Steve at a barbecue there. Best thing I ever did, he thought now, their marriage is a good one, they love each other and the kids are great. But then he frowned, looked down. There was still that black hole in Steve's past life story. Deb knew about it — he and Steve had long since agreed on the 'road accident' lie to account for it, but it didn't worry her, she wouldn't let it. From time to time, however, it still troubled Steve. Joe knew that and he reasoned that the cause of it must have been some seriously bad episode or incident in Steve's past life: a person he'd cruelly wronged in some way, or some appalling

— possibly criminal? — action he had committed. And the hell of it was that Steve didn't know *who* that person or *what* that action had been. That was the really destructive thing, for Steve: having the fear so strong inside him but not knowing.

'Have you had any more of those memory flashbacks, Steve?' he asked. 'Recently, I mean.'

'No.' He answered sharp on the question, then changed the subject. 'Did you put our names down for the squash tournament at the club?'

'I did.' Joe took the rebuff equably: Steve had the right. 'Thank God it's handicapped, at least we'll be in with a chance . . . '

But Steve's 'No' to Joe Anderson had not been the truth. For some while now he had been experiencing more flashback memories than he had recounted to Joe: had kept from him the ones which frightened him the most.

And in the small hours of that night Steve awoke, found himself sweating and distraught and realized it was going to be one of those nights when the hazy, rootless and unconnected memories came alive inside his head: people ghosting them wraith-like, their faces out of focus and then turned aside, gone; their voices making words but the words fading into silence before they made sense to him — and always everything broken up into jagged pieces that never fitted together. Some of the memories were good, but others ... others were black-hearted evil, but in them no reasons for their malignity, or any person he could identify.

And the demons came for him again that night. First, the ones he already knew. Children playing on a beach and a dog with them, then pain in his hand, a car journey, 'It's all right, yes, we'll take you to the doctor now.' Then it's dark and there's trees and water, fast-flowing water. 'I owe you my life', says a voice, boy's voice — his own, is it his own? Now it's darker yet and it's night, trees close around me. 'For the last time', says a menacing voice — then I'm running, running away from — ? 'Sailor, listen', says a new voice, a man speaking and it's a friend voice not enemy like the one before it but he doesn't say any more ...

However, that night the last voice *did* say more. The man with the voice that made him friend spoke to Steve again after all the others had gone away. 'Sailor', he said, 'I'd like you to tell me all you can about your brother.' The words sounded so loud inside Steve's head that he started up in bed wide awake, his mind reaching out for more, more contact with his 'other' life.

But that was all that came to him that night. Nevertheless, from then on Steve Court had cognizance of two completely new facts about himself. First, that to some other man, somewhere, he was known as 'Sailor'. Second, that he had a brother: had no name for him, but knew *he had a brother.*

Holme Lacey, 15 November 2005

'So, they're to marry in December.' Trader, his forearms resting along the top bar of a five-railed farm gate, did not turn to look at Cristin. His eyes were freewheeling across the great sweep of shallow valleys and rolling hills spreading below them, seeking out the scattered farmsteads bedded down within their grazed and crop-rich land, the two villages, the patches of woodland and, in the distance, the city of Hereford asprawl in sunshine. Holme Lacey lay behind them, sheltered from easterly winds by the low ridged hills up which Cristin and he had just ridden, coming out from the riding school which stabled her mare. Hobbled, their horses were grazing nearby: her chestnut and the bay he had been hiring from the school for the last three years.

'Early December.' Cristin's shirt-sleeved

elbow lay touching his on the sun-warmed wood of the gate. 'The way she's been writing about him, I guess I should have seen it coming. Didn't, though. Her letter yesterday was quite a shock. She's so *young*, Matt — '

'Come on, darling.' Trader took her hand and drew her towards a brilliant-leaved copper beech at the edge of the copse covering the top of the hill, 'Let's sit down and talk about it. You've told me a lot about Ansari, but if Melissa's going to marry the guy I'd like to know a whole lot more.' One hell of a lot more, in fact, he decided, considering where Ansari came from and the — open to suspicion? — speed of his capture of Cristin's daughter. He resolved to run some checks on what the Palestinian had done and what he had been in the thirty-five years of his life to date.

They settled down in the dappled shade of the beech, Cristin with her back against its smooth grey bark, Trader sitting beside her with his arms round his knees.

'First, where are they going to live?' he asked. 'Here, or in Bahrain?'

'Here. Apparently everything's falling into place beautifully, Majed's got a good job waiting for him — '

'Computer, electronics buff, isn't he? I remember you saying. Useful trade. Sorry, please go on.'

'He'll be based in Hendon so they'll live there, but he'll have to do a lot of travelling, he'll be a sort of inspector-cum-trouble-shooter, I gather.'

'Sounds interesting. Good prospects?'

'Melissa says yes. I hope she's right.' Cristin had been making finger-patterns in the friable, sweet-smelling soil; now she brushed them away with her palm, dusted her hand clean on her jodhpurs and looked round at him. Found he was gazing out over the valley and suddenly felt a great rush of love and tenderness towards him. I love you, Matthew Kingsmith, she thought. You've grown into me and into my life: we've grown into each other, I suppose. No, that's not quite right. He's loved me since way back, he told me years ago, asked me to marry him. 'Marriage isn't for me, ever', I said to him then. But knowing all that lay behind me saying that, he refused to accept it. 'You're in love with a memory, Cristin', he said, 'and that will pass. Like time itself it will go on by you and once gone it will never return. You'll see.' He went away then. Stayed away for over two years — had another woman during them; I know that, he told me. And then one day he came back into my life. 'I will always come back to you', he said to me that day. Grinned at me then. 'I'm a stubborn bastard,

110

Cristin, you'll never get rid of me'. I can see him saying it now; can see how fiercely he was holding himself in as he spoke because *he wanted me*, he wanted me there and then so it was hard for him.

'What's the matter?' Suddenly Trader turned his head and stared at her, his eyes straight to hers, demanding an answer.

'Nothing.' And at once, she looked away. This wasn't the time; besides, she had to be sure beyond all reasoning . . . Reasoning? You don't need reasons to love, do you? It either *is*, or *is not*: you can reason about it till the cows come home but you won't change anything.

'I don't believe you.'

'You'll have to.'

Trader turned away. Said after a moment, 'Answer me two questions, please. One, how does Melissa feel towards James these days? Two, does Ansari know about him? The *truth* about him?'

Both his questions aroused deep and complex feelings in Cristin, as he had known they would. Scrambling to her feet she folded her arms and, head down, considered her answer, prowling to and fro in front of him — never too far away, though, because she needed him. Finally she stopped beside him.

'Don't look up at me,' she said, 'just stay as you are and hear me out. To your first question the answer is easy, it is the same as it's been every time you've asked it over the years: Melissa feels about her father the way I've brought her up to feel ever since he walked out on us. She loves and respects him as the kind of man he was until then . . . Which, as you well know, is the way I feel.'

'But you've never told her the full truth about what he is now.'

'I only know the little you've told me, and I only believe half of that.'

'You *won't* believe it.'

'Damn right I won't! I believe the bit about him being a married man with three kids — why wouldn't I, one of the things he said to me the night he left was that he wanted a proper married life, wanted a wife and kids. But that he's . . . that under the cover of his proper job he's still secretly operating with a clandestine IRA cadre active in England — no! I tell you, that isn't the Jamie I knew and loved! My Jamie was opposed to the IRA's terror strikes against civilians, and it was because of their continued involvement in criminal activities — ordinary criminal, I mean, money-laundering, intimidation, drug-running and the like, which disgusted him — that he was already in touch with

112

you, with MI5. But then straight after Sean's death *his* James won over *my* Jamie: made him one of Sean's kind again, the lovers of violence for its own sake.'

'Don't hate me for telling you the truth, Cristin,' Trader said evenly, his eyes still down. 'I don't make the rules; I simply play the game by the rules I accept as . . . reasonably good guidance in a dangerous and savage world.'

'God damn Sean Mallory to hell.' The curse low and hard then she swung away from him, stood staring into sun-hazed distance. 'Doesn't achieve anything, though, does it? Cursing a dead man,' she said, after a moment.

The bitterness in her seeped out into the sweet autumn air and, quietly, Trader got to his feet and went to her.

'Helps a bit, nevertheless,' he said, 'Lets some of the steam out.'

Her hand reached for his, held it for a moment, released it. 'Thanks,' she murmured. 'Thanks, Matt.' Then, facing him again, she made a smile and went on, 'As for your second question, the answer is that I haven't asked Melissa so I don't know whether or not she's told Majed about her father. Her letters and phone calls and emails, they're all full of weekends in Jordan, places in Bahrain and so on. There hasn't been time for me to — '

'You ought to make time, you know. Can't you — ?'

'I don't *want* to.' Cristin's thoughts had moved on to other things. Melissa had resigned from her job; she and Majed were soon to arrive in England where they'd marry in December — Registry Office, thank God — and find a place to live: these were the things she wanted to talk about with Trader, so she was impatient with his questions and brushed them aside.

Except for one other he put to her as they unhobbled the horses ready to ride on.

'Are you going to tell James about the marriage?' he asked.

'No.' Her answer was quick and definite. 'He walked out on her when he walked out on me. That choice was his. I've had to live with it. We can go on doing the same; this is no business of his.' Mounting the chestnut, she turned its head to the valley.

'Won't Ansari find it odd not to meet the father of his bride?' Trader moved the bay up alongside her.

'I'll sort it out. It's to be a small, civil ceremony, remember.' Then she lifted her chin, laughed, and set off across the hill. 'Come on, Matt!.' she called back to him. 'The sun's shining, the world's beautiful today; let's you and me *ride!*'

★ ★ ★

Over the last few weeks Cristin had passed on
to Trader various bits of information about
the man Melissa was engaged to and, as he
drove home late that evening, he ran through
his mind all he knew of him. Majed Ansari:
Palestinian by birth; brought up in Beirut
until at age seven he was orphaned by a
bombing in Hamra which killed both his
parents and all three of his uncles. Gifted
with high intelligence and an aptitude for
languages, he was then 'adopted' by a
Bahraini friend of his father's and taken by
him to Bahrain. School there was followed by
university in Alexandria, then four years in
England for English at advanced level and a
degree in IT. After that he had a good job in
Bahrain — with a company which also ran
branch offices across southern England. No
wonder, then, Trader judged, that Ansari had
been able to secure from that company a
transfer to a responsible position at their
London offices. Such a well put together CV
the guy had! Life was working out brilliantly
for him. Such seamless progress to an
excellent appointment over here. Suspiciously
seamless, perhaps? Cristin had told him it

115

was a job which involved a lot of travelling round and about southern Britain; that would be excellent cover for a terrorist working to a secret agenda, would it not? An 'innocent', operating hand-in-glove with others of his kind already established in that part of the country?

The idea caught at his mind — at his MI5-orientated mind-set. And once conceived of, the possibility that some such scenario might be a reality grew into a definite perception of threat. So, on arriving at his flat around midnight he poured himself a nightcap, took it with him out on to the living-room balcony, leaned his forearms along its guard-rail and, sipping his whisky, considered the situation he had envisaged. Below him, the city lay night-quiet, its witching-hours' blackness patterned with the flare-paths of street-lighting, with islands of brilliance where pubs and restaurants were still open for human night-owls to keep their various celebrations going. But he was aware of none of it, he was living inside his head . . . Cristin and Melissa were close to each other, but now their harmony was being infiltrated by a stranger by the name of Majed Ansari. Was, possibly, being *threatened* by him? Could Ansari in fact be a Trojan-horse terrorist with a covert agenda against Britain?

It was a possibility, or at least, and at this moment, an unanchored-in-fact *surmise* which he would ignore at their peril and also, perhaps, that of many others.

Ten minutes later, Trader went back inside, closed his French doors behind him. He had come to a decision. Having no hard facts against Ansari he would have to content himself, at present, with a low-level investigation into the Palestinian's life to date: use long-time sleepers in Bahrain to suss out the man's past.

Streatham, south-west London,
6 November 2005

The man known as James Mallory was alone in the comfortably furnished bed-sitting room at the pad which was his private safe house in the capital. There, he came and went as he pleased, simply one of the two boarders hiring accommodation from Mrs Morton, proprietress of this detached house near to Streatham Common. The other, also male, was a bona-fide 9 to 5 office worker, whose comings and goings were regular. Mallory's true career was known only to Mrs Morton, whose long-dead husband had died in a hail of bullets serving the same Cause as he.

117

Sean had grown into the life and being of his brother James with the speed, dedication and sheer positiveness essential to success in stealing his twin's identity. He had followed through with James's decisions on the night of his death, having no further contact with Cristin or Melissa. And now as he lounged in the big armchair alongside the fireplace with a whisky in his hand, he let his mind dwell for a moment on Majed Ansari, operation SeaSnake's on-site commander for Shakiri's Bahrain-based organization — who would move freely around southern England doing his cover job while, safe within its given freedoms, he synchronized and brought to a head the preparations for SeaSnake's climax.

Then, smiling to himself, Sean tipped his glass towards the unlit fire in a derisive toast: thanks a million, Jay, he thought — But suddenly his memory spun back into childhood and pictured a furious white-watered river and two boys standing together on its bank, teeth-chatteringly-cold and soaked to the skin. '*I owe you my life, Sean,*' he heard James say to him, and then the picture vanished and there was only silence.

For an instant his brother's whispered words ghosted the air about him. Then his mouth twisted in a mocking smile. 'You paid your debt to me, Jay,' he murmured. 'You paid it beyond all reasonable expectations — and only a fool does that.'

Then he forgot his brother entirely. Picking up the four-page decoded report lying on the small table beside him, he sat back to study it. It was from Abu Hamad, Ansari's second-in command, and read thus.

OPERATION SEASNAKE

1 TORQUAY (Shark) Hotel bar.
Suicide bomber(1)
2 BOURNEMOUTH (Marlin) Hotel dining-room
Suicide bombers (2)
3 HEREFORD (Stingray) Tollgate petrol station
Armed assault unit (4)
Suicide bomber (1)
4 BRISTOL (Pike) Templemeads Rail Station
Suicide bombers (2)

There followed details of the action sequence at each target site and the personnel engaged in it, but he flipped through those pages with barely a glance at each. He knew SeaSnake's overall plan by heart: in close co-operation with Ansari he had been, and still was, engaged in organizing the op's entire logistical framework.

Christ, I'm hot for a gun in my hand and combat! As so often since his secondment to Ansari's operation, furious resentment at his purely administrative role in SeaSnake stormed through him and for a moment his handsome face turned ugly, lips thinned, eyes narrowed and angry. Then he controlled his rage. He had known, and accepted, that his life would have to be that way: to the world he was James Mallory, a man known to be reluctant to use the gun so obviously it would take time to alter that perception. Aware of that, he had gone about the process slowly and very cautiously, forcing himself to exercise self-restraint. But now, he judged, his time had surely come; provided he proceeded circumspectly, he might get in on the action of SeaSnake. Majed Ansari held the key to his success: as the op's commander on site the yea or nay to any such request made lay in his giving. Ansari: carefully, and in the light of the nature of the request — the favour — he intended to ask of him later, Sean considered his impressions of the Palestinian's personality. He had not yet met him in person, the business between them had been conducted by mobile, e-mail or special messenger, but already he perceived him to be a touch

120

high-handed but right on top of his job in all its aspects and also — somehow this had come across without his physical presence — a true believer in terrorist clout and the enjoyment and exaltation of delivering it.

So could be they were in spirit two of a kind? Could be that when he put his case to Ansari he would understand what his fellow-terrorist was talking about and give him what he knew he hungered for — as years ago now — Liam had done?

5

Harrow, 2 May 2006

'So, thank God, only two days to go now; the nurse told me you can come home on Monday.' Reaching out to Steve's hospital bed Deborah Court touched his hand where it lay on the covers. 'You were so *lucky*,' she went on, her voice suddenly shaky. 'A few yards to the left with that ladder and you'd have come down on concrete, hit your head on the hard stuff not good green grass.'

'Grass with bloody sharp stones in it.' With a grin he caught her hand in his, drew it to his lips and kissed it, then looked up at her. 'I love you,' he said quietly.

She saw the truth of it in his eyes and for a second was spellbound with gladness that he was alive. She couldn't make words to express her love for him. I don't need to, though, do I, she thought: *he knows.*

Steve did, and watched her hungrily as she stood up and shrugged into her moss-green jacket, flipped her auburn hair free of the collar then smoothed creases from the dark-green trousers fitting so snugly over her hips. Looked up into her face again then: her loved face, the long dove-grey eyes beneath straight brows, the full-lipped mouth that tightened so uncompromisingly when she was angry, the nose slightly beaked and a little arrogant.

'I'll bring the boys tomorrow,' she said, and walked away, turning at the ward exit to give him a fluttery wave.

Christ, Steve thought when she was gone, should what I have now — Deb and the boys, I mean — ever be threatened in any way I would do whatever I had to do in order to remove that threat. So, as soon as I'm out of here, I'll get my project started because I have to keep safe what I have now.

Then, lying back into his pillows he closed his eyes and went over in his mind the course of action he had decided on since recovering consciousness in hospital. Four days earlier he had fallen off a ladder while cutting back a tree near the house, had landed on his shoulder and the left side of his head, close to the scar left there twelve years earlier where granite rock had struck, and had suffered a fairly severe concussion. During the last two days more incidents from his past had been coming alive in his memory. At first, they had presented themselves in fits and starts, people and happenings jumbled together in a chaos

123

of visual and aural memories without connection to each other, no rhyme or reason to them. But then, gradually, they had shifted into coherent sequences and some of those were terrifying evidence of violent things done in which he was involved, so he knew he had to keep them secret — *must* do so if he wanted to hold on to the new life he had made, with Joe Anderson's help.

So now, with Deborah still close to him in his mind, he conned over the plan which, in the light of his newfound knowledge, he had been devising in regard to his past life as James Mallory. Out of the mind-boggling, sometimes sad, sometimes gut-churningly frightening welter of events in that now-remembered life, he had isolated three which, because of the feelings they aroused in him, demanded action. In spite of his present life, he had found that three of the people meshed into those newly recalled happenings laid emotional claims on him, claims he could not deny. He knew he had loved those three and that, if memory was complete, they had loved him. Certainly two of them had, but what of the third? What of *Sean*, his devil-may-care superman brother?

On Sean, Steve's dream-memories remained clouded. He did not know the full truth about

Sean's part in the events which, clearly now, had led to him losing his memory, and everything in him clamoured to discover it. Even if when discovered it broke his heart, it was surely better to know the truth than to live in a dream-world of his own imagining, he had decided. Fast on that decision, he had settled on the course of action to be taken as soon as he was back home.

His first objective would be to find out where Sean was and what he was doing now, and in order to do so he intended to re-establish contact with Rory McGuiness, who had been his best mate back then in Ballymena — best mate after Sean of course. With Rory being a farmer's son and in line to take over the property, it was a fair certainty he would still be over there at the family home. Back then Rory had been running-dog to certain IRA personnel and therefore, hopefully, he would still be sufficiently in with them to know, or find out, what Sean had done after the '94 affair.

His second objective was more complex. Cristin and Melissa had been part of his life until that night in '94; now that once more he was aware of their existence — those two who had been so close to him — a strange and peculiarly unnerving emotion had been born in him; not exactly love, but a strong, all-embracing sense of holding dear, of caring deeply.

'Cristin and Melissa.' Lying in his hospital bed, looking back into his past life and the dream of it on him, Steve Court whispered the two names to himself. He had decided to hire a private detective to trace them; but for the moment, he simply prayed that they were still alive.

★　★　★

'Take a seat, I'll be with you in a minute,' Trader said, working head-down at his desk by the window and hearing Jack Maxwell, one of his senior Middle East Intelligence agents and based in Bahrain since the previous June, close the door and advance towards him.

A quiet-moving, bland-faced man in his thirties, Maxwell did as he was bid, settling himself in a chair facing Trader across the desk, then fixing his eyes on his boss and reflecting that over the eight years they had worked together he had found him a fine bloke; he had a great respect for him. If I was ambitious, he thought now, Trader is the sort of intelligence officer I would strive to be. But Maxwell liked his life well enough the way it was: he got his kicks out of reading human nature, fitting in with other people's aspirations and life style and then making himself sympathetic and therefore eminently worthy of their trust so that they confided in him things which, later, they might find they wished they had kept to themselves. Maybe me and my kind aren't 'nice' people, he thought, but we're bloody useful procurers of info for men like Trader.

'Sorry to keep you waiting, and my apologies for calling you in straight from the airport.' Trader sat back, looked across at him. 'I wanted to hear your latest information on Shakiri face to face, your written report can come later.'

'There's a small thing relating to Majed Ansari I'd like to bring to your attention first, get it out of the way.'

'Go ahead.'

'He's been married before — '

'Good God.' But then Trader dismissed his surprise. 'Only to be expected, I suppose, seeing he's in his thirties. Did he divorce his wife, or what? Easy enough, given his religion.'

'He did not. She . . . died.'

'Was she another Brit?' Trader had barely noticed Maxwell's slight hesitation before he came out with his last word.

'Lebanese, from Sidon. Her name was Tagarid Bedawi. She was nineteen when she was killed, they'd only been married ten months.'

'And how did she die?' Trader saw it now: in the context of the present conversation 'killed' could be very different from 'died'.

Good, he's with me, thought Maxwell, his ever-sunless blue eyes meeting those of his boss. 'She was in Gaza. Got crushed to death by falling masonry during an Israeli reprisal raid on a Hamas supporter's house . . . so it was said.'

'What was she doing in Gaza?'

'Visiting relatives of her husband's. Apparently Ansari was supposed to go with her but when it came to it he couldn't get time off work, said he'd join her a couple of days later. Odd, wasn't it?' he added softly, suggestively. 'Lucky for Ansari perhaps, the way things have turned out.'

'She'd served her purpose, and was best disposed of?'

'Such excessive good fortune does give food for thought.'

'Had she been useful to him — to Shakiri — during the marriage?'

'Yes — as near certain as you can be in the absence of cut-and-dried proof. Owing to her, a certain anti-Syrian activist found himself in the wrong place at the wrong time and got dead. Which solved a problem for Shakiri at the time.'

Trader folded his arms and gazed unseeingly down at his desk considering this last piece of information. Because what had begun in his mind as a slight suspicion that Ansari might be an agent of some Islamist terrorist organization was growing into an acknowledged possibility that the Palestinian had married Melissa for the specific purpose of creating credible cover for himself while he was prosecuting a terrorist mission in the UK. All of which gave Maxwell's new information heightened importance.

'That puts Ansari more securely in the frame,' he said, pushing himself to his feet.

'He's into something over here, sir. I'm sure of it.'

'Proof?'

Maxwell hesitated. 'Not really, sir. But there's a couple more pointers in my report.'

'Tell me.' Turning away, Trader stood looking out over London's highways and byways and heard his agent out.

'Interesting indeed. Still not enough for me to take it higher, yet,' he said, when Maxwell fell silent. 'But I'll shift our undercover ops both here and in Bahrain up a gear or two. As of now.'

* * *

Two days later Trader had a phone call from Rod Evans, a near-retirement inspector with whom he often co-operated. It came at 8.10 in the evening, and he was dead beat having just arrived home after a long and deeply frustrating day on the job. Deciding to have a quick whisky before eating, he went into his living-room, but then as he picked up the bottle his mobile bleeped and he answered it because it might be Cristin. But it was Inspector Evans, and he at once gave him his full attention since he was not the man to make phone calls at that hour just for a chat.

'Evening to you, Rod. What gives?'

'That'll be up to you. I'm at the East Road police station, Hownslow. We're holding a bloke here by the name of Murphy, and I think he may be of interest to you. He's accused of GBH — serious, very — against a civilian. Says he's got information which would be of great importance to MI5, and wants to do a trade.'

'What d'you know about him? Is he likely to have info that might be useful to us?'

'Could be. He was an IRA activist in the past. We suspect he still is, don't have any proof of it though. We have reason to believe that the GBH he was dishing out was a punishment beating ordered by the local top gun.'

'Any idea what he's offering?'

'He won't talk to us about that. He's holding out for MI5, and says it has to be a bloke well-informed on the activities of the IRA, past and present — but mostly past. 'Early nineties', he said; that's what made me think of you — greenhorn, Ballymena area and you still wet behind the ears.'

Ballymena: the name clicked into place in Trader's brain. 'Give me the address,' he said. 'I'll be right over.'

★   ★   ★

Earlier that same evening Majed Ansari and Sean Mallory — known to all men as James Mallory since that night in 1994 — met in person for the first time. Recognizing the need for face-to-face discussion, they had arranged to meet at a safe house in Balham which was the home of one Darren Ahmedy, son to an Irish girl who had married a Jordanian in the 1970s. Ahmedy himself was unmarried and had a good job with the education department of the local council; his mother ran his house — and him. Her name was Patricia. Her father had been a bomb-maker for the Republican movement

131

and had died a violent death in its service, as had her husband. A hard, unforgiving woman, she now served an active splinter group of the IRA.

Ansari had been working in the safe house since midday, collating logistics for Sea-Snake's targets in preparation for his forthcoming session with Mallory. Now, relaxed in his chair at the table in the living-room with the relevant papers neatly arranged in front of him, he was awaiting the Irishman's arrival. Things were going well with the mission, he judged. As UK commander of SeaSnake he was well established in his cover job and, thanks to the freedom of movement it gave him, had personal working contact with each of his four site-captains. As to his private life, it was proceeding according to plan: as newly-weds recently settled in at Hillsdown, their detached house in Hendon set in its own half-acre of garden, he and Melissa were rapidly developing an active social life which provided a canopy of ordinary, alpha-male living to hide him from enemy eyes while beneath it he went about his secret agenda. As to his wife, he had no complaints there; the girl was great in bed and learning fast; she was in love with him, it was easy. Of course, when the time came she would have to be disposed of but meanwhile —

'Your guest has arrived.' Patricia, dressed as usual in one of her elegantly tailored dark-grey suits, was a self-assured woman very aware of her value to the Cause; she withdrew at once, closing the door behind her.

Looking up, the Palestinian watched James Mallory come across the room towards him; saw him tall and handsome, perceived at once his aura of essentially male charisma and, on the instant, gut-reaction dislike of the Irishman surged through him. Suppressing it, he stood up and extended his hand to his fellow terrorist, uttered the required words of welcome then invited him to sit down in the chair facing his own across the table.

His instinctive antagonism towards Mallory was reciprocated. By far the largest part of it, on both sides, was simple male jealousy, but it had its roots in their situation; both being virilely charismatic and arrogant, each resented the fact that he was depedent on the other for the success of Operation SeaSnake. However, recognizing that as an inescapable fact, each now set aside personal feelings and with absolute trust in the other's integrity in all matters relating to SeaSnake they addressed themselves to a thorough check through the logistics Mallory had set in place so far for the four hits. Ansari put forward searching questions on these, and found all of them satisfactorily answered. That done, they discussed the exit strategies yet to be arranged for the direct-action personnel and vehicles involved in Stingray, the assault on Tollgate Garage, situated on Lime Avenue on the outskirts of Hereford. As they worked together, there came alive in each of them a guarded respect for the other: in Ansari, for Mallory's grasp of detail and the high quality of his preparations; in the Irishman, for the Palestinian's knowledge of the topography of the targets and their environs and the honed precision of his overall plans.

Only once were they interrupted. At six o'clock, as asked for, Patricia brought in a tray set with Turkish coffee and a plate on which was a flat, sugary pastry. As she put it down beside him on the table, Ansari looked across at his captain of logistics.

'Would you prefer a whisky?' he asked, 'I am told it is your favourite drink.'

Mallory shook his head. 'Coffee'd be fine,' he said, unsmiling. 'Not the tart for me, though.'

'You should try it. It is called *kunafa* and is delicious. Our hostess makes it especially for me.' He smiled up at the lady of the house. 'Thank you, Madame.'

'It is my pleasure,' she said, but there was no sign of it in her face and with a stiff little bow she turned and left them.

Ansari poured coffee for both of them into the small, handleless bone china cups. 'It comes from the Yemen, which produces one of our finest coffees,' he said, looking up at Mallory as he passed him one of the cups. 'I hope it will please you.'

As Mallory took the coffee, finding its aroma alien to him yet pleasing, memories of the girl Melissa — James's daughter *and this man's wife*, for Christ's sake! — slid across his mind. I can see why you married this guy, he thought, then forgot her entirely.

Half an hour later discussion between the two men was finished, and Ansari rose to his feet. 'I would appreciate a report from you, in person, in four days' time,' he said, 'you will meet me at the Holborn safe house at ten-thirty in the morning.'

His tone and manner were quite plainly dismissive, but Mallory stayed where he was. Looking up into the watchful brown eyes he laid his request on the line. Noticeably, although it was — had to be, given their respective positions within the hierarchy of SeaSnake's personnel — as such a request, his voice and body-language as he presented it subtly proclaimed it to be more of a

135

demand, a demand as of right.

'I want in on the action,' he said. '*Direct action.*'

'You are not . . . qualified.' Caught off guard, Ansari prevaricated: he needed to keep this man on side, readily free with his expertise and his contacts here in England.

'That's not good enough.' Mallory stood up, well-built body ramrod straight. 'I'm as well *qualified* as you are, and you know it. We both learned our trade in a hard school,' he added, eye to eye, and his telling the Palestinian, I'm as tough and experienced as you are, *brother.*

For a moment then, the antagonism between them dissolved. Reading the Irishman's eyes Ansari thought, you and I are both wedded to violence, nothing will ever change that because it runs in our blood. But then his mind probed deeper and he perceived that although they were both hand-fast to violence, as *men* they stood in different worlds: reckoned that he himself espoused violence because he was a zealot and saw it as the best way to advance his cause, the superiority of Islam, whereas the Irishman used it because, mentally and physically, *he enjoyed it* — used it to advance his cause, yes, but it was the violence involved that drove him. He fed on it, needed it to feel fully alive.

On that thought all Ansari's gut antagonism towards Mallory flared in him again and, almost, he cut him down to size, refused his request point-blank and with blistering derision. But practicality prevailed: in the interests of SeaSnake and, of course, his own as its overall commander, he dealt with the situation diplomatically.

'Taking into account your action-experience as listed on your CV, I shall take steps to attach you to the assault unit at the Tollgate target site; Operation Stingray, which is the only one including armed attack,' he said, his voice as cold as his eyes. Then he added, blandly, 'We understand each other well, I think, you and I.'

Too well, perhaps? he wondered, as Mallory smiled and without further words turned and went towards the door. Men of violence both, each of us would trust the other absolutely and with our lives if necessary on the job, but *outside* of that each of us would cheat the other, use him, betray or possibly even kill him — if doing so would be to one's own advantage.

As the Irishman closed the door behind him, he thought; as the Brits say, *it takes one to know one.*

★　★　★

Pulling his Volvo close in against the kerb opposite his sons' school's sportsground Steven Court switched off, hooked one arm over the back of his seat and spoke to his boys, who were already gathering together their cricket gear, eager to be off. As soon as they were gone he was going to start the ball rolling on the plan he had worked out while confined to his hospital bed. He had come home two days ago but, although impatient to get on with it, he had forced himself to carry on normal family life because the step he was about to take had to be kept secret from Deborah and from everyone involved in his present life. The way he saw the situation at that time, he had to fight this thing through alone.

'I'll pick you up at four o'clock sharp,' he said to the boys. 'Be sure you're ready at the gate, OK?'

'Sure, Dad.' Cricket bat and sportsbag in hand Josh got out of the car then waited on the pavement while his brother scrambled out to join him with only a holdall because temporarily they shared the bat.

Dan'll have his new one on his birthday, Steve thought —

'Do I have to wait for my birthday to get my new bat?' Dan was frowning, his grey eyes rebellious.

138

'You do. Yours got broken.'

'Wasn't *my* fault. I lent it to Jacko.'

'But you know he's got a temper — '

'Didn't know he'd bash it against the roller because Josh had clean bowled him, though, did I?'

But then as Steve was about to remonstrate with him, the boy grinned at him, said, 'Steep learning curve, eh, Dad?' then sped joyously after his brother who was already opening the gate into the sportsfield.

Steve watched the two of them pelt across the grass towards the pavilion on the far side, then got on with what he had decided to do. Taking out his mobile he called the number of Rory McGuiness, his one-time mate back in Ballymena: he had found the number inside his head along with many other remembered snippets of information, some of them big things, some little ones, but all of them part of the past life of James Mallory. He tapped in the last digit, sat back waiting. Then, suddenly, a kind of terror seized him. This thing I am about to do, he thought, it's like starting to disinter a body from its grave. What will I find out? *Do I want to know?*

'Hello?'

Only the one word spoken but, recognizing the voice at once Steve said the name in order, as it were, to place himself and Rory,

139

to anchor himself in what was about to take place.

'Rory? Rory McGuiness?'

'In person. Who wants him?'

'James Mallory.' And now, somehow, I've got to sell you the truth, Rory. Because I need your help.

'*Who?*'

Steve caught the utter disbelief in the voice, but something else was in there too, something he could not quite define but for some reason found peculiarly unnerving.

'Jamie. James Mallory,' he said, then forced a laugh and went on quickly, 'Hi there, Rory! OK, it's been years and I should have kept in touch, but — '

'Where are you speaking from?'

'England. London.'

'And what do you want with me? I'm out of the loop now, and you know it. From all I hear you *must* know it, being in the position you've got for yourself over there.'

No mistaking it now: Rory was both angry and *hostile* — and why should he be either? Why speak so aggressively, so . . . accusingly? Apprehension rose in Steve: something was horribly wrong here. Rory and he weren't conversing on the same wavelength.

'Hang on a minute,' he said to him. 'Let me explain. I haven't contacted you in all

140

these years because I was in an accident and lost my memory. I got hit on the head and lost it completely. But I've got some of it back now, just suddenly — '

'When did you lose it? Have this . . . accident?'

'Back in '94.'

After a slight pause, '*Exactly* when? Give me the day and the month.'

'March twelfth 1994. But what the hell does it matter?'

'Jamie. James, listen to me carefully.' Rory's voice was different now: gone quiet, it was shot through with a high-tension urgency which caught at Steve's nerves, shredded them. 'You aren't making any sense to me. On that date you left Ballymena for London. Also on that night, your brother Sean was executed by men we both used to know for 'inexpiable disloyalty'. All I know of James Mallory now is that he commands an undercover unit operating in London for . . . old friends.'

'What are you telling me?' Steve's mind, his very self, were adrift in wild seas.

'Hell to that! What are *you* telling *me*?'

'That . . . that I'm James Mallory.'

'And you're in England, you say. What are you doing there?'

'I've got a job with a big IT company.'

'Are you still with old friends?'

'Christ, no! Rory, I — '

'Listen. Listen to me. Like I said, I've been out of the loop for years. But back in '94 I got to hear things about what happened that night, and what I just told you is what I heard from certain of our *old friends* who were in a position to know. So I'll say it again. On the night of twelfth March 1994 Sean Mallory was executed. His brother James took off for London, is still there. And according to the word around here now, he's still active in the Cause.'

'Sean? Rory, you said he was executed. What became of his body?'

'It was never found. He was reported dead by the execution detail; they said the body had been 'disposed of according to orders'. So I heard. And it's not a good idea to ask too many questions in such situations. As you know.'

Sitting in his Volvo outside the tree-surrounded sportsfield where his sons were at cricket practice Steven Court found that as he and Rory were speaking together some more of the fractured, unconnected bits and pieces of some of his recovered memories were slipping into place. Now suddenly they made one coherent whole.

That night, I saved Sean's life! he thought,

and a kind of exaltation surged through him because his plan back then had worked for his brother, though in a different way from the one intended. Sean must have slept through all that had gone on in his house, then later got news on the grapevine that *Sean* Mallory had been executed, whereupon he'd done what he always did, made the best of the situation as it was,

I saved Sean's life that night. Steve savoured the thought, the joy of it creaming through him. For him, at that time, this one fact was the essence of the entire story; all other considerations, inferences and moral judgements had no significance, they ricochetted off the certainty of his love for Sean as hailstones do off granite rock.

Then, he put the make-or-break question to Rory. 'So we have two men claiming to be James Mallory,' he said. 'Which one will you take for real, Rory?'

'I've done some thinking.' The farmer's voice was grim but very confident. 'Knowing the both of you, I'll take you, the man speaking to me now. Though how Sean pulled off such a trick is beyond me; it's beyond all reasons.'

'Beyond reason or not, it came to pass. I'll tell you how, one day. This isn't the time for it, though. Now, I need your help.'

'Will it involve our . . . old friends?'

'No, it will not. Not in the sense you mean.'

'I'll accept your word on that; never knew you to lie. What do you want me to do?'

Steve told him. Then he thanked him, closed the call and sat back, his mind easy with the knowledge that Rory would get to work on his request at once; it shouldn't take long, the farmer had said, his neighbour Mrs Collins kept up with all local affairs; little news escaped her and she liked nothing more than a good gossip.

I saved Sean's life that night: the glory of it on him, Steve decided to leave Sean to lead the life he'd chosen and himself concentrate on finding out as much as he could about Cristin and Melissa and make sure all was well with them.

Rory rang him that same evening. 'Thought you'd like to know as soon as possible,' he said. 'Cristin's still Daley, but she's moved to Holme Lacey, a village outside Hereford. Melissa's married. No one here seems to know much about them now, but I've got their addresses for you.'

At his desk in the study Steve wrote them down then, noting Melissa's married name, he asked Rory if he had found out anything about her husband, Majed Ansari. But he

144

learned from him no more than that Melissa had met him in Bahrain when she was working there, and had married him within a few months.

From his office next morning, Steve made a phone call to a private detective recommended to him by a colleague at work. Private eye Sam Weaver did not undertake big assignments, this guy had told him when he'd asked him if he knew of a private enquiry agent, but he was a good bet for family stuff.

Weaver took the job on without delay. It had two objectives, each with its own aim but the two linked together. The first was to find out where Majed Ansari was employed and the nature of his work there. The second was to search out and report on any of Ansari's contacts, social as well as job-related, which might be judged to have special significance of any kind.

★ ★ ★

At Trader's request, Inspector Evans had placed an interview room at Hounslow Police Station at his disposal. At the detainee Murphy's request, no other person was present during his questioning by the MI5 officer who, he hoped and prayed, would, in return for certain information contained in

145

the story he had to tell, intercede on his behalf with the police to secure for him some sort of favourable deal regarding his prosecution. Murphy's second request was that the entire interview not be recorded; 'No tapes,' he had stipulated, and flatly refused to give an inch. Evans had agreed to it only on Trader's say-so; but Murphy had won his point in the end, which gave him a kick.

He liked the look of Trader from the moment he entered the interview room; saw the MI5 man sitting on the far side of the grey steel table, looked straight into his eyes and didn't let go of them until he'd sat down facing him and heard the escorting sergeant close the door behind him as he went out.

'Ballymena. March, 1994.' Baldly, Trader placed in context the time and place he was interested in, then waited for Murphy to respond, searching out the man's face and bearing as he did so. What he saw seemed to him quite promising: the gipsy-dark face essentially Irish, black hair, strongly defined eyebrows over blue eyes which were bold and lively, giving as good as they got. Quick on the uptake, Murphy would be, surely also a good man in a rough-house and, almost certainly, a basic honesty in him . . . *unless?* Probably unless his own wellbeing was under severe and immediate threat.

'Whatever's said between you and me today, it's for us alone?' Relaxed in his chair, Murphy gave his question weight. He had already decided to trust this man, reckoning it worth the risk because the returns should be worth having. And what had happened that night way back in '94 — its ghosts had no power to cause trouble for him now; the lead players in it had long since moved on, so he'd best look to grabbing whatever advantage he could to himself because he was in dire need of it.

'I may act on what you tell me,' Trader said, 'but the fact that you were the man I learned it from will always remain known only to you and me.'

Murphy did not ask him to swear on it. Holding his eyes he asked quietly, 'Do you rate me a grass? A squealer?'

'I do not.' Intuiting that his answer was important to the man, Trader folded his arms on the table and told him the truth — part of it, enough to firm up Murphy's confidence in him. 'I believe something very strange happened on the night in question. I believe a false account was given of what took place. I think that, somewhere along the line, things did not go either according to plan or as they were reported: even, perhaps, both of those. I also believe, since you asked for this meeting,

147

that you know facts about this matter that don't tie in with the official, accepted version of events and that for some while you have felt guilty about the whole affair, or, possibly, about one particular aspect of it.' Trader smiled at him. 'I think you want to get something off your chest, Murphy,' he said. 'You want to placate your conscience in what to you is a good cause.'

The Irishman laughed out loud. 'The good cause being *me*, my wellbeing as you might phrase it,' he said. Then the laughter died and he leaned towards Trader and went on, frowning, wanting to get the thing done. 'Ballymena, 1994. I was there. I was one of the men detailed to seize Sean Mallory that night and bring him to secret trial on the charge of treasonable disloyalty . . . 'his oath forsworn'.' He spoke the last three words with a sort of fearful reverence.

'Meaning exactly what?'

Murphy sat back. Eyed Trader speculatively for a moment then said, 'Meaning plain murder — and the bloke he killed paying big money at the time for IRA protection.'

'Surely not! Sean Mallory was no fool, he'd know the IRA would — '

'Leave it! Stick to the point.'

'Which is?'

'That Sean Mallory murdered the bloke

148

because of private trouble between them. That being so, he was up before an IRA tribunal on a capital charge — *aggravated* capital charge, on acount of the disloyalty.'

Trader too sat back. They were in for a long haul here, he could see that. 'I need some coffee.' he said. 'You too?'

'Any chance of a dash of whisky in it?'

'They're not like that here.'

'Uncivilized bastards. Black with three sugars, please.'

Trader passed the order to the sergeant on duty outside the door, then sat down again. 'We'll get down to real business after coffee's arrived,' he said. 'Meanwhile, tell me this: did you know Sean Mallory well? On a personal level, I mean.'

Murphy took his time to answer. 'No,' he said finally, staring up at the ceiling, 'By reputation, yes. I met him a few times. Never worked with him, though . . . thank God.'

'Why 'thank God'?'

Murphy shrugged, then looked across at Trader. 'A cold bastard, Sean Mallory, and bloody arrogant with it. He was admired by the sort who like violence for its own fucking sake; and there's plenty of them in our lot — yours too, I know that for a fact. Personally, I'm not one of them. OK, I've killed to order. Never took pleasure in it,

149

though, and that's God's truth,' he added, then fell silent as a constable brought in two cups of coffee, set one down in front of each of them and withdrew.

'So Sean Mallory was brought before an IRA court on charges which, if proved correct, carried the death penalty.' Trader spoke as soon as the door had closed behind the constable.

'He was.'

'Was he found guilty as charged?'

Now, Murphy's body language changed. Hunching forward in his chair he slid his hands below table level where they could not be seen, and dropped his chin on his chest.

'The tribunal put the death sentence on him,' he answered softly. 'The captain interrogated him; he refused to answer the questions it was his duty to answer, so the captain ordered that the sentence be carried out.'

'And you were there, Murphy. How many in the detail?'

'The captain, two assistants.'

'Of whom you were one?'

The Irishman's head came up; he squared his shoulders. 'Sure I was,' he said, a certain defiance in him. 'The bastard refused to answer the questions so punishment was plain justice.'

Trader was not interested in the morality of the sentence or in the act itself; he sensed himself on the brink of a break-through to long-hidden truths and there was a high-wire tension in him, a grim but invigorating expectation.

'How and when did you arrest Sean Mallory?' he asked.

'From his own house. Past midnight. Me and one other.'

'He didn't resist?'

'Didn't know sentence had already been passed, did he? Besides, we had him at gunpoint.'

'Where did you take him?'

'We drove. Took him to a wood. The captain was there before us, came in his own car. Lonely area, a few farms, houses here and there.' Murphy leaned back again, arms hanging loose at his sides and his head tilted back. He was looking at the wall behind and above Trader but he wasn't seeing it. His mind was turned inwards: his memory of everything that had happened there then was clear and unforgiving; many times he had tried to drive it out of his head but always it slipped back in and curled up quiet and still, ready to strike without warning in the dark of sleepless lonely nights.

Intuiting something of what was going on in Murphy's mind, Trader went on smoothly,

151

'So we have Sean Mallory, the captain, you and your mate in the wood. What happened there?'

'There was an odd thing at first.' A faint frown creased Murphy's brow for a moment, then was gone. 'Something that didn't chime in with what came later. The bastard told the captain he was *James* Mallory; said we'd made a mistake, he'd just been visiting his brother.' His mouth twisted in disgust. 'All that got him was a fist that floored him, then a boot where it hurts most. But that seemed to gear him up somehow. From then on he was brave, was Sean Mallory, I'll give him that. He refused to name his accomplices in Donovan's murder so the captain ordered us to beat him up. We did that, and when we'd softened him up, we stood him up again in front of the captain.' Murphy's eyes were still fixed on the institution-grey wall behind Trader; his voice was without expression as he told his truths. 'Captain said to him, matey-like now, 'You're one of us, Mallory, one of our band of brothers. Why did you kill Donovan, and who helped you? That's all you need to tell us. Give us that information, and you'll go free. Refuse, and we execute you here, now.''

'But he wouldn't tell?' Trader fed it quietly into Murphy's silence.

' 'No comment', Sean said, same as he'd been saying since first time of asking. Then the captain put his face right up close to his and stared into his eyes.' Suddenly, indrawn breath hissed through Murphy's mouth, and when he went on his voice was low and ice-cold. 'I could see the captain's eyes because I was standing right up close at Sean's back,' he said, 'and they . . . they drilled into him, reached right in deep, then clawed about in there until he found what he was looking for. When he did, he stepped back a bit. Didn't speak to Sean Mallory again. Turned to us. 'He'll not talk,' he said. 'Carry out the sentence. I shall return to base. You will report to me there'.' A moment longer Murphy stared at the wall; then he dropped his head and sat silent.

Allowing him a little time Trader drank his coffee, pushed cup and saucer to one side. The story of IRA justice on one of their own who had flouted orders had poured out of Murphy as an exorcism (supposedly) casts out devils, he thought, but what interested him now was not the details of that interrogation, but what had occurred that same night *after* the death sentence had been passed on Sean Mallory.

'What happened next, Murphy?' He put the question suddenly and sharply, saw the dark head jerk up, saw also a shifting shadow of fear in the blue eyes as they met his own. 'What is it you're afraid of?' he asked quietly, desperate not to lose him now, so close to the climax to the story.

'The truth.' Murphy's answer was slow in coming and loaded with guilt.

'Is the truth of that night so dreadful?'

With effort, the Irishman pulled himself clear of his fear. 'Nah,' he said, leaning forward towards the MI5 man with a half smile on his gipsy face. 'You told me that everything I say here will stay known to you alone, and I reckon in you I've got a bloke I can trust. So I'll tell you the whole — '

'Before you do I'd like to ask you a question.'

'Go ahead. What's one more?'

'Do you know *James* Mallory?'

'Sean's twin brother?' Murphy shook his head. 'No, I don't know him. Heard plenty *about* him, naturally. Never actually met him or worked with him, though. Why d'you ask?'

Brushing that aside with a quick 'Just curious', Trader cut straight back to his mainstream interest. 'What actual facts do you have for me about Sean Mallory's execution that aren't already known to our Intelligence?'

'O'Donaghue and me, we didn't kill

Mallory that night.' Murphy shot the words at him with a sort of ferocity, not finding them easy to say.

Trader stiffened. 'How come?'

'We messed up. See, we'd expected the captain to — '

'Leave the excuses. Tell me what happened — *facts*.'

Murphy folded his arms, looked at him steadily. 'Right, mate, you listen up now,' he said, 'Mallory slipped us and took off blind — jumped the captain, sent him flying then sprinted for the woods and crashed straight in among the trees. We fired a couple of rounds after him, but missed. Tried to track him through the woods but . . . '

There in the interview room at Hounslow Police Station Trader learned how, back in 1994, Mallory had escaped execution, the starlit woods his ally as he fled the two men hunting him, trees and bushes colluding with the darknesses of the night to confuse and defeat his enemies.

' . . . realized we'd lost the bastard,' Murphy said and sat back, tight-lipped.

'*Lost* him?' Trader came out of the night-dark woods where he'd been with Mallory running for his life, the way Murphy told it. 'We need some explanation here.'

Murphy shrugged. 'That night, he had all

the luck,' he said, suddenly withdrawn, defensive. 'Me and O'Donaghue, we got dealt a rotten hand; everything that could go wrong did go wrong. And, Mr MI5, there's no one in this whole fucking world can *explain* the way the cards fall,' he added softly, 'no one who walks this earth has the power to do that.' Then suddenly he grinned. 'Come to think of it, you're hell's own lucky yourself tonight, aren't you?' he said. 'Lucky that I'm in a position where I need to make a trade-off, and you're my best bet to get one.'

'True enough. So, Mallory simply disappeared into the night, and you never saw him again?'

'He did. We didn't. Next question?' The mockery blatant; the blue eyes innocent.

Trader sighed. 'Cut it out, Murphy. I came here to get the truth, and asking questions is the only way to do that. These woods the three of you were in, were there any roads nearby apart from the two you mentioned?'

'No. There's just the two. One to the south of the woods which we went in on: the other to the north of them.'

'Which one did he head for when he made his break?'

'The north. He could've circled round though — '

'Unlikely; it would have taken him back to

where your car was parked.'

'I doubt he'd get round to working that out — '

'He wouldn't *work it out*. It'd be an instinctive reaction. If where you came in from is all evil, instinct orders you *away* from there not back towards it. How far would he have to go to reach the north one? Could he have made it, given the state he must have been in after the beatings?'

'Could have. Reputation had him down as able to take punishment then come right back at you.'

'Not many houses in the area, you said. Any near that road north of the woods?'

'Only one, far as I know. A bungalow.'

Trader changed tack. 'When you reported back to the captain, what did you tell him?'

'We went along with what was supposed to have happened. Said we'd cornered Mallory, shot him dead, then called on the blokes across the border contracted to collect and dispose of the body, gave them the info they needed to do it.'

'And the captain accepted your report?'

'Why shouldn't he? No reason not to.'

'But there wasn't a body. How did you square that with your mates in the Republic?'

Murphy's eyes slid away from Trader; he answered obliquely, his voice light and easy, but to Trader both qualities seemed carefully assumed. 'No problem,' he said, 'O'Donaghue and me, we know them from other jobs and we've been in raids based on their farm. They took a bit of a risk: lied to help us out, knowing for sure we'd do the same for them. Besides, lying about it on our behalf like they did put us seriously in their debt and, believe me, the way things were around then it was no bad thing to have a big debt to call in any time you needed heavy help.'

'But wasn't there the danger that the truth of it might get back to your bosses?'

'Not likely, y'know.' Turning to Trader again, the gipsy face slid knowing, secret laughter at him. 'Think on it, friend, and you'll see that every man involved in the deception had life-or-death reasons to keep the truth of the matter strictly to himself for the rest of his days on this beautiful earth of ours.'

After a moment, Trader nodded. 'Point taken,' he murmured soberly. He sat back, linked his hands behind his head and ran his mind over all he had just learned. When he had slotted everything into place he took out his notebook and made a rough sketch-map of the area figuring in Murphy's story, showing on it the wood, the roads bracketing it and the spot where Mallory had been interrogated. Then he marked on it first the presumed route the condemned man had taken on his escape, then the courses taken by his two pursuers.

When it was done he slid it across the table to Murphy and asked him to check its accuracy. Murphy did so, then passed it back without comment.

'That's it, then,' Trader said, as he took it, but as Murphy got to his feet he asked him one further question.

'These men from the farm across the border you and O'Donaghue found so useful,' he said, 'how and where were they supposed to have disposed of the body?'

Suddenly very still, Murphy eyed him coldly. 'That's a whole new ball game, Englishman,' he said harshly and with finality, 'and it's one I'm not playing with anyone. *Ever.*'

Trader took note of both Murphy's answer and his manner and let it pass — for the moment. And as he drove back to his office in central London he considered the Irishman's story and decided on his next moves. In the light of Murphy's version of events, past uncertainties regarding the happenings on that night in 1994 and James Mallory's life since then came storming back to the forefront of his mind. Sean had not died that night — so *where the hell was he now unless* . . . ?

To Trader's way of thinking that was a question which had to be answered because Sean Mallory alive damn sure wouldn't have turned pacifist, he'd still be what he'd always been and took joy in being, a terrorist *activist* . . .

That afternoon Trader called in to his office Jim Robinson and Elliot Dexter, both intelligence-co-ordinating officers with experience in undercover operations in Ulster. Providing them with the requisite maps, he gave them the location of the wood Murphy had identified to him as the place of Sean Mallory's 'trial' — named as Hunter's Wood on these maps — and pointed out to them the bungalow near its northern edge to which Murphy had referred.

'I want you and your moles and sleepers over there to get me the names and if possible the present addresses of whoever lived in that bungalow in March 1994,' he went on, 'and they must do it without arousing the faintest suspicion that it is being done. Can do?'

Nodding, 'We'll get on to it at once,' Robinson said, running a hand over his thick grey hair. 'D'you want our people to interview whoever's living there now?'

'No. The whole op must be done

160

off-the-record and as secretly as possible.'

'Can you give us anything on who's living there as of today?'

'Sorry, no. Hasn't been time.'

'Then God send us a bachelor who's lived there since the year dot.' Dexter, the younger of the two by a good ten years, gave Trader a wry smile. 'What when we've got the names? Do we follow them up wherever it may take us?'

'No you do not. You get them to me as fast as possible.'

'What are you into here, Matt?' Robinson asked. 'Big stuff?'

'Could be. I've got a hunch things are not quite as they seem in regard to a certain individual in one of the IRA cells presently lying doggo here in London. This investigation should help clarify the situation. I hope.'

'Then we'd best get a move on.' Dexter was on his feet. 'You've had similar hunches before, and every fucking one of them's turned out to be on target.'

6

Tollgate Garage, Hereford: the target of
Operation Stingray

For the first time in his life Sean Mallory
— in the persona of his brother James —
drove from London to Hereford, a prosperous,
deep-country city in England's heartland. As
captain of logistics for the entire SeaSnake
mission, he of course knew the location, environs and layout of each of its four assault
sites, including those of Operation Stingray,
the attack on Tollgate garage which was situated on Lime Avenue in the north-western
suburbs of the city. But now that Ansari had
written him into the sharp-end of Stingray he
wanted to spy out the target's layout for himself: to get the feel of the garage, to sense its
work-ethic and observe its daily routine. Passing through the city centre he turned his
dark-blue Fiesta into Lime Avenue at a roundabout, drove on along it and, spotting Tollgate
Garage on his right, pulled in for petrol.

As he stood at the counter in the garage
shop to pay — making visual evaluation of
the set-up inside it the while — he said to the

pretty young blonde who took his cash, 'I'm looking for a secondhand car for my daughter, and I'm told I can count on both a wide selection of vehicles and a good deal here.' He gave her a disarming grin. 'She's just passed her driving test, you see.'

But the blonde barely looked at him. 'Used car lot's at the back, just drive round and park,' she said, putting his change down on the counter then returning to the *Hello!* magazine open beside the cash register.

Sean Mallory followed her advice. 'Just looking at the moment,' he said to the passing mechanic who stopped beside him to offer help. And for the next ten minutes or so he strolled up and down the serried ranks of cars in the parking lot alongside the workshops at the rear. He peered at interiors, inspected wheels, bent down to inspect undersides, looked at prices, but as he did those things his eyes were busy in other directions also, were noting overlooking windows, the comings and goings of staff and customers.

Driving clear of Hereford's suburbs he pulled into the first layby he came to, picked up the plan of Tollgate's premises from the passenger seat and annotated it in accordance with his recent observations there. That done, he sat back and studied it, recalling the

163

proposed Stingray assault. At last I'll get me *armed action*, he thought; and in his mind's eye he pictured the typed outline of the operation itself:

STINGRAY : TOLLGATE GARAGE, Lime Avenue, Hereford N.B.
a) All target buildings are single storey
b) Shoot-to-kill policy in force through-out action
c) The strike requires four vehicles, three crewed by three gunmen plus driver, fourth by suicide bomber alone
d) The action has four parts and culminates in the detonation of the Mercedes car bomb on the forecourt between the pumps and the main buildings

1 VEHICLE A: DAIHATSU
Objective:
    to secure clear access for Mercedes to its detonation position on forecourt between pumps and main buildings
Action:
    armed agents shoot dead occupants of all/any vehicles pulled up at pumps then drive said vehicles clear of pumps and entrance to forecourt

2 VEHICLE B: VOLVO

Objective:

a) elimination of staff and customers present in workshops plus used-car area behind admin buildings

b) destruction of workshops at rear

Action:

a) armed agents shoot dead all hostiles encountered

b) destroy workshops plus all vehicles in used car area (hand grenades)

3 VEHICLE C: RANGE ROVER

Objective:

elimination of all staff and customers inside shop plus admin buildings

Action:

armed agents 'sweep' target area shooting dead all hostiles encountered

4 VEHICLE D: MERCEDES

(bomb carrier)

Objective:

detonation of deep-penetration bomb between pumps and main buildings

Personnel:

Self-drive suicide bomber only

Action:

a) martyr collects armed Mercedes from bomb-maker's house, drives to target site, parks in held slot there

b) four minutes after zero hour for manpower action, martyr drives Merc on to forefourt, halts vehicle between pumps and shop, detonates bomb

5 EXIT ROUTES and POST-ACTION DESTINATIONS . . .

But Sean Mallory left it there. He knew the escape plans for Stingray's action vehicles by heart since logistics dictated their pattern and, therefore, he himself had planned them for Ansari from start to finish. Putting the papers to one side he leaned back, closed his eyes and imagined the entire operation inside his head.

Joe Anderson was tidying up his herb bed when his front doorbell rang. He heard it easily because the French doors of his sitting-room gave on to a broad patio bordered by the herb garden and they were standing wide open to the sunshine and the warm summer-scented breeze. He went to answer it, glad to have a reason for straightening up.

The man he opened his door to was of average height and build, looked to be in his forties and was casually dressed in a navy-blue sweatshirt, jeans and trainers. Nevertheless, there was something about him . . . He looked both meaningful and charismatic, Anderson decided, and asked amiably, 'How can I help you?'

'Mr Joe Anderson?' Trader asked.

Blue eyes were communicating with golden brown ones, and each man liked what he felt coming out of the other towards him.

'I've never denied it yet,' Anderson said, smiling. 'And you are?'

Trader had his official ID ready, showed it. 'Matt Kingsmith, MI5,' he said, saw a sudden wariness come in the other's face and thought that he really might be on to something useful here, that this man might indeed be involved somehow in what he was working on.

Having checked the ID carefully, Anderson handed it back. 'Come in,' he said. 'I've been gardening and I need a beer. Care to join me?'

With a can of lager apiece they sat out on the lawn at the back of the bungalow, one either side of the hand-crafted wooden table shaded from the afternoon sun by an ancient chestnut tree.

'What branch of MI5?' Anderson asked, after his first welcome mouthful of lager.

'Missing persons. Other things too. But basically and at the moment, that's what I'm here about.'

Anderson had always known this moment might come and looked away over his lawn, recalling how he used to argue with himself as to whether or not he should reveal all he knew regarding his man-without-a-memory. Always in the end he had decided to keep the whole thing quiet: but now, with this MI5 man come to ask questions, he knew himself uncertain whether to keep up the deception behind the existence of the man known as Steven Court. It would surely depend on how this bloke Matt Kingsmith was going to use the truth of that night, because it was possible that it might be good for Steve.

'Are you working out whether to tell me something or not?' Trader put it into the silence between them, then leaned back and squinted up at the chestnut tree, sunshine skittering through its leaves as the breeze drifted lazily among them. 'I take it you're an honest man, Mr Anderson. The job you do calls for that and many other admirable qualities — yes, we've checked on you,' he said quickly, looking down again as Anderson began to interrupt then stopped. 'Checked right back to when you were living in Ulster. So I'm going to trust you, tell you certain things. In return, I'm asking you to trust me — '

'Get to the point, please.'

'Glad to,' Leaning forward, Trader went on the attack. 'Ballymena, 1994,' he said, 'Does that place, at that date, have any particular significance for you?'

'I was living fairly near the town, A bungalow — '

'Close to Hunter's Wood.'

Oh Christ, they really are on to him. Anderson did not say it aloud, but his eyes and the sudden tension evident in his face and body gave him away.

So Trader closed in for the kill. 'You picked a man up on the road that night, didn't you?' he went on, searching the blue eyes. He was intent on forcing the truth out of this man, and although quiet his voice was hard, invasive. 'I don't know *how* that happened but I'm damned sure it *did*. And I don't know what happened from then on, but I think it's quite likely you do. Am I right?' Having got his key question out in the open he sat back and waited for an answer. When it came it struck him like a bolt from the blue, but a split second later he realized its implications and recognized it for what it was, a miraculous and priceless gift from a God who had chosen to give to him with both hands that day.

'Are you Sailor?' Anderson asked, and saw the MI5 man look shocked, but then excited.

Of all things, *excited?*

'No, I'm not Sailor.' Trader was smiling at him.

'The name means something to you, though, doesn't it?'

'It does. So you did pick him up? He came out of Hunter's Wood on to the road — '

'And I stopped, helped him into my car and took him home with me.' Anderson nodded, then got to his feet and stood looking across at Trader. For Joe Anderson, the die was cast now: he was going to put his trust in this man Kingsmith from MI5 and give him Steve's story — as far as he himself knew it. He would ring-fence it to secrecy as far as he could; and would trust Kingsmith to keep it that way as far as *he* could.

'I'll tell you what I did that night, and what came of it for me and the man I picked up by Hunter's Wood,' he said. Then he shoved his hands into the pockets of his jeans and, head down, watching his feet tread new-mown grass as he prowled up and down alongside the table, told the tale right through from the moment his headlights caught the dishevelled figure staggering along the verge ahead, to the present day.

Trader did not interrupt; he let the story roll and lived every minute of it with its two protagonists, caught up in and marvelling at the weird and wonderful strangeness of how two people's lives can suddenly collide and alter the course of both for ever.

' . . . and Steve Court has a good life now.' Anderson ceased his pacing and, standing in the sunshine just beyond the circled shade of the chestnut tree, looked across at the man seated at the table. 'I hope and pray he'll be allowed to go on living it,' he said to him, his heart in the words. Then he grinned, worked neck and shoulders in relief from tension. 'I need another beer after that,' he said. 'I'll go fetch us a couple.'

As he watched him walk away towards the back door of the bungalow, Trader thought the whole thing over. He believed all Anderson had told him. It was, he realized, a story that lived on two levels: the personal, and the political — with particular reference to terrorist activity in the UK. It was also a story that carried far-reaching implications for those involved in it, all of them surely deeply traumatic, some of them frankly both appalling and terrifying. As for himself, Trader of MI5, there was much to be considered before action, if any, was taken. There was one certain detail which, if it could be resolved, would inevitably influence future events.

'*Why* was Steve there that night?' Anderson

put a fresh can of lager down in front of Trader, frowned as the MI5 man looked up at his question. 'What had he done to be beaten within an inch of his life and left dead scared of whoever had done it to him?'

'Given the year, the place, and the political situation you must surely have had ideas about that?' Trader searched the blue eyes watching him but they gave him nothing. 'Didn't you ever ask him?'

Anderson's mouth twisted wryly as he sat down again. 'I've asked him a thousand times, over the years. Like I said, he lost his memory. He doesn't remember who he was, his past life . . . No, I haven't been entirely honest with you,' he added after a moment. 'There were long periods when I didn't ask him.'

'Why not?'

Anderson looked down; after a moment he said quietly, 'I was afraid of what the answers might be.'

'The IRA?'

'Of course.' His eyes came up to Trader's again. 'He's never struck me as a man to be involved in ordinary criminality. Would my suspicion have been right?' he asked levelly.

A smile touched Trader's lips. 'He was turning away from the IRA,' he said, and in the privacy of his mind added, *with the help of a certain lady* he was turning away from it.

But suddenly Anderson's face darkened. 'You know who he is, don't you?' he accused. 'What's his *real* name, Mr Kingsmith? If I could only tell him that he'd — '

'No way!' Trader reached out and grabbed him by the arm. 'You listen to me now, Joe Anderson. You will — you *must* — say nothing at all to Steven Court of my visit to you. Is that understood?'

'Why shouldn't I — ?'

'*Is that understood?*' He released Anderson's arm, sat back. 'Forgive the drama. But there's a lot behind my coming to you today and, in the interests of national security, the man you know as Steven Court must for a while go on being just that to himself and to the outside world.'

'Sad for Steve.'

'Not so. In fact, damned lucky for him . . . You'll do as I ask?'

'No choice, have I, after what you've just said about national security? How long will I have to keep quiet?'

Trader eyed him sardonically. 'If I were able to answer that one, Mr Anderson, I'd end up nominated for a medal.'

Anderson smiled. Said after a moment, 'Will you be keeping in touch?'

But Trader had one last question to put to

him. 'Tell me, have you ever noticed a scar of any kind on either of Steven Court's hands?'

Anderson hesitated. He didn't like the question: didn't want to answer it, to do so seemed to be in some way a betrayal of Steve's trust in him. But 'national security' . . . those are words which impose a duty on a man.

'Yes, I have,' he said reluctantly. 'There's a small scar at the base of the little finger of his left hand.' He caught a flicker of satisfaction in the MI5 man's eyes.

'Does he know how he came by it?'

'No. I've asked him but he couldn't tell me.' Then, as Trader began to turn away, he said quietly, 'For that, you owe me, I think. So answer me one question.'

'Maybe. Go ahead and we'll see.'

'Who is Sailor?'

'The man you know as Steven Court was Sailor to me, and only to me. Which, given the circumstances back then, was extremely brave of him. But that was long ago, the fact no longer has any significance. I'll leave a card with you, Mr Anderson. The phone number on it will ensure you can either talk to me or get a message through to me at any time, day or night. Call me, please, if there are any developments you think might, in the light of what's been said, be of interest to me.'

174

He smiled. 'And bear in mind that in cases like this my field of interest is a very catholic affair,' he added.

Nevertheless, as Trader drove home he admitted to himself that he had lied to Anderson. The fact that the man now living under the name Steven Court had been Sailor *did* have significance at the present time: indeed it might yet turn out to be — or be turned to become? — of major importance because there were three crucial, possibly pivotal facts in the story Anderson had told him. The first: that it was *Sean* Mallory, not his twin James, who since 1994 had been working with the covert IRA network in London; *Sean*, who was known to be of the most violent breed of terrorists and was unlikely to have changed his spots. The second: that the real James Mallory had built himself a whole new life and — according to Anderson — remained totally ignorant of his true identity and, consequently, of his earlier life and the people in it, including Cristin, Melissa, and his twin brother Sean. And the third was that quite possibly the real James, i.e. Steve Court, might yet again be of use to MI5.

For surely Sailor's mindset wouldn't have changed? That night in 1994 when Sean stole his brother's identity — God and Sean alone knew how *that* had come about! — James had been on the point of making the final break, changing his allegiances diametrically and becoming an MI5 mole within the IRA. So surely — hopefully — should it come about that Trader found himself in need of Sailor's assistance, all he would have to do would be to reveal Steven Court's true identity to him and then ask him for that help?

15 June

Majed Ansari, well aware of the potential advantage of such a skill to an undercover terrorist agent, had long since taught himself the techniques of rapid and accurate facial recognition; also, he had a very low threshhold of suspicion.

At 10.34 that night he went into his study at his house Hillsdown to catch up on office paperwork, as he often did, leaving Melissa to enjoy a leisurely bath before bed. Following his usual practice, before turning on any lights he went across to the front window and scanned the garden outside for suspicious activity of any kind. He had no reason to suspect himself under surveillance; ever since his arrival in Britain all reports from SeaSnake's intelligence agents had shown the entire operation secure, and to him the act of checking his garden had lost its edge, become routine.

But that night things were different. His study was at the right-hand downstairs corner of the house and looked out over lawn and, to his left, the path leading to the front gate on to the road. The path had a stone sundial beside it, halfway along; the lawn ran the length of the property and on its far side, flanking the road, it was bordered by a broad shrubbery. After a cloudy, sultry day, the hazy half-light of evening hung heavy over the lawn and shrouded the shrubbery into a place of mystery, everything in there soft-focus, indistinct. But then suddenly he glimpsed something amongst the trees just inside the gate — a blurred, man-shaped figure slinking stealthily along the edge of the shrubbery! A shadow among shadows, he was using trees and bushes as cover as he stole along parallel with the house, across the lawn from the study.

Moving in close behind one of the open curtains, Ansari drew the green velvet slightly to one side to get a better view and watched the intruder advance . . . halt opposite him and turn to face the study. Swiftly then, the Palestinian slipped across to his desk and took out the night-glasses he kept in the top drawer alongside his loaded revolver. Standing well back from the window, he focused them on the man who had come out of the night — to spy on him? Or to kill, perhaps, since all things are possible in the no-holds-barred world of the undercover international terrorist.

There was only the owl-light yet, the moon would rise later; and the hazels and rhododendrons of the shrubbery were kind to the intruder; veiled by their foliage he had only to keep his face hidden and he would surely be safe. But his working terms of reference specified that he carry out close surveillance on Hillsdown and report on the activities of its occupants Mr and Mrs Ansari; and in order to get a clear sight of the house he had to push aside the veiling leaves and make a small window for himself. That night he saw no lights showing at the front of the building. On his two previous visits he had seen lights on in the study between ten and eleven o'clock and Ansari at work in there. So now, standing opposite that room, he made his green-leaved window and peered out through it towards where he'd seen lights before.

Ansari saw his face plainly then: through his night-glasses saw it framed in greenery and, smiling to himself, learned it feature by feature. When he had the image fixed in his mind he lowered the glasses, closed his eyes and behind them made a black-and-white picture of the intruder's face, drawing it into existence just the way he'd learned it. You may be merely a thief sussing out my house for a burglary, he was thinking, but you may be enemy intelligence; whichever, *I'll know you if I see you again.*

As he looked out once more the leaves of the shrubs slipped back into place across the spying face and a moment later he saw the shadowy shape of the man steal back through the shrubbery then go out of the front gate on to the road.

Deciding against working that night, Ansari left the study and went upstairs. Melissa was a lovely girl and — he smiled to himself at the thought — she was passionately in love with him. Which fact carried the bonus that, caught up in the physical glory of her love for him, she showed only passing interest in his business activities and asked no awkward questions concerning what he did during the regular overnight stays away from home his job required of him.

The intruder did not show at Hillsdown the following night: Ansari's searching eyes discovered no spy lurking in the shrubbery bordering his property. But then one morning, two days later, he saw that committed-to-memory face again. The central London offices he worked from occupied the fourth floor of a high-rise business block. Late in arriving, he flashed his ID card at the reception desk — on duty there a man he knew and tipped well from time to time — then hurried on towards the row of lifts beyond it, seeing one standing open-doored but nearly full and on the point of departure. Making it inside just in time he muttered 'Excuse me' to the girl who had moved back a little to make room for him, turned his back on her and looked out into the lobby. Then, as the lift doors began to close, he got a glimpse of that same memorized face before the metal doors slid shut and the lift began to ascend. But that was enough: bone structure strong, broad forehead, prominent cheekbones, heavy chin, mouth wide and full-lipped and his ears, unusual for a man, small and lying close to his skull. Yes, *it was him.* The intruder last seen through night-glasses in the shrubbery at Hillsdown was — surely? — spying on him regularly.

That sighting increased Ansari's suspicion that he was under covert surveillance; but he did not know whether it was by enemy intelligence or simply criminal in intent. Whichever, surveillance of any kind posed a possible threat to SeaSnake and, therefore, as he well knew, he ought to report the situation to his Brit collaborator James Mallory, so that the two of them together could decide on the best way to deal with it. However, Ansari chose not to do so. The clash of personalities which had been so immediate at their first meeting had lessened since then. He and Mallory worked together on the four-pronged preparations for SeaSnake because they must, since each desired the success of the mission, and there was professional respect between them, but each went his own way as far as he might do without compromising the operation. So now Ansari decided to deal with his intruder on his own, at least in the first instance. In the light of the possibility, even probability, that the spy might in fact be no more than a common housebreaker sussing out suitable properties and the daily routine of their owners for profitable robberies, he decided to tackle him on his own and force him to name his boss and confess his purpose there. If he brought Mallory into the matter and that purpose turned out to be simple burglary he, Ansari, would lose a certain amount of credibility with the Irishman, and that was a state of affairs he would not tolerate.

Ansari took action hard on his decision

because Melissa presented him with a perfect opportunity to do so. That same evening, a Wednesday, she declared her intention to visit her mother at Holme Lacey over the coming weekend since Majed planned to be working at home on both the break days. After play-acting some resistance to the idea, Ansari gave in gracefully. The arrangement would give him two possible chances: the Friday evening, since Melissa intended to drive up to Holme Lacey straight from work; then, if the intruder failed to appear, there would still be the Saturday.

★ ★ ★

Soon after seven o'clock on Friday evening Sam Weaver concealed himself in the shrubbery bordering the front of the Ansari property, hoping that this time something of interest might occur, even one of the six-strong dinner parties of which there had been two since he started on the job. For he was becoming bored with surveillancing the Ansari couple: he wasn't getting anywhere, their life together was obviously going splendidly and at work Ansari simply got on with things, did what he had to do. After this weekend, Weaver had decided, he'd quit, call it a day. He saw Ansari get home and let himself in at 7.45. There was no sign of the girl, though, so he assumed she'd come home earlier.

At 10.50 Weaver, tired-eyed and feeling rather stale by then, looked out again at the window of the ground-floor room at the right-hand corner of the house, which he had decided must be Ansari's study since he worked there most evenings. The lights had come on in there ten minutes ago —

Whipping out from the half-darkness behind him a man's arm locked iron-hard around his neck, jerked his head back and held it prisoned cruelly tight against the assailant's shoulder.

'*Make one sound and I'll slit your throat!*' The man's voice was quiet, the knife in his right hand was doing his work for him.

Its point was digging into the flesh below Weaver's right ear and, as he felt blood trickle down his skin, he stopped clawing at the arm clamped around his neck, half choking him. Play this cool, he told himself. You've got no weapon. He has, so you've got to let the bastard call the shots till you're ready — then go for it, fight him for the knife, you know a trick or two —

'That's better,' Ansari said, as his prisoner's arms dropped to his sides. 'Now, you answer my questions. First, who are you working for?'

'I'm not telling you that.' His voice was half-strangled, hoarse from the pressure on his throat. He was thinking, if he knifes you you can't answer, can you? He knows that as well as you do so keep talking and *watch for your chance.*

'You'll have to tell me if you want to stay alive.' The knife pricked a little deeper but Ansari loosened his arm lock slightly so the man could talk more easily. 'Who's your boss?'

'I don't have one. Work on my own.'

'Work at what?'

'Shit, what d'you think? Thieving. There's good pickings round here — '

'In which case there'll be a gang.' Ansari moved his knife in flesh. 'Who's your boss?'

Blood ran warm against his skin. Weaver gritted his teeth then got the words out. 'No comment.'

Ansari recognized the often mocking phrase from TV cop shows, and anger flared. 'Don't play games with me!' he snapped, but then realizing he would have to use stronger methods to get answers he said with quiet menace, 'We'll play our games my way and inside the house, where you'll find the dice loaded in my favour. I think that after you and I have been in there together a little while you will decide to, as you put it, *comment.*' Then his voice sharpened again. 'Now put both hands behind your back. I'll hold them together there and, side by side, so we look friendly because even though it's late someone might chance to see us, you and I will walk across to the path then go along it and into the house. And don't make trouble as we go: I'm very fast with the knife.'

Got to do something soon, Weaver thought, as they stepped clear of the shrubbery and, shoulder to shoulder, set off across the lawn towards the path, because once we're inside he'll get it out of me — and then he won't leave me alive to tell the tale, will he? So I'll go for him, *have to.* The knife's in his right hand. I'll break his grip on my wrists — jerk round and bull my full body-weight into him as I do it. Grab for the knife with my left hand, smash my right into his face, knee him in the balls as he doubles over — then bloody *run for the front gate.* I'll make my move when we're level with that sundial halfway down the path.

The square-topped yellowstone sundial was set into the centre of its flagged surrounding base. As the two men drew close to it, in one swift violent action Weaver broke Ansari's grip on his wrists, pivoted on his heels, grabbed for the knife with his left hand, drove his right fist at the dark face and caught it a glancing blow, but lost his balance as he struck out, stumbled and half-fell against the sundial. Ansari kept his hold on the knife and came back at him fast — grabbed his shoulder as he scrambled upright, swung him round and struck for his heart, driving the blade in deep, feeling it slide in smooth and easy, slicing through the living flesh. Weaver hunched over the wound in agony, but then, as the knife was pulled out, he gathered the last of his failing strength and turned to run, lurched a step forward but collided with the sundial and held on to it, face distorted with pain, left hand clenched over the wound and his blood running over it. Sensing Ansari coming at him again he pushed himself upright — but the Palestinian dived for his legs and brought him crashing down. As he fell, the base of his skull struck an edge of the sundial. He collapsed on the paving surrounding it and lay spreadeagled on the pale stone, his face upturned to the starless sky.

Ansari had fallen with him. Scrambling swiftly to his feet, he moved closer to the still figure lying on the ground, stood looking down at the man who had come to his house to spy on him. Saw him sprawled with his shoulders against the earth; saw his blood seeping darkly from the back of his head, creeping out across the yellow stone in an uneven, widening circle.

7

Holme Lacey

Cristin and Trader had been gardening together all afternoon, he repairing the fencing on the south side of her property while she weeded the rose bed. Now, showered and changed, they were in her sitting-room having a drink, one either end of the window-seat overlooking the pond at the side of her house, which was surrounded by sward wherein meadow flowers ran riot.

'Getting a bit, well, undisciplined out there, isn't it?' Trader observed, eyeing the brilliant ex-lawn with a certain amount of disapproval.

Cristin laughed, leaning back into the cushions behind her. 'But that's the *point* of it, my darling order-obsessed martinet,' she said. 'It's *natural*. Besides, it saves an awful lot of work, which is no bad thing.'

Trader's eyes left the flowers, went to her. When I first met you over ten years ago I fell in love with you then and there, he thought. Still am in love with you, also love you deeply. Made a serious effort to put you out of my life a couple of times because you wouldn't marry me and I thought life was passing me by. Always came back to you, though. And over the years you've given me . . . almost everything. Bloody word, *almost*; you won't marry me or live with me on a permanent basis. And, like a vagrant, I take what's on offer, visit you, sleep with you, make myself useful —

'Cristin.' He sent her name at her, a hardness in his voice.

She turned to him, sea-green eyes direct to his. 'I know what you're about to say, Matt. The answer's still the same . . . I'll tell you something else, though.' But then she was silent; picked up her glass of wine, sipped it, looked out of the window again.

'I'd like to hear this something,' Trader said after a while.

'It's . . . things I said to Melissa, years ago. She was seventeen and I'd realized she was beginning to . . . to hate her father because as she went out and about more she was hearing things about Jamie, rumours of him being active in clandestine IRA affairs here in England. But as you know, when he left us he was starting to move away from belief in the IRA, in the path it was taking. So when she began speaking to me of hating Jamie, I tried to explain to her that the change in him had happened because everything had gone bad for him on account of Sean's death. How with him and Sean being so deeply close, losing him *broke* something in Jamie, killed it off just when it was growing into . . . was becoming really meaningful.'

Trader sensed the tension in her. 'What . . . what words did you use to her, to do that?' he asked. 'How did you put it?'

'I told her she should keep loving the father she'd known before that night in 1994.' Cristin's voice had slipped into the monotone of someone whose entire self is caught up in reliving the event being recollected. 'I said to her, 'Keep loving the man you knew then, Melissa. I do. The man friends in Ulster still send me rumours about from time to time, the one they whisper runs with splinter groups of the IRA in London — that man is not the sort of man your father really was. For you and me, I said, your father as it were *died* that night he left us, the night Sean was executed by his IRA masters. Don't let your memories of what your father truly was die too, Melissa. Don't do that — ''

'Cristin! It's a terrible waste of a life — of *lives*, because there's yours as well as hers — to live for and inside memories!' Trader held his despairing anger in on a tight rein, but it showed in his voice. And only after the words were said did he wonder whether they were against her or against himself; because although he had for a while now believed that her 'Jamie' was in all likelihood alive and well (*knew* only that he had not died at the IRA's hands that night in 1994), he was deliberately keeping that fact from her and intended to go on doing so until the need for the subterfuge ceased to exist, if it ever did. And he was doing so because, through Melissa, she was tied in with Majed Ansari, who was under suspicion of terrorist connections — very tenuously suspected; as he well knew, the Intelligence Services had no proven evidence against him.

Suddenly, and smiling, Cristin faced him. 'With you in my life, it doesn't seem a wasted one to me,' she said. 'Forgive me for . . . well, for all there is to forgive between you and me.'

Their eyes held for a moment then he broke the sad/sweet tension between them, drained his lager and got to his feet. ' 'Half a loaf', as they say,' he remarked to no one in particular. 'Bring your wine, let's go cook supper. I want to hear the latest about Melissa.'

But what Trader was really after was knowledge/ information through Melissa regarding Majed Ansari, an insider's knowledge, which is surely the best way to get to the truth of a person.

190

'Melissa was up here with you last weekend, you said. How was she?' he asked, as he prepared a salad to go with their cold ham.

'Positively euphoric.' Cristin was setting the table in her big, full-of-light kitchen at the rear of the refurbished farmhouse that was her home.

'Last time I saw her, she said it was about time you and I got married as she'd love me for a dad.'

'What did you say to that?'

'Told her I wouldn't mind her as a daughter — could manage to survive it, anyway.' Heart-ache in him, buried deep.

'It's lovely to see her so . . . so well-loved and happy,' Cristin said after a silence. 'Makes me feel good.'

Trader saw that his feeble attempt at humour had passed by her unnoticed; there hadn't been room for it inside her head as Melissa lived in there, only Melissa. Sometimes, anyway.

'And how's Majed?' he asked. 'Presumably he's in the same state of married bliss?'

Catching a flick of bitterness in his voice, Cristin considered her own happiness more carefully and found in it a slight cause for concern.

Watching her face, Trader tensed suddenly,

191

feeling his scalp prickle. She didn't like Melissa's husband, he intuited, she didn't trust him, had reservations about him. And he realized he might be on to something: there must be some sort of ambivalence about Majed Ansari that disturbed Cristin, caused her, perhaps, to fear for Melissa's future with the man.

'He gives every impression of being happy,' Cristin said, turning away and setting about mixing their favourite salad dressing. 'They're good together. He seems crazy about her, does all the little things which show a man's in love with a woman. But . . . ' Her voice trailed off into silence.

'But to you it doesn't always ring quite true, and that troubles you.' He stopped what he was doing and went to her, laid a hand on her arm below the short sleeve of her peacock-blue summer dress.

'You're right, I don't quite trust him.' She turned and looked up at him, frown lines between her brows. 'Stupid, really, isn't it? Has to be, he's — '

'I've never known you do or think anything that was actually stupid. Tell me more about him. What's really behind that 'But' you came out with?'

Moving away from him Cristin folded her arms across the back of a chair at the table, leaned on them and cast her mind back over the times she had been with her son-in-law either by himself or with Melissa.

Trader waited without impatience. He knew her for one very perceptive lady; she was good about people, sympathetic, intuitive. And the reports he had received the previous day from one of his Bahrain agents had been interesting to an MI5 man such as himself. Nothing therein of crucial importance, but one or two pointers.

'Don't get me wrong, Matt.' Suddenly, Cristin was with him once more. 'I *like* Majed. He's a super bloke, he's cool and damned attractive. Besides, he makes Melissa happy which has him in superclass for me. *But.*'

'But, you don't like the feel of him, now and then?'

She nodded. 'It's just that sometimes I get this weird idea that, when the three of us are together, he's sort of *assessing* Melissa and me. Also, that he's laughing at us in some obscure way. As if he's looking in at us from another world. And, Matt, at those times it gives me the shakes. I feel afraid of him. You know? I get to thinking he's *against* us somehow.' Then she blinked, gave a small toss of the head as if to throw such black thoughts out of it. 'But then, you see, he smiles at me and it's all gone,' she went on almost apologetically. 'Majed is back as my utterly charming, clever son-in-law whom my daughter loves to bits and who gives every impression of feeling the same way about her.' Pushing herself upright she went to the refrigerator for the butter. 'So forget it,' she said. 'Let's eat.'

As they did so Trader soothed her fears, assuring her that surely all was well, reminding her that as a Palestinian married to an English girl and now domiciled and working in England, Majed Ansari would have passed through all the required security checks. Nevertheless, certain of the words Cristin had used stayed in his mind: 'gives every impression of' — 'he's sort of *assessing* us' — 'looking in at us from another world'. Strange turns of phrase to use of one's so recently — and so, *rapidly?* — acquired son-in-law?

'Tell me, how's his job going?' he asked. 'Doesn't Melissa get lonely with him having to be away from home so often? It goes with the job, of course, as IT troubleshooter for his company he has to — '

'I think she does, a bit. But there are only four places he has to stay overnight. And she's settled into her new job. Gets on well with her neighbours, too.'

194

'It can't be pleasant for her, though, being alone at night.' Trader knew those four places at which Ansari's job required him to stay over: Torquay, Bournemouth, Bristol, Hereford; as area inspector for his company he doubtless had plenty of work to do at each of them.

'I do worry a little about that. Specially after the burglar thing last Friday — '

'*What?*' Trader put down the wine glass he had just picked up. 'You didn't say, on the phone! Is she OK?'

Cristin's face registered both contrition and a touch of amusement as she looked across at him, 'Oh Lord! You had to go over to Amsterdam and were away for a couple of days, remember? So I guess I forgot to tell you when you got back. Melissa was here for the weekend, came up straight up from work and stayed over till Sunday. The thing could've turned out worse, I guess, but Majed — '

'What happened?' His fear for Melissa's safety quickly controlled, Trader relaxed physically but not mentally.

'It seems Majed was working in his study — '

'What time was this?'

'Latish, eleven maybe. He heard a suspicious noise outside — '

'Where, outside?'

'Crikey, how should I know? Look, stop interrupting and just *listen*. You asked, and I'm telling you. OK?'

'Sorry. Sure, OK. Go on, darling. I've lost the power of speech.'

'Temporarily, I hope?'

He smiled at her, loving her with his eyes. 'So do I,' he said.

'There isn't much to tell, in fact,' she went on. 'Majed went out to investigate — used the back door, hoping to take the noise-maker by surprise — and saw a bloke standing opposite the study window. Unfortunately — or fortunately, who knows? — said bloke heard him coming and took to his heels, ran across the lawn towards the front gate. Majed went after him, caught up with him by the sundial, tackled him and brought him down. But the intruder was first up, and took off like a bat out of hell, as they say. So Majed left it.' Coming to the end of her story Cristin sipped her wine, then set the glass down and searched Trader's face. After a moment she said quietly. 'Attempted burglaries are two-a-penny nowadays in that sort of area. Why do you want to know all this?'

'Has he reported it to the police?'

'No. I asked him that. He said it would be a waste of time since all he'd get would be a lot

196

of questioning, statements, and stuff, but they wouldn't be able to actually *do* anything as he didn't get a good look at the bloke, wouldn't be able to identify him.'

'But he told Melissa. That was a bit stupid, wasn't it? With him being away from home quite often, and regularly?'

'He said he told her in case some neighbour had heard the commotion that night. Better for him to tell her what actually happened, he said.'

But Trader's question had done what he wanted it to do. By changing the drift of the conversation he had avoided a repetition of her 'Why do you want to know all this?' question, so he was content.

Cristin did not repeat it; talk of their own affairs washed over it, drowning it.

★   ★   ★

At 8.30 the following evening, from the first-floor office of a safe-house pub near Oxford Circus, 'James' Mallory made a mobile-to-mobile call to Ansari. There was in him a degree of *schadenfreude*: as commander of SeaSnake Ansari's hand had been fairly heavy on him to date, and now for once Mallory was — according to the accepted rules of procedure within foreign-assisted operations, so far

197

as he was aware of them — as such 'on top', with Ansari the one who was out of order. And about to be called to account.

'Yes?' It was Ansari's voice.

'Viper.' He gave his code name.

'Secure here. Proceed,'

'Last Friday night, Ansari, you abused your authority by your actions; as captain of logistics I demand an apology — '

'*Enough!*' Whiplash fast, it stopped Mallory dead. But when Ansari went on his voice was quiet. 'Do not be a fool, my friend,' he said. 'An accusation like that, unless fully substantiated, can have fatal consequences. For the moment, because at this stage of SeaSnake I have great need of your expertise, I admit to exceeding my authority, but certainly not to abusing it. My actions that night were consistent with the requirements of the situation.'

'You and I are supposed to be working together as a team, yet without authorization you used two of *my* agents — sleepers, both of them — to organize and carry out the disposal of a body — '

'The prevailing circumstances demanded swift and secret action.' Ansari's interruption was incisive. 'Had the wounded man been found on my premises that night, SeaSnake itself might have been compromised by the

198

resulting police enquiries, might even have had to be aborted. Such possibilities are obvious and incontrovertible; it was on them that I based my decision to use your agents.'

Mallory shifted his ground slightly. 'I'm not questioning the act itself, I'm questioning the way you went about it. You should have informed me of the situation and requested my assistance in dealing with it: you don't have the right to give orders directly to my men.'

'You are wrong. In climactic emergencies, I do have that right. Consult your orders for this mission, Mallory. You will find there — '

'I know what I'll bloody well find! In furtherance of SeaSnake's operational matters, you're top gun. But to my mind there's more to terrorist ops than standing orders: there's an unwritten commitment to honour your co-ordinating cadres, Ansari. *You should not go over my head and give direct orders to my men!*'

Where I come from the mindset is not like that, Ansari thought. But then it was bound to be different, wasn't it? The cause Mallory and *his* kind fought for had lived through and derived its continuing strength from — what? — at most 200 years of bitter strife. While the cause he, Majed Ansari, and *his* kind fought for had lived through over a thousand years of

it, and their ethos was the harsher for it
— was more battle-hardened, more vulpine
and more devious.

'They did a good job that night, your two
sleepers.' Ansari had no intention of apologiz-
ing, but he judged it wiser to placate the
Irishman at this stage of SeaSnake. 'Their
response time was excellent, and they had
their plan worked out by the time they
arrived on the scene: the two of them would
sling the body in the boot of their vehicle,
drive to an area of London they knew well —
a lawless warren of a place, they told me
— and in a certain street would arrange
everything so that the intruder on my
property appeared to be the victim of a
mugging which had turned violent and
developed into a homicide. One of those men
of yours is ex-SAS, I gathered. Certainly it
was no problem to him to kill the
unconscious intruder there and then, give
him the swift death which leaves no sign of it
being intentional. Please compliment him on
my behalf — '

But there, Mallory cut the call.

★ ★ ★

Shakiri's house in Bahrain was an old, very
beautiful residence outside the village of

200

Janousan in the north of the island, two-storeyed and spacious. His three-acre property was enclosed by a white-painted wall banded on the inside by a broad swathe of date palms; between them and the dwelling, landscaped gardens pleasured the eye. His wife was daughter to a Qatari diplomat, and as a teenager had lived in England while her father was serving at his country's embassy there. The love of all growing things that blossomed in her during those years had stayed with her, and in the gardens of her married home she had created a lush paradise decorated with roses and hibiscus and bougainvillea and brillianced with the flashing life of exotic birds and butterflies. Nowadays, she found solace in the lovely place she had made: for many years now her husband had in all things lived his life apart from her, allowing her no part in it. A garden gives back to you all you put into it, and more, she thought in her loneliness, and counted her head gardener, an erudite horticulturalist, her friend as well as her henchman. A Syrian in his early forties, he loved her, and between them flowered a love which perforce remained platonic.

The ground floor of the house was given over to reception rooms, dining-room, and accommodation for senior staff; its upper floor was private to himself and his family. Now seated at his desk in his study there, he was reading through a report just received from Majed Ansari which had been decoded by his confidential aide-de-camp. It read thus.

1. No further action has been taken re incident three as reported previously therefore assume intruder NOT Brit Intelligence.
   ID of intruder remains untraced.
   Media coverage of incident: local, minimal, short-lived.
   Will continue to monitor this situation.

2. Preparations at target sites: all on schedule.

3. Reports from moles in place at target sites: all positions secure, no impediment to action identified to date.

4. Suicide bombers visited and tested by me personally at Training HQ.
   Assessment thereof: excellent (detailed individual reports attached).

   NB. For your personal attention: Accompanying personal report on logistics captain JAMES MALLORY (A-listed for decoding).

Your comments on same looked for at your convenience.

Coming to the end of the report Shakiri nodded his satisfaction with the information it contained, then put it aside and turned his attention to Ansari's data on Mallory, the IRA activist seconded to SeaSnake. As he read through it his gaunt frame stiffened with anger, for what Ansari described was indeed insubordination. In itself, such behaviour as that detailed was deplorable; that Ansari had suffered it from such a source was not to be tolerated. The offender must be severely disciplined, but not, naturally, before SeaSnake had been brought to a successful conclusion. Until then, it was imperative that Mallory be kept actively loyal.

After a little thought, Shakiri conceived a plan he felt sure would achieve that purpose.

★ ★ ★

Half past ten, and Trader was in his office catching up with paperwork when his phone rang — the yellow one, so he answered at once.

'Your caller gives the name Anderson, sir, Joe Anderson.' The monitoring officer on duty was a woman, she had a slight Scottish accent which Trader found very attractive.

'Right, put him through. Good of you to call, Mr Anderson. This line is scrambled so you may talk freely. What have you got for me?'

'Steve doesn't know I've contacted you.' Anderson was uptight: it showed in his voice, which came across the line loaded with doubt — also with what seemed to Trader a certain foreboding.

'You haven't told him I came to see you? He doesn't know you've — ?'

'Christ *no*! You said not, so I haven't. But with what's just happened, I think I'll have to.'

'What *has* happened?'

Anderson told him, his sentences short and sharp. As Trader listened, questions about what he was hearing formed thick and fast in his mind; grim-faced, he lined them up for later since Anderson was obviously desperate to get his story across because it was threatful stuff and he feared for Steve on account of it.

The facts Anderson then gave him registered hard and clear in Trader's brain. Steve had told Anderson that from his flashbacks of memory he'd learned that in 1994 he'd had a lover named Cristin Daley and, by her, a daughter called Melissa. Then, he'd found out that the girl Melissa, now

204

twenty-three years old, had recently married a Palestinian named Majed Ansari. Worried by this fact, Steve had hired a private detective, Sam Weaver, to run surveillance on Ansari at work and at home, and report his findings to him, Steven Court, at the end of each day. This, Weaver had done until, two days earlier, he had failed to telephone in as usual. Late that night Steve had called Weaver's office to check, met with his Ansaphone again and again so given up; had then called next morning, spoken to his two-hours-a-day typist and learned that he had not been home to his bachelor pad the previous night.

'Weaver's *vanished*, Mr Kingsmith,' Anderson said, the fear now plain in his voice. 'And then the police went round to Steve's place — '

'*Sent by who?*' Trader could not keep the questions bottled up, things were on the move, and dangerous.

'Not *sent*. Weaver's typist reported him missing, the police searched his records, found Steve listed as a recent and ongoing client of Weaver's — '

'He's a lone operator?'

'Yeah. Has access to a wide pool of operatives, some straight, others far from it, apparently.'

'Thank God he's not with a big firm. I'll

get on to this immediately, we'll take it over from the police.'

'So will Steve have to know I . . . betrayed him to you?'

Given the situation re possible terrorist strikes in Britain, Trader had no time for personal scruples, personal guilt. 'What you've done here is no *betrayal*, Mr Anderson,' he said. 'National security may be under threat. Get focused. I'll be in touch with you again.'

★   ★   ★

As Melissa preceded him into their sitting-room and flicked on subdued lighting, Ansari went across to the drinks cabinet in the far corner and poured out a long gin-sling for her and a weak whisky and soda for himself.

'That must have been a bore for you at times, darling, all those suits talking shop,' he remarked, as he carried the drinks across to her. 'Sorry there weren't many wives and girlfriends.'

'It wasn't boring at all, hardly any of the suits talked shop. I enjoyed the whole evening.' Sitting down on the *chaise-longue* by the curtained window she eased off her strappy gold sling-backs. They had been to a cocktail party given by Harry Garner, whom

206

Ansari had known while studying in London and who was now a non-executive director with the company Ansari worked for. They had stayed on to dine with him after the other guests had departed. 'Did *you* have to talk shop all the time?' Gathering together the skirts of her jade-green silk and chiffon dress, Melissa leaned back into the cushions behind her.

'Actually, tonight I was well pleased to talk shop.' Ansari sat down beside her. 'One of Harry's friends is head-hunting an IT specialist. Harry thinks I'm just the man for the job; he set this evening up for the two of us to meet.'

'What a thing, being head-hunted.' Melissa was smiling, pleased at the thought because Majed had been discontented of late, his present job was too routine, he said, it was beginning to bore him. 'Did he offer you anything?'

Ansari, of course, had no intention of changing his job. His suggestion to Garner that he was on the lookout for a move upwards had been a ploy to add substance to his persona as a newly-wed eager for any opportunity to make a progressive career move.

'Nothing was promised there and then, naturally,' he answered, 'but the omens are good.' Then he put down his glass. 'There's something I want to talk to you about, darling,' he said. 'You're not tired?'

Melissa smiled into his eyes. 'Never could get tired of talking with you.'

You little fool, Ansari thought, reaching out one hand to caress her arm. 'And I never tire of talking *about* you,' he said, feeling her skin warm under his hand, 'I want to know all about you — how you think and what you believe in, to know your mind and self as well as I know your body.' You young and lovely little fool, I'd like to take you to bed right now but — first things first.

'And I yours, Majed.'

As have several women before you, and as other women will after you have served your purpose, he thought, and withdrew his hand. Kept that train of thought out of his eyes and went on, 'I would like us to talk about your father — '

'We already have.' Suddenly she was frowning.

'Indeed we have, and that's partly the point, darling. You've told me the facts of it, but I still do not understand why you and your mother have gone on all these years refusing to let him back into your lives.'

'I don't see how I could put it more plainly than I've already done. To summarize and re-state: point one, he's a committed, active-service undercover terrorist hiding behind his day-job; and point two, since he left us he's not shown the slightest sign of wanting anything more to do with us. You don't know him, Majed, and I hope and pray you never will,' she added quietly.

Ansari let that pass. 'What really interests me is how — no, *why* he changed so dramatically that night his twin brother was executed by the IRA.' Getting to his feet he sipped his whisky then stood glass in hand, his head down. 'From all you've told me so far the two of them seemed very close, the way I understand identical twins often are, so for him the death of his brother must have been traumatic in the extreme.'

'My mother says it altered him . . . altered him *deep down*, changed his whole mindset in a way that made him want to be more like Sean.'

'Almost as if that way he could as such keep his brother alive.' Then suddenly a bizarre and half-formed possibility entered Ansari's head. Turning away from her he swiftly developed it into a complete scenario. Identical twins sometimes played tricks on people by pretending to be each other, did they not? So, what if in this case one of the Mallory twins had played the trick for real?

But why should he do that? demanded reason. Besides, how *could* he do it? It would almost certainly require the co-operation of the twin who was going to die, and plainly that was not —

'Finish your drink and take me to bed.' Slipping off the *chaise-longue* in a swirl of jade-green chiffon, Melissa went to him. 'I don't want James Mallory in our life and I'm damn sure you don't.'

But he's already in it, thought Ansari, as he put down his glass and took her in his arms. And much later that night, as she lay sleeping at his side, he decided it would be worthwhile to initiate a speculative search into the events of the night in 1994 during which Sean Mallory had met his death and his left-alive twin brother had *altered*, as Melissa's mother had put it, 'because he wanted to be more like Sean'.

8

29 June

Sitting in the back of an unmarked police car being driven to an arranged mid-morning meeting with MI6 officer Superintendent Martin Reever, Trader looked out at the crowded, lively London streets without his brain registering that vivid passing scene at all. He was harried by a sense of impending disaster, of a terrorist attack somewhere on his home territory already in the making, its climax possibly even imminent; and with that sense increasing every day that passed without his officers and informers discovering any solid reason for it, he had to decide how much of the present situation he should divulge to Reever.

He had known the MI6 officer, who was near retirement now, for many years; first as mentor, then as friend and, when called on, trusted adviser on professional matters. Now, he was about to seek his advice on — or to put it more honestly, his approval of — a certain course of action he was considering, a last-resort ploy which if successful would surely resolve all doubt regarding the truths of Majed Ansari's bona fides.

Their meeting took place in one of the small leafy squares still to be found in some areas of London. Often comprising little more than an acre of railed-in land, these are usually quiet places; within are lawns, flower beds, trees and blossom-giving shrubs, with wooden seats set back from the paths winding through them.

Arriving five minutes before the agreed time, Trader sat down in one corner of a seat on the far side of the square, pleased to have grass and flowers around him and the sun shining. Early birds get the best seats, he thought inanely, then caught sight of Reever coming along the path towards him, the wiry dark-suited figure striding along purposefully, grey-haired head bent. Reever looked up and saw him, quickened his pace, raised a hand in greeting.

'Good morning to you, Matt,' he said, sitting down beside Trader. 'What's on your mind?'

So there with the sun shining on them and a bed of yellow roses in full bloom opposite them across the path, Trader related to Martin Reever the story behind the twin Mallory brothers, Cristin Daley, her daughter Melissa and her recently acquired son-in-law

Majed Ansari. The MI6 man was a good listener: when the narrative was presented as straight fact he stayed quiet and let it run, sure that everything Trader put forward was exactly as stated, no more and no less. When the account digressed into supposition or personal opinion he often interrupted with probing, sometimes caustic questions. From time to time people passed by them, men, women, and young children, some of them leisurely, some in purposeful haste. Once, a passing small boy miskicked his scarlet football — it struck Trader on the shin and he picked it up then as the boy came towards him after it, tossed it back to him.

'So you've mapped out the towns Ansari spends time at in the course of his job, and surveillance has provided you with the timing and duration of those visits of his and, in some cases, with information on the contacts he makes outside office hours,' Reever observed thoughtfully, as Trader sat back, silent. But then he turned to him, sliding one arm along the back of the seat. 'Why have you told me all this, Matt?'

He had to wait for his answer. Trader sat quiet for a full minute, considering. Then all he said was, 'There's enough in it to make a bloke suspicious, seems to me.'

Reever's lined, severe face broke into a

grin. 'I'd say it's a fair guess that old intelligence hands like you and I would find their minds moved to a degree of suspicion,' he agreed. But the grin swiftly faded. 'I ask you again, Matt: why have you told me?' he persisted, dark-blue eyes invasive, searching Trader's.

What are old friends for, if you can't trust them with . . . if not exactly your life, with all the things in it that you hold dear? 'I love the lady,' he said.

Reever smiled at him. But all he said was, 'And you want me to tell you how I would proceed were I living, like you are, in the middle of the situation you've just outlined to me.'

'Got it in one. Thought you would,' Trader said. Then added sombrely, 'I need moral back-up, Martin. Honest moral back-up in a situation fraught with ethical highways and byways.'

But Reever did not find it easy. Sitting in the sunshine with his head bent in thought, he isolated and assessed the implications and ramifications of the information Trader had given him. There were too many unquantifiable risks involved for his liking, too many not-quite-proven assumptions in Trader's given scenario. Yet at the same time there were, undeniably, strong grounds for suspicion in it all: grounds which sketched in a picture so threatful as to make it near criminal to take no action?

'I think I know how you would like to handle this,' he said finally.

'I'm sure you do. You've always been able to read me like an open book, you bastard.' Trader looked up at the sky, narrowing his eyes against its brilliance. 'And many's the time I've been glad of that,' he added quietly. 'It saved my life once, remember?'

Reever waved it away. 'That was in the course of a single, straight-down-the-line operation. This one's different: this one's iceberg stuff, bits of it can be seen above the surface, but God knows what's lurking below the water-line. I don't like the sound of Ansari. This could land you in deep shit, Matt, if it goes wrong.'

'But look at t'other side of that coin. If I'm right, but don't do anything about it, how many people might die because I failed to act? I'd rather take the putative shit than have to live with the answer to that.'

'I'm with you there.' Reever stood up, ran a hand through his thatch of grey hair. 'I suggest we repair to the pub I passed on my way here, it's just round the corner,' he went on. 'Over a glass I'll tell you how I'd handle it, and you can see how it fits in with your line of thinking.'

Over beer and ham sandwiches Reever laid out the course of action he would take were he wanting to discover — covertly, of course — more about Ansari's activities and contacts in the cities he stayed at overnight on business. And Trader found that, as he'd expected, the MI6 man's ideas on the best way to achieve that aim coincided with his own.

'You'd better get to work on this fast, Matt,' Reever said, as they parted outside the pub, his eyes moody, haunted by inner fears and memories. 'If Ansari *is* here on a terrorist mission . . . Well, he's already been here several months so suppose the groundwork for an op had been completed before he arrived — lines of communication established and secure, *matériel* assembled and ready for use — then it's only too appallingly possible that the strike's close to climax. Don't waste time.'

Calling Cristin that afternoon, Trader asked if he could come and visit her that same day. And *yes*, he told her when she asked, it was very urgent and very important indeed. As he put away his mobile he gave thanks that it was her day off; he would be with her by teatime and together they could work out something so that she could go down and stay with Melissa the next night

216

Ansari would be away from home on one of his business stopovers.

* * *

Superintendent Reever called Trader the next day. 'Via the good offices of a friend of mine,' he said, 'I've dug wide and deep into Ansari's times in the UK. Didn't find anything really important, but there was one lead that might be worth following up if it's new to you. In 1997, when he was on a two-year course at a London college offering advanced electronics and IT, he developed a close friendship with a Lebanese gentleman by the name of Hamed Mansoor. That friendship has continued up to the present day, and, in 1998 Mansoor was convicted for money laundering with terrorist connections to Iran and Syria. He escaped custody last year, present whereabouts unknown. No big deal there, but it does show that at least one friend of Ansari's was involved in terrorist activities, does it not?'

* * *

Ansari kept fully detailed plans of the four strikes which together comprised SeaSnake double-locked in the bottom drawer of his desk in the study at Hillsdown. That evening,

217

as was his habit on returning from one of the overnight trips his job entailed, after dinner at home with Melissa he spent an hour or so checking through those plans to up-date the data they contained in the light of new knowledge acquired during his time away. He brought his desk keys with him — they were kept in a secret small recess behind a sliding panel at the back of the bureau in the sitting-room — and now opened the bottom drawer.

Inside it lay a pile of A4 soft-cover files, each of a different colour. Lifting out the top four he placed them in front of him and worked through them one by one. Written in English, each had the name of one of SeaSnake's target cities printed on its cover, and contained a fully detailed summary of the action plan for its named city — only the identities of its active personnel were encoded. All except one consisted of three pages of closely typed notes; the exception was the one referring to the attack on Tollgate Garage on the outskirts of Hereford which, since it required armed-assault personnel in addition to a suicide bomber, ran to four pages.

Rapidly, Ansari updated each of the four files in accordance with information he had received during his latest inspection trip. That done, he pushed aside those files, and took out the fifth from the bottom of the drawer. On its scarlet cover a white sticker identified its contents in black capitals:

OPERATION SEASNAKE
ACTIVE LIST

He did not open it at once. Laying it down in front of him he leaned back and ran his mind over SeaSnake's action as summarized in the files he had just annotated: Torquay, the bar at the biggest hotel laid waste by a suicide bomber; Bournemouth, the auditorium of the Odeon Cinema brought to screaming chaos and destruction by another two martyrs; Templemeads Rail Station in Bristol, devastated by two others of The Chosen — brothers those two were, sons of a noted fanatic who presently had three more such being prepared. And at Tollgate Garage on the fringes of the deep-country city of Hereford — the armed assault strike he himself would take part in, as would Mallory — one more martyr who, as soon as his comrades had blasted their way through its premises, would detonate his bomb on its forecourt.

So, SeaSnake was on course. Good. A narrow-lipped smile on his face, Ansari opened the scarlet-covered file in front of him on his desk. The four pages it contained carried encoded information. Neatly centred on each was a rectangular block of figures and letters printed small, compactly, and without spacing of any kind. But he only leafed through it — he knew all that was written therein by heart. The file with the scarlet cover named each and every agent engaged in SeaSnake, and gave full details of both his personal and his business life.

★　★　★

Later that night Ansari took an emergency call from the leader of the team of agents he had sent to Ulster to investigate the events surrounding and during the execution of Sean Mallory in 1994.

'This is probably no more than a bit of moonshine, sir,' his agent said, 'but I've come upon an old story, a rumour really, that I think you should hear.'

'From more than one source?'

'No. One only, and could be he's not to be trusted, I couldn't rule that out. But there's something in what he says he saw on the night in question which corroborates what I learned from someone else — '

'Give me the gist of it.'

'That in '94 Sean Mallory escaped execution.'

'And?'

'Was picked up, nursed back to health, fled to London and built himself a new life.'

'Doing what?'

'No one here knows — or if they do, they're not telling and for sure never will. Do you want me to follow up on this?'

Ansari was silent for a moment, thinking things through.

'No,' he said then, 'No further action required; return to base.'

★　★　★

As a result of his discussion with Reever, Trader was a man in a hurry. His old friend's robust reaction to the Ansari story had added fuel to his own suspicions and fears that Majed Ansari had had ulterior motives in marrying Melissa.

Reaching Cristin's house on the outskirts of Holme Lacey just after four o'clock that Wednesday he found her picking strawberries at the side of the house. She looked up as he called her name.

'You got here fast!' she cried, putting down her almost full bowl of fruit and going to him, flushed and smiling. 'I'd planned on greeting

221

you arrayed in silk and smelling of roses but — ' Seeing his set face she broke off. 'What's the matter?' she asked, quietly, tensely.

'Come inside, Cristin. We have to talk.'

'*Melissa* — is she all right?'

Trader took her in his arms. 'She's fine,' he said, kissed her hard then stood back. 'This is about the job I'm working on, not her.'

'We're mixed up in it, though, aren't we? Melissa and I, we're involved in it some-how — '

'You are. That's what I've come to talk to you about.' Picking up the bowl of strawberries he took her hand and led her towards the house.

'No, Matt. Not inside.' On the terrace she pulled her hand free of his. 'From your expression I'd rather stay outside in the sunshine,' she said, and sat down in one of the chairs at the garden table where terrace met lawn.

Taking a chair facing her, he was silent for a moment, his eyes loving her: her blonde hair catching sunlight, the sea-green eyes anxious, questioning.

'If it's about you, I want to know everything you know,' she said to him tightly. 'Don't keep bits of what's going on from me like you did with that drugs case last year, saying afterwards that it was better for me not to know — *safer*, you said. You risk your life sometimes, working in anti-terrorism, and if there's danger in what you're doing I want to be right in there with you. I need to know *why*, to *understand*. It's part of your life, Matt, so it's part of you and I . . . Don't shut me out. Please don't do that.'

It was the nearest she had ever come to saying she actually wanted to live with him and for a moment it drove everything else out of his head. He reached for her hand where it lay on the table. 'Cristin, I've always wanted — '

'That's for later. Now is for telling me what brought you up here in such a hurry.' Nevertheless she closed her fingers around his hand, drew it to her and brushed her lips across it before releasing it and sitting back, eyeing him steadily.

So get on with what you have to say, Kingsmith: *do it!* Slamming back his chair, Trader stood up and turned away, knowing he had got to go on accepting the fact that the Jamie Mallory Cristin remembered still held her from him — and also, that he would find it easier to declare his truths about her son-in-law to her if he couldn't see her face.

'*Tell me*, darling.' Her voice was quiet from behind him and there was a lot of love in it.

223

He was not ready to look her in the eyes yet but he got it said, stark little words to make absolutely clear to her certain facts.

'I believe Majed Ansari married Melissa for the sole purpose of entering Britain under cover to carry forward a terrorist operation against this country,' he said.

For a split second then it seemed to Cristin that warmth went out of the summer air and sunlight lost its life-brilliance because terrorism had come into her sweet beloved garden and it had come for her. Then the world slid back into focus: the air *was* honey-sweet, the sunshine *was* golden-bright.

'I realized earlier that you had suspicions about him,' she said evenly. 'Do you mean they're certainties now?'

'No, they're not certainties, but they have been strengthened. That's why I'm here today.'

'Please, explain. And come back and sit down while you're doing it,' she added with forced lightness. 'Your back's very nice but I like your front better.'

Trader turned to her then, but he made no move to sit down. He was engrossed in working out how best to phrase his coming assault on her loyalties; he had to admit it would be no less than that.

'I need your help,' he said, across the space

between them, 'MI5 suspicions — mine alone, mostly, but recently given a little more credence by surveillance reports — have hardened. But they are still no more than suspicions and, as such, do not empower my department to take action against those we suspect. To do that we need *factual proof* that a mission is being planned. Well, so far we don't have it. And, Cristin, there is only one way I can think of which might access that for us. If it's there, of course.'

'*If* it's there.' Her bright head was down.

'Yes.' What else was there to say? He wished she would look up at him so that she might see in his face his probity in all this, his good faith.

But she did not. ''Action against those you suspect'.' She repeated what he'd said slowly, giving it weight; then suddenly looked up at him. 'Say it plain, Matt!' she said sharply. 'Do you *really believe* Majed is a terrorist?'

Now he wished she had not looked at him because there was a coldness in her eyes that distanced him from her. Put the words on the table, he ordered himself. *You have to do that. Now.*

'I do. I believe Ansari is a terrorist and that he has been, and is, involved in the planning of a terrorist strike in this country.'

'Dear God.' She looked down again, and

Trader was glad of it.

'He doesn't love her. He never has,' he said.

'But she loves him.'

Her voice bitter and despairing, but Trader rejoiced to hear it so because it meant she was turning against Ansari. 'Cristin, his courtship of her, the marriage — the whole thing was engineered to have him appear innocently resident here in England, new wife, new job — '

'You say. But is it true?'

'It's the truth.'

'Swear it — '

'You need that, *from me?*'

His flare of anger burned into her. 'Forgive me,' she said. 'It's . . . difficult.' Then she leaned back in her chair, raised her face to the sun, closed her eyes and was silent, her arms hanging loose at her sides. Trader sat down again and watched over her with love, intuiting that she already had some idea of the nature of the help he was going to ask of her and was clearing her mind and spirit ready to learn more and dare to work with him against Ansari.

After a few moments she sat forward again, her eyes seeking his and alight now with determination.

'Tell me what I have to do to help you,' she

said. 'But first answer this question: is there any suggestion that Melissa is involved in whatever it is Majed's doing?' She grimaced, then added softly, 'Christ, what a sad thing to have to ask about one's own daughter.'

'Sad, yeah, sure. But you need to know, and the answer's no, she is not.'

She smiled — a little. Turned away from him to look over her garden. 'Go on then, Matt.'

'Right. Here it is. I believe Ansari is masterminding an op here in England. I've no idea what form it will take, when it's planned to climax, or what or where its target is, but from the fact that the job he was parachuted into over here requires him to travel regularly to certain cities, at four of which he stays overnight, I think it's possible that it comprises several separate hits, one at each of those overnight stopovers. Whether or not I'm right about that, one fact remains more or less indisputable: he'll have in his keeping documentation recording the location of his targets; and details of the personnel, logistics, timing and so on of each strike.'

'Documentation? Wouldn't it be more likely he'd store such information on a computer?'

'I don't think so. Too dangerous, too

vulnerable: hacking in is highly sophisticated nowadays, and hard drives don't keep secrets from experts.'

Cristin sat quiet; first getting her head round what she already perceived as the inevitable conclusion to all he had told her, then *accepting* that conclusion, together with all its implications for herself.

'It's all right, Matt,' she said finally, when she was sure of herself. 'I'll do it. If I can, and with your help and advice, I'll do it.'

Trader looked at her and for a moment their eyes held, each acknowledging total commitment to the other. Then he grinned, shook his head.

'You are one amazing lady and I love you beyond all things,' he said to her.

'You want me to go into Majed's study and search for that documentation, don't you?' she said, planting both elbows on the table and resting her chin on her clasped hands.

'I do. I thought of putting it to Melissa but — '

'Thank God you didn't. She's besotted with him, wouldn't have believed a word against him. Might even have told him the whole thing, which would have been a disaster. What I don't see, though, is — suppose I do find stuff like that . . . well it'd be no good stealing any papers, Majed would — '

'You photograph them. We've got miniature high-tech cameras that will suit. Of course it'll take time but we'll plan for that. Our real problem will be access.'

'No difficulty there, I think. His study's never locked — it'd look distinctly odd if it were, wouldn't it, in his own home? When he's out he leaves the keys to his desk in a so-called secret place in another room which Melissa told me about once.'

'*All* his desk keys are there? You mean you'll be able to open any locked drawer in his desk?'

Cristin nodded. 'Surely. And Majed's often away over Friday nights — you know that, it's why since that attempted burglary at their place I often go down then and stay with her.' She frowned. 'How soon do you want this done, Matt? You're in a hurry, I think?'

Reaching across the table he took her hand in his. 'Today's Wednesday. Can you make it this weekend? Because could be we've no time to waste. I can't know that for sure, but later might be too late. Too late for God knows how many people.'

'Majed will be away this Friday *and* Saturday night; there's a conference he has to attend. Melissa rang me a couple of days ago and asked me to go down then but I said I couldn't make it. Well, I can now. I'll fix it at work and call her tonight, tell her. She'll be pleased. How long will this photography take? If there's anything to photograph, that is?'

'If you don't find what you're looking for ten minutes should cover it, just enough to make a thorough search. But if you *do* hit pay-dirt it could take up to an hour or more. It'll depend on — '

'*If I* hit *pay-dirt.*' Suddenly very still, she stared at him; and he saw in her eyes a certain doubt as, now, she fully comprehended the appalling horror of the terrorism-in-the-making which, acting as Trader's catspaw, she would *if he was right* uncover at her daughter's home.

'Cristin. I honestly believe that everything I have told you about this is true,' he said. As he spoke there came in him a feeling, a *belief* that this undertaking was to be a catalyst in their long relationship: that if she changed her mind now and refused to act with him in this, something, some vital quality in that relationship — he couldn't find a name for it but knew he would give his all to keep it alive — would wither and die away out of his love for her. Whereas if she went with him, it would show that she was willing to share fully in his way of life and therefore — surely? — would give him hope that very soon she would live with him, marry him.

230

'So, I'll allow for it taking at least an hour,' Cristin said, smiling at him. And Trader knew then that his love for her remained intact — no, more; it was enhanced beyond his dream of it.

9

Hendon, Westside Country Club, Saturday afternoon, 4.00 p.m.

'Your daughter should've won that, you know,' Melissa's next-door neighbour remarked, turning to Cristin as she stood up, smoothing the creases out of the calf-length skirt of her elegant sharkskin summer two-piece. 'She's the better player by far, obviously.'

'Plenty of style and flair but lacks the killer-instinct, that's Melissa's trouble.' And not only in tennis, either, Cristin added in the privacy of her mind, slightly annoyed with her daughter for losing in the Ladies Singles Final at her local tennis club. Its four courts — two grass, two *en-tout-cas* — were situated along the south perimeter of the grounds and now, as she and Natalie Morton made their way to the clubhouse to meet Melissa for tea after she had showered and changed, she listened politely as her neighbour regaled her with the latest gossip.

Forty-two years of age, outgoing and sophisticated, Natalie was married to a wealthy entrepreneur considerably older than

232

herself. Articulate and shrewd, she possessed a quirky sense of humour and a sometimes cruelly witty tongue. She was fun to be with, but, as they walked along the well-tended paths, Cristin listened to her with the surface of her mind only, contriving to laugh in the right places and come up with a leading question when a silence threatened. Beneath that surface, sombrely, her mind was brooding over what she planned to do a couple of hours later. For, after the leisurely tea together, the plan was for Melissa to follow Natalie home in her own car to a meeting there of the local theatrical Society, scheduled to start at six o'clock and last for at least two hours. Meanwhile Cristin was to walk to Melissa's house just over a mile away. 'No, I don't want you dropping me off before you go on to Natalie's,' she'd said earlier, rejecting her daughter's offer, 'I need the exercise, I really do,' Later on she would get a light supper ready for herself and Melissa around 8.30.

I'll do us a Spanish omelette and salad, she thought, walking smooth-raked gravel at Natalie's side, comfortable in her blue linen trouser suit; that'll give me plenty of time to do what I have to do. Time to get Matt's neat little digital camera from my locked suitcase upstairs, take the keys to Majed's desk, then go into his study, open the drawers in his desk and —

'Indoors, or outside?' Natalie asked, halting at the edge of the broad terrace running the length of the many-windowed bar inside the clubhouse.

'Outside would be nicer. Let's go in the shade, over on the far side.' Stay anchored in the real world till it's time for you to leave it for a while, Cristin counselled herself, leading the way to a table for four she had spotted beneath the big sycamore shading the opposite side of the terrace. But then, suddenly she was engulfed in a rush of sheer terror because which *was* the real world? This one of sunshine and club tennis tournaments and afternoon tea, or the one where he was 'Trader', not Matt? Trader's world, which had her son-in-law Majed in its sights as a terrorist engaged in a mission against her country —

'You all right, Cristin?' Beside her, Natalie laid a hand on her arm, concerned for her.

'Yes. Of course I am.' Realizing she had stopped dead in her tracks and was standing stiff and still in the grip of the utter horror of her thoughts she caged them tight, shook the beautifully manicured hand off her arm and walked on. 'I was just wondering which table would be best . . . '

It was cool beneath the sycamore. In the light summer breeze, sunshine filtering down between its leaves cast light-and-dark shimmering patterns on the paving of the terrace. The two women chatted together until Melissa joined them, young and lovely in a sleeveless shift dress of jade-green linen, her hair slicked back from her face, still damp from the shower — and telling them she had ordered tea and cakes on her way through. A few minutes later a waiter arrived with a loaded tray, and when he had gone they drank tea to the toast 'You can't win 'em all, all the time'. Then, laughing, Melissa said, 'I'm glad Majed wasn't here to see me lose' and they joked that she played better tennis than he did, anyway. But Cristin perceived that even as her daughter laughed, a certain disquiet slid in behind her eyes as she spoke her husband's name; and seeing it, she recalled that, to her, Majed had seemed somehow different just recently. Different as in self-assertive, even arrogant towards both Melissa and herself. Also, from time to time, his manner towards Melissa had betrayed an offhand impatience which, after a moment, he quickly smoothed over.

'If you stayed an extra night, Cristin,' Natalie said, 'you could come to our barbecue with Melissa and Majed. My husband's eldest son and his wife will be with us and I'd love you to meet them . . . '

So easily the talk flowed that afternoon at the club where Melissa and Majed played tennis. With effort, Cristin masked both her unease regarding her daughter's happiness and the nervous tension in her which increased as the hour drew near when she must begin the betrayal — she could think of no other word for it — the devious, profound betrayal of the man her daughter loved and was married to. She felt no guilt regarding what she was about to do, felt only regret, a certain fear and a terrible sadness because even if Matt was wrong and she found nothing that incriminated Majed, thereafter she would never be sure of him: the doubt would always be in her so she would never be able to take him to her heart.

Soon after 5.30 Natalie and Melissa went off to the car-park together then drove away to their meeting, each in her own car. At the same time Cristin made her way through the club's grounds then out on to the road, and set off at a brisk walk for her daughter's home. As she went, there came in her a calm self-confidence. Soon now I'll know the truth about Majed, she thought. Thank God for Matt in my life. He would never lie to me, any more than I would lie to him: we both would stake our lives on that. Smiling to herself at the beautiful simplicity of the way it was between them, she quickened her pace.

Majed Ansari's house (for Cristin at that time, Melissa was no part of what she was doing) stood bathed in early evening sunshine. Going in through the front gate she closed it behind her, walked swiftly along the path, passed by the sundial and went in through the front door using the key her daughter had given her. As she put it down on the hall table she caught sight of her reflection in the mirror above it and stood transfixed, staring at her own face. *Thief*, she whispered to it, and caught her breath, momentarily ashamed of what she was about to attempt, sneak-thief come to steal the soul out of a man. Then the world swung back into place and faith in herself returned. If Matt was right, *Majed* is the thief in this situation, she told herself; and there came in her a baleful hatred of the man Melissa had married. Because she believed that Matt *was* right: Majed Ansari was a terrorist, a practioner of the arrogant, life-despising pitiless credo she had loathed *and feared* ever since she became old enough to think for herself. That revulsion had been against the IRA, for her personified by Sean Mallory, its most violent disciple known to her. A quick shiver shot through her at the memory of him, then she dismissed him from her mind. Go find the truth of *this* man, she told herself, and hurried on through the house.

She encountered no problems. The camera Trader had provided was ready to be collected from her suitcase in the spare room; the keys to Majed's desk lay in their place in the bureau in the sitting-room; and when she took them into her son-in-law's study the required key slid smoothly into the lock of the bottom drawer of his desk. Pulling open the drawer she saw inside it a small pile of soft-covered files. The top one had a white sticker on its scarlet cover and on this was printed in large black capitals:

OPERATION SEASNAKE
ACTIVE LIST

Lifting this one out she opened it and began to do what Trader had asked of her . . .

★ ★ ★

On the afternoon of that same day Mallory and Majed Ansari were sitting facing each other across a table in the studio of a safe house on the outskirts of a village in Sussex owned and lived in by a long-time artist friend of Mallory's, an Irishman who had never committed himself formally to the IRA, but who unremittingly travelled with them in his soul. With most of the floor space given over to artists' paraphernalia, the table was tucked into one corner. Between the two men stood a bottle of Irish whiskey, two glasses and a cut-glass carafe of water. Coming to the end of the plans for the armed assault and car-bombing at Tollgate Garage which they had been discussing, Ansari looked across at Mallory.

'Tell me, are you satisfied with your part in this operation?' he asked him.

The question came quietly, and the voice carried no particular overtones. Nevertheless, as Mallory met and held the dark eyes he perceived in them a certain longing which he had not previously been aware of: a hunger he understood, a hunger which lived in him also and which suddenly made them brothers under the skin — bizarrely, in the light of the jealous rivalry that lay between them.

He smiled. 'You're itching to be there, aren't you?' he said softly. 'We'll build into a very good partnership, you and I; I can see it now.'

Abruptly, Ansari's manner changed. Putting down his glass he sat forward and looked sharply across at Mallory.

'SeaSnake is not the format I would choose

were I masterminding an operation; multiple attacks each on a relatively small scale — that has never been my preferred option.'

'It has its advantages, though.' Carefully, wondering where such talk was leading, Mallory followed the change of subject. 'The shock factor it generates hits several areas of the target country, not just one — '

'None of its advantages compares with the extreme national and international impact of one massive strategically-aimed assault which produces truly monstrous casualties.'

'Like nine-eleven.'

'That was in a class of its own. But we can all dream, can we not?' Getting to his feet Ansari began to prowl around the room, a certain excitement in his voice and body-language as he went on. 'The organization my group is affiliated to has a big operation in the planning stages, Mallory. Its groundwork has been in progress for two years now. Climax is scheduled for 2009.'

'What level of destructive potential?'

'Treble all SeaSnake's put together.'

'Target?'

'Heathrow, and all of London that lies below its flight-paths. A worthwhile target, is it not?' he added softly, sliding it across Mallory's silence, questing.

Mallory looked up at him and Ansari liked

what he saw in that handsome face.

'Are *you personally* involved in that mission?' asked the Irishman.

'I am.'

'Why have you told me this?'

'Because you can be part of it.' Ansari had stopped his pacing and now stepped closer to Mallory. 'It is a mission which will resonate across your world as well as mine; any true terrorist would give his eye teeth to be part of it,' he added, an exaltation in him.

'If that's so, why me?'

'For the same reasons you and your cadre were chosen by us for SeaSnake as our logistics experts and local executants: because our research proved the high quality of your past work and because of your contacts within Britain, the fact that you and your comrades are already well established here.'

'And what's in it for me apart from the kudos attached?' Mallory's eyes were diamond-hard.

Sitting down again Ansari hooked one arm over the back of his chair, looked across at him. 'For you, there would be direct action,' he said. 'I shall be commander of one of the mission-sections in what is to come. I choose my own combat teams, and I would like to have you with me.'

'In what capacity?'

Knowing what he wanted, Ansari promised it to him. 'Leader of one of my four six-man assault units.'

'Then I'd be glad to.'

Ansari nodded, sat square to the table again. 'Good. I will contact my chief of operations in Bahrain and request his confirmation.'

'Is there any question of it?'

'The final decision on all such matters is his.' Ansari relaxed. 'Have you time now for us to discuss our Heathrow — *spectacular* is the word, if I remember rightly?'

'Best to leave it until I've received that confirmation. Meanwhile, tell me this: after SeaSnake, what do you intend to do about your wife?'

Ansari stiffened. 'What is that to you?'

'I'm interested to see how you handle these things.'

After a moment's deliberation, Ansari decided to tell him enough of the truth to satisfy him.

'Immediately after SeaSnake's climax I shall return to Bahrain, where all trace of Majed Ansari will be lost to the outside world,' he said. 'As for my wife . . . I think you know the answer to that, Mallory.'

He nodded, but probed deeper. 'Why do you want her dead? It seems . . . unnecessary.

And unnecessary fatalities can cause trouble.'

The Palestinian took his time to answer; half turning in his chair, he sat staring out of the window. Mallory folded his arms and waited without overt impatience, feeling certain that when he got his answer it would be the truth — a truth, at least, though not necessarily the whole of it.

'When I was ordered to sweet-talk and then marry the girl, I thought little of it,' Ansari said when he was ready. 'These things are needed sometimes. Meeting her, I found she was young and attractive — sexual attraction between us was immediate. And her personality pleased me as I got to know her. I found her intelligent, well informed and articulate. Also, she fell deeply in love with me and that is . . . very pleasant for a man.'

Again Mallory waited for him to go on, but he did not; so, after a moment, discovering himself quite interested in the situation though not particularly in the people concerned in it, he moved the conversation on himself.

'Then the two of you married and settled here in England,' he said. 'So have things deteriorated? Does she bore you now? Sexually?'

'No, she does not bore me, sexually or otherwise.' Ansari turned to face him and

243

Mallory saw in his eyes a kind of . . . ? He sought for the right words, found them, instinctively rejected them, but then realizing they were the only ones reflecting a brutal reality, accepted them: passionate *hatred*.

'I want her out of my life,' Ansari went on harshly. 'I find myself in danger of desiring to stay with her and live her kind of life, and that is a state of affairs I will not tolerate. I will live my life as a terrorist devoted to the Islamist cause. For me, that is the purpose of living, there is no other way to be truly alive.' He sat back. Said quietly, 'So, make it easy for me, Mallory. As soon as SeaSnake is done, kill her for me.'

He saw the Irishman look at him with comprehension, heard him say he would arrange for the thing to be done when the time came. Then, having agreed on a meeting place for the following afternoon, they left the house, and each went his separate way.

★ ★ ★

That evening, as arranged, Trader called Reever on his mobile.

'She got what you sent her for?' The MI6 man did not bother with preliminary chat, he wanted in on developments in the Ansari case and was hot for news of it.

244

'Up to a point.'

'So presumably you got something.'

'She got enough to make it clear that a four-pronged operation over here is in the planning.'

'What went wrong, Matt?'

'She opened up a locked drawer in his desk, saw five files in there. The top one had a sticker on it saying it was the active list for an op code-named SeaSnake; and stickers on the other four each named a town in southern England. The active list file contained four pages of encoded information, and she photographed those. Then she found that the other files, each of which presumably had contained details of the strike at the town named on its cover, were absolutely empty.'

'Good God! *All* of them? Every bloody one?'

'That's right. Ansari must have taken their contents with him, needed them at the towns he'd be visiting.'

'Those target towns, Matt. Their names again, please.'

'Torquay, Bournemouth, Bristol, Hereford.'

'*Christ Almighty.*' Reever's voice was a horror-struck whisper. 'And we're in the dark about the timing of the attacks, the ancillary personnel, assault strategies and so on. You took the situation upstairs, Matt? To Stoddart and co?'

'Sure. But they want more evidence; won't move in any big way unless and until I come up with more.'

'So our next step's obvious, isn't it? You have to have more info, and it's a fair bet the only way we'll come by it is by accessing the contents of those other four files. So that girl of yours will have to have another go, won't she. I only hope she's got the bottle to — '

'She's all set for it. On Monday, Melissa and Ansari are going up to Town — some big dinner he doesn't want them to miss — so Cristin's driving down then and will stay over for a couple of days. It's been arranged for ages. Ansari doesn't like leaving the house empty overnight since that burglary scare they had. Lucky for us, eh? Means we're in with a chance.'

'The sort of luck one dreams of.'

'Usually to find it remains the stuff of dreams.'

'Hopefully not so in this case.'

'Meanwhile, we should get something from those encoded pages soon. I sent them for decoding but Simon just called, said it's going to be a tough one to crack.'

10

Monday 7 August

At his desk in his central London office Trader pushed aside the report he had been reading, folded his arms and thought about Cristin. Already she would be with 'Lissa and there was surely danger in what she planned to do this second time. Why the hell had he let her do it?

Slamming back his chair, he stood staring down at his desk and told himself the truth: Cristin wasn't about to try to steal Ansari's secrets again because he had let her; she was doing it because now she'd had *proof* that her son-in-law was a terrorist and had 'used' and was continuing to use her daughter in furthering his undercover terrorist agenda. She was afire with fury and an elemental desire and intention to defeat and then destroy him: to discover that terrorist agenda of his, by fair means or foul, so that it could be used to annihilate not only his mission but also the man himself. And now Trader recalled her face as she had given an answer to him when he'd asked her — as a supplicant almost — if she would consider having a second go at photographing Ansari's documents. She'd told him she had already planned how to do it. As she spoke, he'd seen his real Cristin — and had understood on a deeper level her fierce determination to follow whatever path she had chosen to its end however bitter that end might turn out to be. Exactly as, years ago now, she had acted about James Mallory. Having refused to marry him unless he turned his back on the IRA, she had stood firm on that one point until he couldn't stand it any longer and had walked out on her and Melissa.

The red phone on his desk shrilled and he answered it, his mind immediately back in his office.

'Gold here. We've cracked that code, Matt. Shit, it was a devil, but we're — '

'*Give*, Simon.' Trader spun his chair round and sat down. Simon Gold, bossman in coding, had as requested afforded top priority to deciphering the four pages of encoded material in Ansari's file, and Trader was avid for its plain text.

'You'll like it, Matt, damn sure you'll like it. A copy of the complete thing is already on its way to you by secure messenger, but you asked me to let you know pronto should the name Ansari figure in the text, so I'm telling you now — *it does*. Prominently. The text names the A-class agents involved in the SeaSnake mission.'

'Thanks, Simon. I'll catch up on that when I get your transcript but right now I'd better — '

'Wait on, boy, wait on!' The two men were roughly the same age but Gold had called Trader 'boy' since a particular incident many years earlier and it had become a sort of joke between them but at that moment it annoyed Trader, he hadn't the time for it.

'*What?*' he demanded tersely.

'Something that'll have you pulling your finger out sharpish. There's a man named in that text as active in SeaSnake who both you and I have had serious truck with in the past, but who's contrived to stay off our action-required radar for years. You got time to hear his name?'

'Yeah, sure. I'd very much like to hear it, as you well know.'

'It's Mallory,' Harry Gold said. 'James Mallory, code-named Viper.'

★ ★ ★

Trader received Simon Gold's decoded transcript of the contents of Ansari's active list file at 11.30 and at once he put aside the memo he was reading and gave it his full attention. It ran thus:

Operation SeaSnake. Location: England. Targets; as listed individually in separate files. Overall commander: Sheikh Shakiri (operations USA, Spain, Afghanistan). Presently based: Bahrain. Field commander: Majed Ansari (operations Iraq, Afghanistan, Bahrain, Lebanon). Presently based: England. Co-opted personnel (UK): James Mallory (operations Holland, Ulster, England). Presently based: England (London) . . .

Trader's mobile rang so he stopped reading, answered it — and at once knew from her voice that something had gone badly wrong.

'Hell, Matt, it's no good,' she said bleakly, 'I don't see how I can possibly do it.'

Christ, no! he thought, then took her at her word and asked tightly, 'Can't you stay down there? Try again later?'

'Not a chance. There's been — '

'What's happened?'

'It's Melissa. She's ill. She's got gastroenteritus, was sent home from work. She was in bed when I arrived so I was hoping everything would be OK but then she

250

improved fast and she's up and about now. The doctor says she's to stay home for a couple days at least so she'll be around all the time and I won't be able to do it. I thought of telling her everything so she'd *understand* and let me use the keys, but it wouldn't work, Matt. She . . . she wouldn't believe me. I'm so sorry, Matt. So *sorry*.'

'These things happen.' The platitude came out without him thinking, and the triteness of it appalled him. Yet it was true, he thought; like with a lot of hackneyed sayings, there was a kernel of truth in it, accidents *did* happen, people *did* fall ill at drastically inopportune moments.

'So I'll be leaving today, there's no point in me staying now, is there? Majed'll be back home; he won't be away overnight again till Friday.'

Cristin rang off soon then, leaving Trader harrowed by apprehension. He could get authorization to mount an armed raid on Ansari's house and take the documents by force. But do that, and clearly the greater part of SeaSnake's personnel would be able to escape arrest because such an action couldn't hope to be kept secret beyond its execution, knowledge of it would spread like wild-fire along SeaSnake's lines of communication — and at once the majority of its agents

251

would either go to ground to take flight. The photographing had to be accomplished without arousing suspicion in Ansari's mind and, with the way things now stood at Hillsdown, that could only be done by getting Melissa's consent to using the keys. But how could that be achieved? *How* could he persuade the girl to betray Ansari? She was in love with him, so how the hell could he, Matt Kingsmith, ever hope to do that?

That night Trader slept badly. His mind would not permit him to relax; it persisted in working out possible ways he might access SeaSnake's secrets only to then pick holes in their fabric until the whole thing fell apart. As dawn broke, he flung himself out of bed and crossed to his open bedroom window, threw back the curtains and heard a blackbird calling. Then, as it fell silent, he found a name singing loud and clear inside his head: *Steven Court.*

Steven Court: born to the name James Mallory, and twin brother to Sean, thief of James's identity and now in that persona operating in SeaSnake in co-operation with Majed Ansari. And to complete the chain-link of possible advantageous circumstances, Ansari himself. He is married to Melissa who is Steve's daughter and who, *erroneously*, believes her father to be an activist in one of the IRA's splinter groups embedded in London.

There was his line of attack, Trader realized, blinking in the morning sunshine flooding in through his bedroom window. Surely he could gain access to Ansari's papers by using Steven Court, Melissa's real father. Like Cristin had said, simply showing her the transcript of the encoded pages from Ansari's desk would be unlikely to win her co-operation since of the two men named therein as being involved in the terrorist strikes they referred to, one was her *beloved* husband, and the other was the man she believed to be her fondly remembered father to whom she would almost certainly stay loyal; while if he used the key without her permission she'd find it unthinkable not to tell Ansari.

But surely, if he could prove to her that the Mallory with whom Ansari was working on a terror op was not in fact James but was actually *Sean*, who, back in 1994, had knowingly allowed James to go with the execution squad in his place and submit to the death sentence meant for him — surely then she would hate Sean with vengeful intensity and, therefore, consent to do the one thing that would enable Trader to destroy him? Could be she'd agree to that even though it would mean her husband being taken out as well, once she knew the truth about them both?

Leaving his flat at 07.00 Trader drove to the address Joe Anderson had given him. It was Tuesday morning and he had decided to ride his luck: he would take a chance and, he hoped, Steven Court would still be on the same wavelength as the man he had known as 'Trader'.

★　★　★

By custom, the Court family ate breakfast together in their big, airy kitchen on holiday mornings, and now, of course, the boys were on holiday. Nevertheless, that day they were going to their school for a lecture plus discussion at 10.30, and Steve had taken the day off on their account. By 8.30 they had all finished eating but still sat on, Deborah and Steve enjoying a leisurely second cup of coffee while talking over the school-organized adventure holiday in Canada the boys would be going on at the end of the month. That was the subject of the meeting Deborah was taking the boys to; one of the two lecturers was the manager of the company running the enterprise, while the other was an activity leader in Canada with stories to tell and pictures to show.

'Well, time you got ready, boys,' Steve said, after a glance at his watch. 'The best seats'll go to the ones who get there first — ' He broke off as the front doorbell rang.

'I'll get it,' Deborah was on her feet. 'It's probably Megan from next door. You stay and finish your coffee, Steve.'

On opening her front door Deborah saw standing in front of her a fortyish, well-built man, a stranger, bareheaded and casually dressed in chinos, his fawn jacket open over a black polo-neck.

'Good morning,' he said to her — a pleasing voice he had, and golden brown eyes smiling in a square-jawed, frank-looking face. 'I'd like to speak to Steve, if he's in.'

If you're a friend of his I'm sorry I haven't met you before, Deborah thought; but she did not ask him to step inside because Steve had said never to do so straight off unless she knew the person asking to see him.

'Yes, he's home,' she said. 'We're in the kitchen; just finished breakfast. I'll go tell him you're here. What name shall I say?'

'Tell him . . . Say I've come to speak to him about Sailor.'

Taking note of his slight hesitation Deborah too paused for a moment, wondering if he was lying; then deciding he wasn't, she gave him a half smile, turned and went back to the kitchen.

Very different from Cristin, is Steve Court's Deborah, Trader thought, watching her walk away from him, a slender woman, easy-moving, her head held high, shoulder-length auburn hair.

She was back within a minute. As she faced him he saw her dove-grey eyes were . . . puzzled? Annoyed? No, neither of those. She was on edge, he decided, and liked her for it; it spoke of a true closeness between her and her husband, for there surely hadn't been time for more than a look and a few words to pass between them before she was back.

'Do please come in,' she said quietly. 'I'm sorry I left you standing outside.' Trader closed the door behind him, and followed her as she led the way along the corridor to the kitchen.

On its threshold he stopped dead, his eyes going straight to the man he had last known as Sailor.

Steve had risen to his feet and was standing stock still, staring at him. '*Trader*,' he said, the one word harsh out of a dry throat as he fought to keep his mental balance in a world that on the instant had swung wild, sending the life he had built for himself sliding away from beneath his feet.

'I'll . . . I'll go upstairs with the boys.'

Deborah put the suggestion into the silence building between the two men. 'I'm taking them to a meeting at their school so they'd better smarten up a bit,' she added, turning towards Trader but not looking him in the eye and already moving towards the door. 'Come on, you guys,' she said over her shoulder.

Josh and Daniel had been sitting tight, their eyes going from their father to the stranger; sensing conflict and danger in the nervy high-tension binding their father to him, they were half excited, half frightened by it.

'Go with your mother,' Steve said to them. But he did not look at them and they realized he had as it were left them, they knew that somehow this stranger had some sort of power over their father. Moving quickly and quietly they got to their feet and made for the door.

'See you later, Dad,' said Dan, pausing in the doorway to gaze back at his father anxiously. But then his brother pushed on past him with a muttered, 'Come on, Dan, Dad's got stuff to do, he doesn't want us hanging around,' so he turned and went after him to pick up on their own young, thrilling affairs.

'Sorry to do this to you, Sailor.' Trader spoke from where he stood, and he was indeed sorry, deep inside himself where memories dwelt. But he was not about to let that get in the way of what he had gone there hoping to bring about, having long since learned to control emotional deterrents when the chips were down.

'How did you find out?' Steve was holding himself ramrod stiff, one white-knuckled hand gripping the edge of his kitchen table. His voice was very quiet, flat; but his eyes were haunted by demons and riven by conflict as, inside his head, ghosts out of the discarded shell of a past he had hoped he had escaped from for ever fought to re-establish themselves within him.

'We have ways. You know that.'

'Was it Joe?'

'Does it matter who it was?'

'*Doesn't* it?' Bitter-voiced.

'Personally, maybe. But there's a bigger world out there and, as you well know, to live in it the values you have in mind sometimes have to be put aside in the face of bigger issues.' Trader gave him a brief, tight-lipped smile. 'So, stop playing for time, Sailor; could be that's something we don't have a lot of. National security is at risk and I need your help.'

'I don't belong in your world!' Violence running sudden in him, rip-tide strong. '*I'm not your kind now!*'

At that, Trader moved: covered the distance between them in three strides, stared him in the eye and laid into him. 'So are you *Sean's* kind?' he demanded, his voice savaging him. 'Worse still, are you so damn' happy and self-satisfied in your domestic bliss that you're content to anchor yourself into it and let others burn *because you did that*? To stand by while Sean's kind do the things they do, so long as you and yours stay safe? Are you that kind of bastard now, James Mallory?' He stepped back, 'Christ, I never thought I would live to see this day,' he said, his eyes diamond hard.

'*Sean?*' The rest of Trader's attack had passed him by, the name of his brother had sunk its teeth into his mind and hung on. 'How does Sean come into this?'

Turning away, Trader pulled out the chair young Josh had tidily pushed back under the table, and sat down, folded his arms on the blue-and-white checked tablecloth and looked up at Steven Court. 'That night in '94, he let you take his place in the full knowledge that the men who'd come to seize him were an execution squad. Sean knew it, Sailor! He *knew* it, and let you — '

'No! That's not so, he was asleep upstairs; he'd never have let it happen if he'd woken up and heard what was going on — never in a million years would Sean do that!'

'You're wrong! He heard, and realized what it meant.'

'How can *you* know? You can't be sure of that.'

'I know relevant facts. Facts that prove the truth of what I've just said.'

'You do? So come on, then: give me them!'

'OK. Sean was seen that night; about an hour and a half after you were grabbed, your Renault pulled in for petrol at that all-night garage south of the village. Its driver paid with a Visa card in the name of James Mallory.'

'That doesn't prove anything.'

So Trader laid his hands flat on the table, held his eyes and told it all straight and simple, the story cut to the bone.

'The Visa card was James Mallory's. The car was James Mallory's and in the back of it were a couple of suitcases with James Mallory's clothes inside them. Later that night a man who gave his name as James Mallory — and who subsequently was identified as James Mallory from photographs — used a passport in that name, boarded a plane from Belfast to London. He let you be led away to interrogation and execution, Sailor. And that same night he discarded his Sean persona: from then on he's lived as

'James Mallory' — and made him one of his own kind, a committed terrorist.'

'No. No, I won't . . . He could've woken up much later — not till early morning maybe — found me gone and done the only sensible thing to do.' He forced the words out, but there was a dreadful hopelessness in his face; he was falling apart inside.

'The timing shows it didn't happen like that, Sailor.' Deliberately, Trader used the code-name again, hoping it might help to bridge the years since James Mallory had begun to work with him against everything Sean embraced so wholeheartedly. 'Sean had both his mobile and yours; the commander of the enforcement detail had one also and Sean would have known the emergency number to put him in touch with that commander, fast. Face it, Sailor; face it, and *help me*! I *need*, your help, badly. Against him and all he stands for.'

In that moment, Trader saw Steven Court accept that his twin brother had sent him to die in place of himself. Not an easy thing to witness, Trader found it: the breaking of a man, the destruction of a trust (of a *love*, he corrected himself, facing the word with a certain cynicism), that had been the bedrock solid foundation on which, until now, that man had built his life.

'We're off now, darling.' Deborah's voice was light and easy from the hall, she and the boys were on their way to the front door.

''Bye, Dad. Don't work too hard!'

'See you later, alligator!' That sang out from the younger boy, to be followed fast by his brother's scornful put-down, 'For goodness' sake, you still got *that* on the brain? It's — it's *prehistoric* . . .'

The voices from the hall faded. The front door slammed. Silence continued in Steven Court's kitchen and, again, Trader waited. He had told Sailor the salient facts and he was sure that, since they came from him, Steve would accept them as die-hard truths. They were enough to give him now; to go into the details of Sean's sustained continuation of his betrayal might confuse the issue; so all that was left to do was to wait for Steve to make his decision.

However in that, Trader was wrong. Steve needed one last question answered before he chose his path.

'Melissa,' Steve voiced his daughter's name stiffly, reaching back for it through the years; let it lie alone in the room for a moment, then asked, 'Does she think Sean — Sean the terrorist masquerading as me — is her father?'

'Yes. There's no other way for her to think, is there?'

'*Jesus.*'

Trader's scalp prickled. He should have realized, he thought, he should have *known*. Said, looking down, 'She figures in what I want you to do, Steve. If you come in with me now, she will know the truth; she'll have to,' he added, because Steve had a right to know.

'Will Cristin have to, also?'

Trader heard him speak her name as if it belonged to a stranger. Deeply glad of that, he answered quietly, 'To know the truth about you will make both of them very happy,' he said, 'happy for you as much as for themselves. You've got a good life here, Sailor, and they have both got their own lives.'

'I know that.' Steve came and sat down facing Trader across the table.

Trader's bent head came up fast. 'How come? And how much do they matter to you now?'

For the first time since Trader had come into his house, Steve smiled. It was a narrow, closed smile; and noting it, Trader knew he had won Sailor to his cause. 'The answer to your question,' he said quietly, a new confidence in his voice, 'is that I have a friend from the old days who still farms out Ballymena way. When I told him my own story, he believed it — believed I'm Jamie — and he told me a bit about Cristin and

Melissa. Not a lot, just the local gossip over there, but enough to know they're both happy. The answer to your second question, though, is that it's no business of yours how much they matter to me; you've got no right to ask; it doesn't have bearing on what's up for discussion here between you and me, it's not relevant.'

'You're going to help me? Come in with me?'

'You know I am, saw it in your eyes.'

'Then I must tell you that what you just said is wrong: my second question *is* relevant, or rather, your answer to it will be.'

But then Steve leaned across the table, stared him in the eye and asked him a question he had not been expecting. 'You and Cristin: you're lovers?'

'In both senses of the word.' Answer followed hard on question, but Trader's mouth tightened.

'How long has it been that way?'

After a moment, Trader sat back and laughed. 'To quote a friend, 'That's no business of yours' and 'it's not relevant' to what you and I are about to discuss. OK?'

'Sure.' Steve relaxed, the tension in him fading to a quiet smile. 'You've made your point as succinctly as this friend of yours made his,' he said, then stood up and regarded Trader with a certain eagerness — an excitement, even — in his body language now. 'So, let's start work. There's a hell of a lot you'll have to fill me in on, so I'll make us some coffee and we'll settle down to it.'

★ ★ ★

First over coffee, then over ham, rye bread, cheese and a lager apiece, Trader had put him in the picture regarding Sean, Ansari and Melissa, and SeaSnake; then they had worked out and agreed on plans which, hopefully, would result in Steve winning Melissa's consent to them accessing Ansari's desk and photographing the information held there.

'Christ, I need this,' Trader said, leaning back in his chair at the kitchen table as he took a second cold can of Foster's from Steve's hand. 'I've talked myself dry.' Over ten years is a long time in a life, long enough for people who initially began working together in close understanding to grow apart. But these two men were indeed, deep down inside themselves, two of a kind.

'You know,' he went on, 'there was an awful worry in me that I'd find you'd lost your edge,' he said, 'that you'd become a nine to five conformist — '

'And would turn you down flat; that being happy in my own life I wouldn't care the way I used to and would refuse all part in this Operation SeaSnake.' Steve sat down facing him. 'Well, I'm happy all right, Trader. Wonderfully so, incredibly so. But Christ! I can't sit back from this one. I'm *part of it*, aren't I, because Sean's working with the enemy and it was me who presented him with the opportunity to be in a position to assist in a terrorist op against this country.'

'Indirectly, it was you. Only indirectly, though.'

'The result's the same, isn't it? He's into SeaSnake because I let him free to live his life. Christ! If I had my time again I'd let him die!'

Steve's last words came at Trader charged with gut hatred, and glancing at him sharply he saw him staring down at his own hands clasped tight round his can of lager.

'Well, I'm going to do something about it now,' Steve went on quietly, the words spoken to himself alone. 'Something decisive and with permanent results.'

Was he referring to the part he had agreed to play in the photographing of SeaSnake's operational plans or — perhaps? — to some move against his twin brother who had intentionally betrayed him to death and could therefore be branded a murderer? Trader wondered; and inside his head the old phrase said itself over, insidious, suggestive, 'blood for blood'.

'Will you and Cristin marry?' Steve asked abruptly, looking up and his face simply interested.

'I've been asking her for years,' Trader said blandly, achieving swift transition to the change of subject.

'So you've come up against the same brick wall as I did years ago? She won't marry you because you're a bloke whose life's given over to the hard stuff? Violence — '

'Something like that.' Trader cut off discussion on that, this was not the time for it. 'I live in hope: since this SeaSnake op sucked in her and Melissa she's been different towards me.' He drank the last of his lager, stood up. 'It's time I went,' he said, slipping his jacket off the back of his chair and putting it on then heading for the front door with Steve following. 'So, we're ready to swing into action, you and I,' he said as Steve opened up. 'I'll call you later like we said, give you the final times then and check through exactly how we play this.' Turning his head he looked out through the doorway: the sunshine out there showering down over green grass and a brilliance of flowers. 'Nice garden,' he remarked.

'Good luck to you, Trader, with Cristin. May you win what I lost.'

'Having seen what you've got here I wouldn't say you lost anything.'

'Guess you're right at that,' Steve said, but then suddenly gave a brief, vicious little laugh. 'You always were, weren't you, about things that mattered?' he went on, his voice rough and a raw anger riding it. 'Even back then, you were right about Sean. You saw all the way through to his bastard black heart, told me to watch my back with him — '

'That's all done and gone, Sailor. Leave it lie. We've got a job to do, you and I, so stay focused.' But turning to him, Trader saw the expression on his face and was appalled by the sheer malevolence corroding it. He had awoken a monster in this man, he realized. Steve had loved his brother, and now that Trader had ripped the heart out of that love hatred had roared in and filled the emptiness inside him.

'It's possible SeaSnake's close to climax,' he said to Steve sharply, urgent to cut him clear of Sean-remembered, 'so keep your eye on the ball, Sailor; don't be tempted to go after any one of the players because of personal hatred. What you've just agreed to do tomorrow — going to Melissa with me — is something no one else *could* do, no one.

268

And provided we get from it what we hope for, we'll break operation SeaSnake. Then Sean will be caught in the net like all its other agents.'

Slowly, Steve's face cleared. 'Sure,' he said. 'Justice will be done, and all that . . . So, you'll call me later, then. And — thanks, Trader. Seems a funny thing to say, maybe. But I mean it. From the heart.'

'If you pull this off, the debt will be all on my side,' Trader said sombrely. Then throwing a quick, 'You've got a family to die for there, Sailor. Lucky man,' over his shoulder he turned and walked out into the sunshine.

Steven Court's eyes followed him, but he was not thinking about him, or about SeaSnake, or about his daughter Melissa. He was thinking about his twin brother, and the tenor of his thoughts ran thus: out of my love for you, Sean, of my own free will I took your place that night, assuming I would be taking a beating, and banking on going free when they realized they'd got the wrong man. I didn't know the punishment was already decided, and was death. But *you* knew that, Sean. You knew, yet let me take your place.

And that is an act which places you in a world peopled by the lowest of the low and for which I will make you pay. Soon now, I will make you pay.

11

As arranged, Ansari and Mallory met in London, at a café-bar near Victoria Station. Catering largely to passing travellers Chico's was spacious, bright without being gaudy and during the daytime, with the exception of two wise-cracking, brawny barmen, was staffed by attractive, efficient women in their mid-twenties. Arriving at the bar at eleven in the morning, separately but within seconds of each other, they threaded their way between tables and seated themselves in an alcove on the far side of the room. Their waitress was beside them almost at once, took their order for coffee and two cheese sandwiches then went off to fulfil it, a half smile on her pretty face. 'Lucky you,' murmured her friend Vicky behind the counter as she passed the order across to her, 'those two look interesting blokes. Friendly?'

'Very polite, nice. You know, behave like they've actually noticed you as a person, 'specially the Arab . . . Thanks. See you in the break.' Her name was Lucinda Smith.

270

Pleased to be serving two youngish person-able men unencumbered with women and kids and piles of luggage, she would remember them well when, a few days later, she was interviewed by Trader.

'That OK you got from Bahrain for me to work with you in your Heathrow op: I'm disappointed it's on hold until SeaSnake's done.' Sean's eyes were cold and searching as he looked across at Ansari. 'And the proviso put forward — surely that's unnecessary?'

' "That between the final confirmation of the agreement and the operation itself there shall be no alteration to outside matters affecting either party to it, or the target".' Word for word and an edge to his voice, Ansari voiced the proviso stipulated by Shakiri. 'It seems reasonable to me.'

So Mallory left it at that for the moment because they had met to discuss the operation in Hereford — code-named 'Stingray' — which would see them in action together.

'Your recce trip to Tollgate Garage — you didn't find any ways our assault strategy might be improved?' he asked.

'You mean find any errors, I think.' Pushing aside his coffee Ansari leaned his forearms on the table. 'Your plans for it could not be improved upon,' he said, keeping his voice down, mindful of other customers

271

although the nearest table to theirs was a good four yards away and was occupied by a family of seven, kids and their parents all fully and noisily engaged in eating, drinking, and exchanging argument and banter.

'And the getaway vehicles?'

'Well placed for swift departure, destinations known.'

'Arrangements for arms collection prior to action?'

'Good planning there . . . I congratulate you, Mallory.' The last words stiff, formally spoken.

Mallory responded in kind but more expansively. 'As you are yourself to be congratulated on your skill in structuring the four attacks. That you've brought such a multi-faceted mission so close to climax without British Intelligence being aware of its existence is a brilliant achievement.' And that was no empty compliment, Sean thought, as he fell silent. Then he smiled wryly at the strange dichotomy in his feelings towards the Palestinian, the way in which his admiration for Ansari's expertise on the job was constantly at war with his gut-felt antagonism towards the man himself.

'Why the smile?' Ansari asked, instantly suspicious.

Sharp-eyed bastard; maybe he feels the

272

same way about me.

'I was just thinking you're the kind of bloke it's better to have as a friend than as an enemy,' he said, blandly.

Impatient to get back to business, Ansari brushed it aside.

'Reports received over the last four months from our agents surveillancing the degree and nature of staff and customers' activity inside Tollgate's administrative offices, retail shops, repair bays and used-car area, taken in conjunction with reports from local sleepers, all promise well for us,' he said.

'In plain speak, a good body count should result from our assault.'

Ansari gave a slight shrug. 'We are committed to the shoot-to-kill policy,' he said quietly. 'There will be no survivors.' He sat silent for a moment, then looked across at Mallory, a glint of curiosity in his dark eyes. 'That I have total confidence in you,' he went on, 'is something I find surprising, for I have learned the hard way to beware of placing trust in a fellow-combatant unless and until he has proved his right to my loyalty by his courage in action *with me*.'

'I'd go along with that.' Sean shifted his gaze to their attractive, dark-haired waitress who, bearing a well-laden tray, was approaching the noisy family party who were their nearest neighbours. But then he realized the implication of one possible corollary to what Ansari had just said — looked back at him quickly and added, 'Nevertheless my trust in you regarding our imminent action together is absolute. I bloody well wouldn't be here if it weren't.'

Ansari smiled faintly, but said nothing. He had taken note of that limiting phrase 'regarding our imminent action together', but had decided not to make an issue of it before SeaSnake had climaxed successfully. And he had lied by omission to the Irishman: until he had seen him in action not only during an operation but also throughout its *immediate aftermath*, he would not place absolute trust in him.

Suddenly, Mallory felt oddly ill at ease in the company of the Palestinian. 'So your final recce at Tollgate — there's no changes you want made?' he asked, thrusting the question into the thickening silence between them, anxious now to bring this meeting to an end and be on his way.

'There are none.' Ansari spoke coldly, he also suddenly aware of . . . not exactly *discord*, rather a *dissonance* between them, as if the mind of each had abruptly gone off to — or back to? — some place in himself kept entirely secret. He did not like the feel of it

274

and, pushing back his chair, got to his feet.

'So, until tomorrow, Mallory: our meeting with the captains of our other three strikes.'

'Final briefings.' Mallory also stood up.

Ansari picked up the bill, slipped a pound coin down on the table then looked across at him. 'May you travel in safety,' he said, standing slightly aside and with a smooth gesture indicating that the Irishman should precede him on their way out.

Lucinda Smith watched them go, sighing to herself. Then she dismissed the daydreams and got on with her job. As she cleared their table she found the sandwiches untouched on their plates, each still pristine in its clingfilm sheath — and thought, what a pity; if they'd been ham I'd have liked them with my coffee break at eleven. Then she slipped her customers' largesse into her apron pocket and forgot them.

However Lucinda was to remember them well a few days later when plainclothes policemen arrived at Chico's. It all came back to her then: the two blokes in their early forties, interesting-looking, their clothes designer-casual, cash no problem obviously, good tip. Media chaps, maybe? And a girl can dream, can't she? 'Sure, that's them,' she said the minute they showed her the photographs.

12

Melissa was working in the sitting-room at Hillsdown. Comfortably dressed in a sapphire-blue shirt blouse and jeans, she was sitting at the bureau conning over the case notes from the file delivered to her earlier that morning by a messenger from the law firm she worked for.

The front doorbell rang. Startled and also slightly annoyed at the interruption she looked at her watch, saw it was nearly eleven, muttered 'Shit' to herself then went to answer the bell.

'*Matt!*' On sight of him standing in front of her as she opened the front door annoyance vanished and, all smiles, she went into his arms, gave him a hug then stepped back. 'What a lovely surprise.'

'Let's go inside.' Trader suited the action to the words, taking her arm and leading her back into the hall. Closing the door behind them, he turned to face her. 'I haven't come to see how you are though I'm glad to see Cristin's reports are right and you're in fairly

276

good shape,' he said, holding her eyes and speaking with hard urgency. 'You know the job I do. Well, I'm here to ask for your help in a matter of national security. I want us to sit down together and talk, because I have a story to tell you. You're in this story, my darling, much-loved almost-daughter, and it's a dark and very terrible story. Some parts of it you'll find hard to believe — they are hard to believe. Also, parts are going to hurt you very much. But it has to be told and you have to listen to it, because as a consequence of it, fallout you might say, big things are at stake now; quite possibly many lives.'

Melissa's eyes had not left his as, starkly, harshly, he stated these truths. He saw fear and a desolate uncertainty come to life in them. As he stopped speaking, her right hand moved out towards him as though to hold his, but then she snatched it back.

'We'll go into the sitting-room,' she said, and walked past him without a backward glance.

'I'm sorry,' he said; but then as he followed her, wished he had kept quiet, such pointless words best left unsaid.

'Majed won't be back till seven o'clock and I'm not expecting anyone else, so we've plenty of time,' she said as they sat down one either end of the cushioned window-seat.

'Tell me this . . . this story, Matt.'

'It's hard to know where to begin.' In fact Trader was finding it hard to begin at all: sitting looking at him with one arm resting along the windowsill she seemed, he thought, too young to be told that, first, her true father had been *knowingly* sent to die by his own brother to save his skin; and secondly, and perhaps even more soul-destroyingly, that the man she loved and was married to was a terrorist presently engaged in masterminding an operation against her homeland . . .

'To be effective it's usually best to start at the beginning,' Melissa observed against his silence.

'If I did that in detail I'd be here talking to you for a year and a day,' Trader said. But from then on, the telling of it became for him simply part of his job. 'So I'll give you the bones of it first and we'll discuss it afterwards.'

To his surprise, Melissa heard him through the facts of what had taken place on that night in 1994 and thereafter without interruption. And when it was told he moved on at once, got down to business.

'Earlier, I told you I'd come here today on affairs relating to national security. Actually that was a euphemism. Now, listen to me, Melissa; listen, and wait before you jump to

278

conclusions. The man whom since 1994 you've known as James Mallory, your father, is in fact *Sean* Mallory, his twin — no, don't interrupt me, just listen till I've finished this bit. At present, as James, Sean is closely involved in a terrorist mission in progress in southern England, and you are in a position to help me gain vital information about the targets and timing of that operation.'

'*Me*? How the hell can *I* help?' No longer able to contain her anguish and sheer incomprehension, Melissa was on her feet, staring at him, her face chalk white, her eyes dark with fear.

'Majed Ansari is commander of the operation I spoke of.'

'*I don't believe you!*' The gut-reaction came out fierce and fast. Turning her back on him, she stood tense, hands clenched at her sides.

'I have proof of Majed's involvement at the highest level.' He stated the damning words coldly and saw a shudder pass through her entire body as they knifed in to her, killing all hope.

'Show me the proof.'

'This was taken from Majed's desk.' From the breast pocket of his shirt Trader produced the first page of a photocopy of the decoded information from Ansari's scarlet covered file naming SeaSnake's Active List agents, unfolded it and passed it to her.

She read it through. Coming to the end of it, she stood head down and very still. 'Ah. Well. Operation SeaSnake,' she murmured, but the words were no more than meaningless sounds dropped into the silence gathering in the room. The silence grew oppressive but neither she nor Trader broke it for what seemed to both to be an eternity but was in fact no more than half a minute.

'What is it you want me to do?' she asked quietly, looking across at him.

Searching her face he found it empty. What a dreadful thing to see in the face of someone you love, Trader thought, and for a moment felt an Arctic coldness sweep through him. Then it was gone: world affairs closed over it, occluding it.

'I want you to give me the keys to his desk,' he said evenly. 'When that page you've just read was photocopied the contents of four other files with it in Majed's desk — which we think gave details of the attacks, their timing, their strategies — were missing, the covers were in the drawer but not — '

'Yes, sometimes on his overnight stopovers he takes loose papers with him in his briefcase, their covers would make them too bulky, he said . . . ' Her voice trailed away into silence, but her eyes still held his as she fought her way through the horror engulfing her. 'It all falls into place, doesn't it? Makes a disgusting, horrible sort of sense. I see that now . . .'

'So give me the keys, Melissa,' he said.

But her face had changed; it was not empty now; a kind of wild undirected anger was ruling her and Trader realized he was in danger of losing her.

'No!' she cried. 'I *can't do that*. I won't *betray* Majed like that — '

'I have the authority to break his desk open if necessary.' Swiftly Trader stood up and grabbed her arm, throwing at her words to break her resistance, loaded words to get through to her older loyalties. 'But if I have to do that then as soon as Majed comes back he'll see the damage, draw the obvious conclusions and alert every single one of his network of agents engaged in his operation! Sure, we'll be spared those particular strikes *for now*, but — don't you see? — all his personnel from sleeper to suicide bomber will *escape* us! They'll live to fight another day. Go to ground, then regroup and mount another hit!' Letting go of her arm he stepped back a pace. 'I want *all* those men behind bars for a long, long time, Melissa,' he said. 'Give me the keys to his desk!'

'Do that, and I'll lose everything. *Every-thing.*' Her anger was gone. Her refusal came hard and . . . lifeless; she saw it as all she had left.

'You'll lose Majed, but you'll gain — '

'There's nothing for me *to* gain.'

Trader had got what he had played for: his way ahead was clear to him now. Stepping close, he took her hand in his.

'Yes there is, Melissa,' he said, his voice different now, it was Matt Kingsmith's, not Trader's. 'There's the best thing of all: your father.'

'What?' Disorientated, she frowned at him, but her fingers closed around his hand, seeking his closeness.

'Think back to the story I told you. It will be *Sean* who will go down with Majed. *Sean*: the man who, in full knowledge of what the result of his action would be, let your father go with the IRA death squad in his place. But it didn't work out the way he had counted on: Jamie escaped death that night, Melissa. He lived and he's no terrorist now, I promise you that. Also, he loves you still and wants to meet you, wants to be part of your life again.'

'How can you know such things? You — '

'I know because he told me so.' Trader smiled, scenting victory as he saw hope come alive in her eyes. 'He told me, and he's come here with me now to tell you himself.'

'*He came with you?* You mean he's — he's here, now? But how on earth — no, wait. Wait, Matt! How can you be sure he isn't Sean?' Then, with a half laugh on the edge of hysteria, 'Oh *shit*. Even *I* remember that Sean and Jamie were dead ringers one for the other, so how can you — or me — ever be sure?'

'James had a scar on his little finger. It's still there — '

'The dog fight! *Yes*! Oh God I remember, there was a dog fight on the beach. Cristin told me about that years ago — and Jamie showed me the scar, I can see him doing it, I can see the scar!' Trader saw a wonder coming to life in her eyes. 'Is it true, Matt? The man you've brought here with you — the scar's there on his hand? You've seen it?'

'I've seen it.'

'Then even Sean won't be able to get round that — he used to try sometimes, when they were kids and he'd done something bad, Cristin told me . . . *God*! How incredible. And how marvellous. I can't believe it — '

'You will. He's outside in the car. Shall I call him in?'

Melissa sobered. Stood quiet. Said after a moment, 'No. I'll go out to him. I don't want to meet him again in *Majed's* house. Is that OK?'

Trader nodded. 'I'll stay here, do what I came here hoping you'd allow me to do. Come back in when you're ready. Don't be too long, though,' he called after her as she made for the door. 'There's a lot to be done.'

A hand already on the doorknob, she turned to him for a moment. 'You know where the keys are; just take them, Matt,' she said and then was away, out into the garden and along the path, blonde hair flying.

Trader did as she had suggested. Fast. And an hour and a half later had contacted Chief Superintendent Chase and was about to drive back to London to meet him, his photographs of the contents of Ansari's files on the passenger seat beside him, packed into a briefcase Melissa had lent him.

'SeaSnake's scheduled to climax in less than forty-eight hours, at twelve-thirty on Friday the eleventh,' he had said to Chase, getting through to him without delay on the hot line. 'I've photographed the files. They give us blow-by-blow information on the attack strategy of each strike and — '

'Right. Get yourself up here and to me at once, with those photographs. Meanwhile I'll contact top brass and set up emergency briefings . . . '

13

Chase's immediate task was to formulate and then kick-start the overall plan for the frustration of SeaSnake by such strategies as would ensure that its agents were caught redhanded and, therefore, would be arrested in circumstances likely to support and further their conviction on serious terrorist charges when brought to court. To that end, hard on Trader's call, he had informed his superiors on the new situation, then summoned to conference at 18.30 hours the departmental heads of MI5, MI6, Rapid Reaction and Armed Response units, together with certain advisers and other high ranking police and military officers. And although Trader would be present at the conference, he had been ordered to report to him as soon as he arrived in London for an immediate one-to-one session on his fresh data re SeaSnake.

Trader had done so; and now, alone in the conference room, the two men were sitting side by side at the long table on whose polished surface lay five piles of papers: each

285

of the first four contained full details of the planned assault on one of SeaSnake's targets as garnered from Ansari's files, plus sketch maps of that target and its environs. The fifth contained the information given in the encoded file also found in his desk. Chase had worked through the four assault plans with Trader, discussing with him the counter measures to them which he had drafted in preparation for the conference; now, with that done, he sat back and clarified one particular point regarding the counter attacks on SeaSnake which caused him concern,

'We have less than forty-eight hours before these strikes come to climax,' he said, 'and we want to acquire rock-solid evidence against all hostiles. Therefore I've decided to take certain risks. During the next twenty-four hours we shall put in place close surveillance on all the SeaSnake agents named in Ansari's files. Security during the period will be maintained by instructing local forces in the target areas at their highest level that, working in conjunction with our special forces units, they are to make preparations for arresting said agents — *on order from our officers only*.' He paused, looked down at the notes he had in front of him.

'Risks indeed.' Quietly, Trader slid it into the silence, knowing what was coming next and giving thanks that such dread responsibilities were not his.

'That done,' Chase went on, 'we put the entire procedure on hold for approximately twenty-four hours. Then, just prior to SeaSnake's zero hour, all units swing into action and we take all hostiles *in flagrante*.'

'Leaving the bastards no place to hide when they're brought to trial, however tricky their lawyers may be,' said Trader, grimly.

'As you say, Kingsmith. So, we're ready for conference, I think.'

But Trader had one further question stored up.

'Sir, do you have information on SeaSnake from any other source?' he asked.

For a moment Chase stared at him, gun-metal grey eyes piercing, sharp-boned face wiped clean of all expression.

'Why do you ask?'

'I'm sure you know why, sir, but I'll say the words if you wish. I ask because of Jean Charles de Menezes, and two other cases recently. Both incidents involved — given hindsight — over-reliance on single-source evidence.'

'Rest easy. Those documents from Ansari's desk preclude all doubt.' But now Chase himself had a question to ask. 'One other matter, Kingsmith,' he went on. 'It's a personal one. You don't have to answer if you'd rather not. It's about the Hereford counter-op on Stingray. I see you've put yourself forward to command it. Tell me, why d'you want it?'

Trader met his eyes. He did not want to give his reasons; was loath to give them the clarity of honestly-spoken words. Then, suddenly, his thoughts homed in on Sean Mallory and he dropped his head; ran away from Chase's eyes as, deep inside him, raw, red hatred against the Irishman boiled up inside him for the appalling thing he had done to James and, through him, to Cristin.

'Kingsmith?'

Swiftly calling his mind to order, he looked up. 'Personal reasons, personal interest, sir,' he said stiffly.

'You know it's for me to grant or withhold command of our Hereford operation?'

'Of course.'

'Personal interest . . . ' Chase sat back, considering. 'That can be dangerous to the success of an armed-assault op.'

'I know that, sir. I can handle it.'

'Have handled before now, probably; it can happen in our job as much as in anyone else's.' But Chase still wasn't satisfied. 'Elucidate, Kingsmith. Personal interests is an extremely wide-ranging phrase, would you narrow it down a bit for me?'

'I'd rather not, sir.'

Chase eyed him for a moment, then sat forward, smiling — a real smile, and the austere face was transformed. 'I'll give you Stingray, you've earned it,' he said. 'You will not take part in person in the direct action, however: it's radio control for you, that's where you'll be most useful.'

'Thank you, sir.' Looking into his eyes, Trader understood why people found Chase an inspirational leader and were willing to trust him — some of them with their lives.

'And one more point about Stingray, Kingsmith, before I call the others in.'

'Sir.'

'Remember it's vital that we take Ansari *alive*. Egypt wants him too, but we'll put him in the dock first by right of seizure.'

★ ★ ★

Chase conducted the conference with consummate skill, handling the sometimes aggressively disparate points of view regarding the strategies to be employed with his highly valued and respected authoritative diplomacy. The men and women present were all top-ranking in their own particular field of expertise — arms, logistics, communications or whatever — and their opinions were informed and strongly held, so, inevitably, arguments occurred; but they had all received a preliminary briefing on SeaSnake so they understood what was at stake and appreciated the need for rapid decision-making.

Early on in the session, Chase had appointed one commander to set up and thereafter control the counter-attack at each of SeaSnake's targets; as it came to an end he called upon those four to remain with him for further discussion.

Chase stayed where he was at the head of the table while the four commanders moved to sit two either side of him, bringing with them the notes they had made during the conference. He knew them well, those four: Charlie Romero and Susan Remington from police college days ten years ago when he had lectured the new intake on undercover work, and both Matt Kingsmith and Will Mason from recent operations.

'It's thanks to Trader we've been lucky with this one,' he said, his eyes drawing together his four movers-and-shakers. 'However, we have one other useful — though much more limited — source of information. Ansari's papers gave us Sharif bin Hamad as mentor and master to all the suicide bombers dedicated to SeaSnake. Bin Hamad has been known to us for some months, he's been under our surveillance. Access to info on him is available to you, usual channels . . . '

★   ★   ★

To Melissa, that day seemed to go on for ever. She and Jamie — no, not 'Jamie', the name was *Steve*, and she *must* remember to use it however alien it felt in her mouth — had sat together in Trader's car outside her house for a long time, leaving him to photograph the SeaSnake plans. Much had been said between them then: the lost years had been bridged, remembered love had been rekindled. Nevertheless both of them were greedy for more time together: each knew and accepted that it couldn't all happen at once; that words came fast to the tongue but *feelings* . . . feelings were bound to take a while.

At Melissa's suggestion they went into the house after half an hour or so; she would make coffee for them, she said. She'd take a cup in to Matt and then she and Steve would drink theirs in the sitting-room where, with him there for her to touch and see, they could go on talking alive the dream of the real Jamie returned to her and Cristin.

That they had done, she and Steve Court

together. But although she was half lost in the wonder of regaining her father, fear and apprehension prowled relentlessly around the edges of her newfound happiness, waiting their chance to break in and tear it to shreds. And when at 1.30 Trader's work was done and he joined them in the sitting-room, one look at his grim, self-absorbed face as he came in killed stone dead in her throat the words of greeting; she said nothing. Trader went straight across to Steve and ordered him to his feet and the two of them left her then, with only the briefest of farewells.

Left her not only in the flesh, either, she thought, hearing the front door slam: Matt could reach Steve easily across the years, there was such a strong bond between them. And the thought made her feel closer to Matt than ever because, surely, with both him *and* Steve in their lives she and Cristin would have the best of both worlds.

But soon, present loneliness closed in on her. The house so quiet but in a few hours Majed would be home! Majed — now exposed as a terrorist. Proved a terrorist by *Matt!* For her, she knew, incriminating documents alone would not have been proof enough of that fact even if Majed's name was on them. But there was *Matt's* word for their truth, so no escape was possible: none now, and no hope of any to come. Majed was a terrorist and Matt and Steve had taken with them the evidence of it.

Three times since they left, Melissa had checked the study to make absolutely certain it was exactly as Majed had left it that morning, each time more frantically than the last because she knew her husband for an obsessively observant man. But as promised, Matt had left the room as he had found it in every detail; she herself had returned the keys to Majed's desk to their usual place of safe-keeping.

She went out into the garden to fill in the time, did a little weeding among the lettuces beside the greenhouse; went back inside after that and prepared a light evening meal of omelette and salad, as Majed would have lunched out. But all the while, *Majed* was inside her head, and — now — she was afraid of him. Nevertheless, when he was home she would have to behave as though everything was the same as usual. At the thought of that she was glad of her recuperating patient status because it meant they couldn't make love, but then she recalled that, just recently, there had not been much inclination to doing so on Majed's part. He had been different, a coldness in him, a distancing of himself from her. Which would make it easier, she thought.

Besides, she wouldn't have to keep up the pretence that everything was normal between them for long: the climax of SeaSnake was only two days away, Matt had said before he and Steve left together. She could live a lie through two nights.

14

Thursday 10 August

Lime Avenue was a long, broad road on the western outskirts of Hereford. The middle-income houses bordering it were set well back from the carriageway. Richard Carter's dwelling stood halfway along it and on the opposite side to Tollgate Garage which was 700 yards further on, away from the city. His neighbours knew him as a self-contained but amiable man, quiet-living and law-abiding: a chap who enjoyed friendly acquaintanceship with them, who in summer played Twenty20 cricket with them on Sundays, and took prizes at the local garden show — but who never invited their close companionship. They also knew him to be an IT buff and — most winningly of all, perhaps — one who was always ready to use his expertise to put right their various electronic appliances when they went wrong. He had lived amongst them for the last ten years: had come there from London when, he told them, his wife had died of cancer.

Sean Mallory, however, knew him for an

embedded sleeper central to the reception and transmission of encoded orders and information on behalf of clandestine IRA groups, also for the strategies of Stingray, the Tollgate strike. It was in the workroom at Carter's house that he and Ansari met the day before Stingray was scheduled to climax for a final check through their plans. It was a small-windowed room illuminated by strip-lighting and starkly furnished with a square table and, set out on benches and shelving against its walls, Carter's state-of-the-art electronic equipment.

Ansari was the first to arrive, bringing with him a briefcase full of maps and notes. Sitting down at the table he began setting these out in front of him.

Mallory came in as he was finishing, sat down facing him.

'I didn't bring my notes,' he said after a moment.

'There will be no need for them. You deal only with the logistics of the operation, and today we are concerned only with the action. Logistics obey mathematical rules. Action is different; being subject to human behaviour it may be volatile in practice; therefore, commanders have to be ready to adjust it in such a way as to counteract any alteration to that already planned.' He picked up the top page of the pile of reports he had set out. 'Before we discuss Stingray I will run through SeaSnake's other three actions — '

'No need.' Mallory made no effort to hide his impatience. 'I know the lot. We've been over it before.'

'SeaSnake is a composite action,' Ansari said coldly. 'Six servants of God will give their lives to it. For my part I admire their courage and dedication — '

'For mine, I respect them. But you've checked those other three srikes already today and that's enough for me — No, wait; one thing before we move on to Stringray: the suicide bombers at the cinema and the hotel — are you sure there's no chance of them being spotted for what they truly are before they get to their prime positions to effect detonation?'

Ansari gave a narrow smile. 'There is no danger of that,' he said. 'All are long-serving members of staff at the establishments they will destroy.'

'Whoever produced their IDs and CVs must've been a maestro in the forger's art.' Grinning, Mallory got to his feet and went to pour himself coffee from the flask Carter had left for them on a nearby shelf.

Watching him, noting the strength in the lithe body and aware of the precision and cunning of his mind, Ansari acknowledged to himself that he was glad to have the Irishman with him on the mission, but was also aware that Mallory's ultimate loyalty was to himself alone. A bitter twist came on his lips then, because he knew from cruel personal experience that in the heart and head of even the most dedicated terrorist there may exist one core priority which, in moments of extreme tension or danger, may claim his fealty, may subject all other loyalties to its will. Was James Mallory such a man? he wondered. Because if he was —

'This the final sketch map for the Tollgate strike?' Coming back to the table, mug in hand, Mallory picked up the three-foot square chart and spread it out in front of Ansari; resumed his seat beside him then, put his coffee down.

'It is.' As he answered, Ansari took up the Action Plans lying beside him on the table: four sheets of typed notes which detailed the positions of the Stingray attack vehicles prior to the action at the garage and gave all information relevant to it. Then, referring to these and the sketch map as they did so, the two men traced through that assault (following on from the Daihatsu's 'clearing' of the forecourt) with Ansari reading out information from the notes and Mallory following it through on the map.

' . . . At 12.30 hours all assault operatives depart their target areas *whatever their situation at the time.*' Coming to the end of the action Ansari looked up at the Irishman, and finished without further reference to his papers, 'And at twelve-thirty-one the Mercedes is driven on to the forecourt, our martyr positions his vehicle between pumps and shop then detonates his bomb,' he said.

Mallory smiled at him.

'I salute you, Ansari,' he said. 'It's brilliant. An op on their home territory, and you've got them beat.'

'I long since came to the conclusion that whether one is operating in hostile territory or on one's own ground, success is best achieved by keeping all documentation to the minimum and under one's own close safeguarding.'

'Yeah.' Putting his elbows on the table, Mallory half turned to the Palestinian. 'I resented you insisting on doing that at first, thought it might put us all at risk.'

'As you said at the time, and quite forcefully. So now I in my turn salute *you*, James Mallory, for accepting that policy of mine as valid. Coming as it did from a foreigner, that cannot have been easy for you.'

' "Under one's own close safeguarding".'

Shrugging off Ansari's compliment, entirely sure it had been insincere, and rather taken with the phrase, Mallory repeated it. Then he asked, 'How did you ensure 'close safeguarding' at home? Married man, wife around all the time — '

'My wife is young and relatively ingenuous: as yet in her life she has not encountered the level of lies and deceit at which men like you and I operate.'

'And, she's in love with you?'

'She is. Also, she believes that I am in love with her and I have taken great care to preserve that illusion.' Ansari smiled into the slate-grey eyes. 'Do not have doubts, Mallory,' he went on. 'I know her; know she has moral attributes which have been, and still are, of great value to me in this mission of ours. First, she is deeply and comprehensively honest: if I lock my desk, it will stay locked; she would never steal my keys to open it in secrecy. Second, she is a respecter of other peoples' — what is that phrase? — of other peoples' *living space*.'

'Whatever, she hasn't *done* anything, has she?' Mallory pushed himself to his feet. 'Stingray's in the clear.'

'As is SeaSnake in its entirety.'

15

Thursday 10 August. Afternoon

'Dad, you're not *trying*!' Young Josh Court scowled down the back-garden cricket pitch at his father, rubbing sweat off his forehead with his free hand, mouth mutinous. 'I *told* you I don't want dolly-droppers, I want *leg-breaks*, that's my weak point and how'm I ever going to get better at them if you keep lobbing kids' stuff like that at me? It's fucking boring — '

'Don't swear.'

'*You* do! Sometimes, anyway, I've *heard* you, and you probably do it a lot more when it's not in front of us.'

'Hey, come on! Let's play cricket, eh? Take guard! I'm about to send down my killer leg-break; let's see if you can lay a bat on it.'

'Bet I can.' With a quick grin Josh turned to his brother who was fielding on the boundary over by the two sheds. 'Hey Dan!' he yelled. 'Wake up, there's one big hit coming your way! Dad thinks he's Shane Warne but I'm going to *get* him — '

'Ste-eve. Phone!'

301

Hearing his wife's call from the back door, Steve was at once beset by anxiety. 'Coming, love,' he shouted back. And telling the boys to clear up then come in for tea, he hurried indoors, thinking it might be Trader with news of some crisis in the SeaSnake operation which called for his attention and involvement. For by going to Melissa with Trader, he had become part of that action: the story behind all that had happened between himself and Sean back in 1994 had been the catalyst to turn Melissa against both Majed and Sean and give Trader access to those devastatingly incriminating documents held by her husband. Although harrowed by the frightening magnitude of the situation he had so precipitously been drawn into — and also by his personal dilemma as to how he might 'marry' together the components of his own two lives, might hold Melissa close without losing his wife and the two boys — Steve had realized and accepted that Trader might be likely to call him in, pull him deeper into the counterstrokes being put in place to nullify SeaSnake's threat.

'I want you at my place, Steve.' There was that in Trader's voice which at once commanded his total commitment to assisting in that many-faceted counter attack. 'There's something I have to discuss with you, *now*.'

'Right. You gave me your address. Be with you in half an hour.'

★　★　★

However circumstances — fate? — decreed otherwise. Ten minutes into his journey Steve found himself stuck in a traffic jam: some half-dozen cars ahead of him the badly secured rear doors of an overloaded delivery van had burst open, and half of its cargo, tumbling out across the carriageway, now blocked it completely.

No one was hurt, and police and breakdown services were on scene quickly, but clearing up took some time and, like several of the other drivers held up by the accident, Steve got out to find how things were going and then returned to his car, resigned to the estimated fifteen-minute delay. Deciding it was not worth calling Trader to explain his lateness, Steve relaxed behind the wheel and began to go over everything Trader had told him about SeaSnake.

But then, suddenly, those thoughts fell away and one alone winged through them out of the blue, cleaving fierce bright passage of its own: he must ring Melissa, must ring her now.

303

'Hello?' Her voice hesitant, uncertain.

'Melissa, this is Steve. I just . . . I just wanted to talk to you. Is . . . is Majed there?'

'He's not back yet. He rang me, said he was running late and wouldn't be home till around eight.'

'Are you all right?'

'Not really. How could I be?' She gave a brief, tight little laugh. 'But I suppose in a way I'm all right because now I know it all, so . . . I mean, it can't get any worse, can it? So I've sort of accepted that things are as they are. I have to, don't I? Because it's all fact: it *exists* and I've no way to change any of it.'

'Can you handle it?'

She gave no direct answer to that. 'I'm scared, Steve,' she said. 'I'm sure I'll be able to do everything OK when he's home, I can manage that, but . . . ' Her voice was rising and he sensed she was on the edge of hysteria. 'Steve, I'm scared about what'll happen *afterwards*, after he's been arrested. He'll know it must've been me who . . . who sold him out; he'll know that for certain so — '

'There was no *selling out*! Get that into your lovely head, my much-loved daughter,' he interrupted, suddenly seeing her face and consumed with both fears for her safety and simple love for her.

'Much loved?' That got to her in a way he had not intended; for a moment everything else went out of her head and, coldly, she threw his words back at her father because in spite of everything he had said to her the previous day he had not succeeded in giving proper answer to her agonized, pleading question of '*Why*, Steve? Why *so long*? Why didn't you claim Cristin and me as soon as you discovered who you really are?'

'Yes: truly much-loved and truly my daughter. I . . . ' But then suddenly he realized that full explanation spread for the moment — maybe for always? — too wide and too deep for full understanding, for all of its complex component parts to be herded together and caged in words. 'Forgive me, Melissa,' he said, low and from the heart. Then there was a silence between them. Slowly, it grew into what both of them felt to be a good sort of quietness, a new closeness.

'You . . . you must have loved Sean very much.' Coming out of the deeper comprehension and sympathy that had flowered inside her, it was softly spoken.

'It was a love which died a very sudden death when I discovered the truth of what he did that night — and *continues* to do.'

'So, did you hate him then? *Do* you hate him?'

'James Mallory' answered her with a lie, to spare her. 'I don't really know,' he said.

'That's probably because deep down you don't *want* to know; in fact would probably rather *not* know.'

How sad that she perceives things like that so young, he thought. And said, 'I'll come down to you tomorrow, after Majed has left, stay with you till all this is over.'

'You promise?'

'Cross my heart and hope to die, I promise.' He spoke her childhood catchphrase with a flick of laughter in his voice but almost at once his inner laughter died. 'And Melissa, forget Sean,' he said grimly. '*Forget Sean*: he is what he is, and he has no place in the world you and I will live in when this is done . . .'

'What are your two sons doing now?' she interrupted. Her voice was sharp with a kind of desperation, and Steve intuited that she was reaching for his other life because therein normality ruled, not terrorism and the murder of conjugal love.

'We were out in the garden playing cricket when I left,' he said. 'They'll be in the house by this time.'

'Go on, Steve.' No edge to her voice now. 'Tell me about them and you, and your wife.'

So Steve started to do that — but half a

minute later the cars ahead of him began to move forward.

'I have to go,' he said to Cristin's daughter. 'Don't be scared, Melissa. Just play Ansari carefully, but not so carefully that it shows. He's no fool. It's not for long, he'll be off early tomorrow morning, that's for sure. Don't be afraid, I'll come down, be with you.'

'I'm not afraid now.' Melissa said. But both she and her father knew her denial for a lie.

★   ★   ★

With the exception of his study, Trader's bachelor pad was a model of its kind. His sitting-room, bedroom, kitchen and bathroom were kept in a state of immaculate cleanliness by his non-resident housekeeper, but his study, save for a vacuuming when asked for, was his alone and was both comfortably crowded and extremely untidy. He understood his own untidiness, though, could swiftly lay his hands on any map, reference book, document or whatever he required.

He came straight to the point as soon as he had Steve Court installed in one of the two capacious armchairs facing each other in his study with a glass of whisky in his hand. He seated himself in the other.

'As I see it,' he said, putting his own drink down on the table beside him, 'you've got a right to know more about our measures to deal with Stingray. Without your help, we'd have been mounting it dangerously blind, but thanks to you Ansari, Sean and all their hard men involved will be ours for the taking.'

'Providing everything goes according to plan.'

'Obviously. Equally obviously, we've taken various possibilities into account; back-up is in place all along the line, available if needed.

'Never can tell, though. Things can blow up in your face. Sometimes. Maybe some happening you've never reckoned on.'

'True. What started off as one thing can end up as something entirely different, turn into a situation that's light years away from the original intention. Whatever, Steve, by this time tomorrow Sean will be out of your life for — '

'I'd like it better if by this time tomorrow he was dead.' Although his voice was quiet there was such underlying violence in it that Trader glanced at him sharply, but his head was down, his eyes hidden. 'So, Trader.' Steve looked up, and there was nothing in his eyes but a lively interest. 'Give me the plan of action, blow by blow.'

Sitting forward Trader talked at him

straight and hard. 'As you already know, Tollgate Garage is situated on the outskirts of Hereford with four pumps on the forecourt and a used-car lot at its rear together with repair shops. I'll give you the bones of their assault first, then our counter to it. Stingray has three prongs and these are driven home by three vehicles, Range Rover, Volvo, and a Mercedes carrying a hand-detonated bomb, its driver a designated martyr. The Rover and the Volvo carry gunmen. The Volvo blokes shoot up all staff and customers in the used-car lot and repair sheds at the rear. Those in the Rover do likewise on the forecourt and in the shop and the adjacent sales rooms. They get three minutes shoot-to-kill action, then drive clear to getaway cars parked nearby and proceed to designated safe houses. Four minutes after start of assault the Merc speeds into the space between pumps and shop, driver parks it there and blows her.'

Trader fell silent on that; for a few seconds there was a taut silence as each man, visualizing the described assault, assessed it for effectiveness and its vulnerability to counter attack.

Then Steve asked, 'Sean and Ansari: where do they figure?'

'Both are in the Range Rover: working with

one support gunman they shoot up forecourt, shop, admin offices etc.' Getting to his feet Trader, stood by his chair, hands in the pockets of his chinos as he went on. 'All three assault vehicles have to be positioned fairly close to the garage's access road leading in off the highway. In order to ensure they can do this, Stingray positions three holding vehicles in suitable parking spaces well in advance: these move out as the action cars approach at the given time. Thanks to Ansari's files we now have all the info necessary regarding those vehicles and, consequently, we'll have all three bracketed by or targeted from close to by unmarked Special Forces transport — vans of various sorts — manned by armed marksmen.' He looked across at Steve. 'You get the picture so far?'

Steve nodded. 'Yeah. There's two points you haven't brought up.'

'Name them.'

'One. What's your back-up?'

'Two armed response officers in the Tollgate shop, two in the repair area. Should Stingray hostiles somehow manage to get within striking distance of targets, they'll be eliminated on sight. Officers will know who to look out for. Second point?'

'Armed lookouts outside in mobile contact with — ?'

'Thought you'd pick that up.' Trader smiled. Then he sat down again and went on telling Steve how Stingray was — God willing — to be frustrated. He intuited that, since Steve had met and talked with Melissa, his emotions and his mindset had harked back to the old days, and memories of his own past subversive activities had stirred him to . . . not *direct* action, that was not available to him, but to an urgent and aggressive desire to find out all he could about the plans so that when the time came he could visualize the action, with Sean and Ansari caught in the thick of it and arrested. Sean, his brother who'd sold him to buy his own life, and Majed Ansari, the man who had made such arrogant, pitiless use of Melissa.

'We'll have plainclothes officers on all junctions to Lime Avenue, the highway alongside which Tollgate is located,' Trader went on, 'they'll be on the lookout for the arrival on scene of the Stingray vehicles. They call in to command centre — I'm in charge there, holed up nearby — as events unfold, so that if anything goes wrong it will be dealt with immediately. We'll also have a number of plainclothes men around in the area; they may seem to be simply on their way to the local shops, walking the dog, clipping their front hedge or whatever, but they're all armed and in radio contact with me. When we're done talking you can take a look at the maps on the table back there if you like' — he jerked a thumb behind him — 'every officer's position is shown, and all relevant details as to vehicles, friendly and hostile, are in the notes at the side. Feel free.'

'Tell me the rest of it first.' Steve's face had closed in on itself. To him at that moment Trader was no more than an information-providing machine. 'What about the Mercedes with the bomb on board? Hairy that'll be, timewise.'

'Hairy, indeed. But Ansari's papers detail the progress of the Merc second by second from point of starting out. Its driver has orders to leave both his front windows open — '

'Sounds stupid, the weather we're having?'

'Not really. He'd look eye-catchingly weird if he's sitting in there with all his windows closed.'

'Air-conditioning?'

'We assume the vehicle doesn't have it. Anyway, those are his orders and it gives us an edge. We take him when he's parked in Lime Avenue prior to going in, the bomb on the passenger seat beside him, done up to look like a large square parcel. At his given time the armed driver of our van already parked behind the Merc gets out, approaches the suicide bomber, leans down to the open window with a 'Hey, mate, you got a light?' or whatever, and puts his gun to the man's head.'

'Shoots him dead if he makes a move?'

'Does just that. Then within seconds his three-man team are there too, plus bomb disposal personnel.'

'How's the bomb detonated?'

'Electronically, by a switch inside the glove compartment.'

Steve looked down, sat quiet for a moment. Then he stood up, eyed Trader moodily. 'And you? Where exactly will you be?'

A faint grin came on Trader's face. 'At the garden centre a hundred yards or so along the road; my radio van will be in the car-park at the rear.'

But he got no answering grin. Steve turned his back on him, looked out of the window. When next he spoke it was to change the subject to one not to Trader's liking.

'It was good, finding Melissa after all these years,' he said quietly. 'But you know something, Trader? It's you she loves, not me.'

'Not really.' His tone was cynical and there was a wry twist to his mouth. 'It's only that . . . well, I've been there for her during 'all those years'.'

313

'And I haven't. But — '

'Leave it for now, Steve. Stingray's bigger.'

'On one level yes, obviously it is — '

'And this is no time to talk of levels of emotion.'

'You're right, I guess. But she's scared, Trader. She's gut-scared.'

'Of?'

'*Christ — of the whole bloody thing!*' It burst out of him and he swung round to face Trader as, suddenly, the well of bitterness against his twin brother turned gusher and spewed out. 'The whole mess, the stinking mess of all the lying people in her life, the rotten bloody *evil*.' But realizing he was in danger of losing the plot entirely he broke off, exerted his will and forced himself to give reasoned appraisal of the situation as he saw it.

'Understandably, she's dead scared of Ansari now,' he went on, holding Trader's eyes. 'But also . . . It's *Sean*, Trader. She hates him; hates him with that deep-down visceral hatred that eats out your heart. She hasn't ever *said* it to me, but — *Christ*! From her I don't need the words. Now she knows what he did to me that night — did in his soul as well as physically — she hates him. OK, things didn't work out the way he expected them to — I stayed alive. But the

point is, she knows now that Sean is
. . . What's the word for it, Trader?' Trader
saw his eyes turn diamond hard, with a kind
of death in them. 'What word does the
English language have for a man who,
deliberately and of his own free will, sends his
brother to die in his place? Is there one?
Or — '

'Steve,' Trader cut in, incisive, hard. 'You've
got a life. Live it.'

'I fully intend to. But if he crosses my path
in that life, I'll kill him. For Cristin and
Melissa as well as for myself, I'll kill him.' For
a full minute Steve let the threat lie in a
silence all its own, then he gave a grim little
laugh, shrugged, and suggested that he and
Trader go over the counterattack again with
reference to the maps on the table.

Trader was glad to do so, but later he was
to recall Steve's threat against Sean — and
himself act accordingly.

16

Friday 11 August

As area inspector, Majed Ansari arranged his own work schedules. For the day SeaSnake was to climax his diary committed him to a staff meeting in Bournemouth at 11.00 so he was on the road early, leaving Hillsdown at 07.00 hours. His presumptive destination, Bournemouth: his intended destination, a safe house in the suburbs of Hereford.

As Melissa heard the front door close upon his going, relief welled up inside her and she lifted her head, closed her eyes and let the tension drain out of her. He was gone, the long hours of having to watch every word spoken, every nuance of expression shown in his presence were over; she was alone, free of him.

When next — if ever — she saw him he would be a prisoner of the law of her land: the thought stood clear in her mind, and the resultant sense of liberation created an elation she had never known before. It seemed to her as though she had lived through a little death and now had come alive once more. With hours to kill before she could expect Steve to arrive she dealt with the household chores as fast as possible, then went out into the garden and set to work clearing undergrowth in the shrubbery at the front of the house. The whole ambience out there was summer sweet; it kept at bay the looming horrors of Stingray and the involvement in it of both Trader and Majed, the one man loved as her stand-in father for many years, the other so recently her beloved husband, but now, and with appalling suddenness, a man both loathed and feared.

An hour before midday she went back into the house and changed into fresh kingfisher-blue jeans and a black cotton overblouse patterned with golden-yellow flowers. As she came downstairs there was a knock on the door. When she opened it Steve was standing outside.

'You're early, but how lovely!' she cried, giving him a quick hug as he stepped into the hall, then closing the door behind him and leading the way on through the house into the kitchen. 'Beer or coffee?'

'I'd prefer a beer, I'm parched; it's already stoking up out there on the roads.'

'Sit down at the table and I'll bring it over. The traffic was hell, I imagine — ' But then abruptly she was still. Standing with one hand on the half-open door of the fridge, she turned and looked at him. 'Steve, I'm so very glad you're here,' she said quietly. 'Thank you for coming.'

But Steve wanted to have one thing clear between them. 'Melissa, answer me this. Would you rather it was Matt Kingsmith here with you?' he asked, and even as he spoke realized sadly yet with absolute certainty that he hoped her answer would be Trader, because he had so much more to give her than it lay in Steve's power to offer with the lost years like a barren chasm keeping them apart.

To Melissa it was a big question. Taking a can of lager from the fridge she gave it to him. 'Would you like a glass?' she asked, standing at his side (fleetingly, noticed the narrow white streak in his dark hair and remembered Sean).

'Like it is will do fine. Better in fact — feels good in the hand, cool.'

She sat down and gave him her answer. 'If you'd asked me that say nine years ago, and I was in a hard place like I am now, I'd have wanted Matt,' she said, holding his eyes. 'But it's not nine years ago and I'm a grown woman, so the way I see it, I count myself lucky to have either of you with me when things are getting rough.'

There was a silence. Breaking it, 'Maybe you should consider a career change, try for the diplomatic corps,' he said lightly, but his eyes were saying other things to her and she was content. Then he gave her a quick grin and changed the subject. 'I hope you've done as I suggested on the phone, got a stack of man-sized garden jobs for me to do while I'm here?' he said.

'You bet.' She returned his grin. 'Specially as you come for free, gardeners cost gold-dust in these parts.' But then the grin went, and she in her turn changed the subject. Sure of herself, and of him, now, she moved without preamble into sensitive territory.

'Your wife, Steve, have you told her yet?'

For a second he stared at her, disorientated and a little angry, but she met his frowning stare with a steady wide-eyed frankness which he found rather beautiful and utterly disarming. 'Yes,' he said, then smiled, and said, 'Thanks for knocking down the barriers so unceremoniously.'

He got no smile back. One forearm resting along the table, Melissa searched his face.

'And your sons? Have you told them too?'

'Not yet. Deborah and I decided we'd do that together — later, after she's got her head round the whole thing.'

'I'd like to know . . . well, how it came

about. What she said when you told her.' She gave a painful grimace, realizing the magnitude of what she was asking him. 'Will you tell me, Steve? If you refuse, of course I'll back off, it's your right to. But if you let me in properly I'll . . . ' She fell silent, unable to find the right words.

'Respect me more?' He offered it tentatively.

'No! Please don't think like that, it's not what this is about. I'll come to know *her*, is what I mean; know her a little, anyway. And maybe . . . she and I might like to know each other more. Later? Perhaps?'

Reaching out Steve covered her hand with his own, pressed it then released it, and gave her a true account, wanting her to understand the kind of person his wife was.

'Deborah's very direct in her dealings with people,' he said. 'I remember exactly the words she used when I'd told her — told her the part of it that really matters.' Then, leaning back, he stared up at the ceiling and, as he recalled his wife's words, made pictures inside his head of her face as she'd spoken them. 'She got up and came to stand in front of me, and she looked me in the eye. She's auburn-haired, grey-eyed. 'Steve darling, you're an idiot', she said to me, with love. 'Why on earth didn't you tell me these things years ago? Not early on, when we first met, I don't mean that. I didn't know you well enough then and I might have said stupid things like never darken my door again, and then you and I would never have become what we are. And, my beloved, know this: what we have been, and what we are now, and what we will be — *that's my life*. So let's move on and make that part of your life part of ours'.'

There was a brief silence; then Melissa said, 'You and she must be very close.'

'We are.' Steve Court's voice was quiet and very sure.

17

Friday 11 August. The Lion Hotel, Hereford, 0800

On Sean Mallory's bedside table, his mobile rang. He answered it. 'Viper'.

'Shark,' Ansari's voice thin and hard. 'Are you secure?'

'Secure.'

'Our strike at Tollgate is severely curtailed. Our suicide bomber has been killed in a road accident. He was on his way to take charge of the Mercedes. He died instantly.'

'*Christ!*' Mallory breathed the one word, shaken to the core, but then swiftly recovered. 'Of course we go ahead with the rest — '

'Our other assaults will proceed unchanged. Stingray will lack its grand finale, and one courageous agent.'

'We'll do enough, shoot the place up. There'll be plenty of casualties; it'll make one hell of an impact nationwide.'

'The comrade is dead.' Cold as Siberian permafrost.

'Yeah. Well, sure. I'm sorry about that, but it goes with the territory. And with the car bomb denied us, all the more reason to press home the rest of the op and bloody well make sure it hurts. OK?'

After a pause, Ansari's response came quietly to him across the line.

'You are a man after my own heart, Mallory,' Ansari said. 'We meet in the Range Rover after I have checked with Carter. May we go with God this day.'

★　★　★

Trader had received the news from Superintendent Chase twenty minutes before it reached Ansari. The martyr scheduled to drive the bomb-carrying Mercedes on to the forecourt of Tollgate Garage was — as was each of the suicide bombers at SeaSnake's other three target sites — being shadowed from his place of residence to that of his bomb-maker by three armed anti-terrorist officers. Consequently these men witnessed the death of their mark who — running late so jay-walking across a busy road to make up lost time — was struck square on by a speeding motorbike overtaking a parked car and was dead before he hit the ground twenty yards away.

Keeping a low profile on the fringes of the fast-gathering crowd of bystanders, one of the officers made sure he was dead, then all three slipped away from the scene and within a couple of minutes found sufficient privacy to report in to Chase.

'Jesus.' Gobsmacked and hardly able to credit his luck, Trader switched off his mobile, looked across at Mike Miller, the IT analyst monitoring the computers ranged along the opposite wall. 'We've got a major break.' he called to him and, as he turned, went on exultantly. 'The car-bombing — *it's out*, Mike! Their bomber for the Merc is dead! He got killed in a road accident on his way to pick up the loaded Merc. So that crucial, worst-possible element of Stingray is dead in the water!'

'Could be they'll put in a reserve?' A short, wiry man in his late thirties, dark and intense, Miller was experienced in co-ordinating anti-terrorist ops; to him, computers were part of his very being, he lived with and for his work — was married to it, his friends said.

Trader shook his head. 'I just put that to the Super, and he was ninety per cent sure they won't do that. It'd be almost impossible at such short notice,' he said.

Miller nodded. 'I agree. Suicide bombers don't grow on trees. Leastways, not in this country. Thank God.'

'Get new info and changed orders out fast.

If the vehicle holding space for the Mercedes drives off early, the officers assigned to deal with it are to follow and arrest its occupants as soon as both they and it are well clear of the sensitive area. If the holding vehicle stays put, they take it out as planned for the Merc. All other officers on site are to proceed in accordance with their given instructions. Get back to me as soon as that's done.'

'Sir.' Miller began to turn away, but then swung back to Trader. 'God is on our side today,' he said to him, softly and with absolute sincerity.

'I'm glad of it.' Trader held the steady grey eyes for a second, then got down to repositioning certain of his forces in the light of the changed situation.

The black Transit radio van he and Miller were working in had been parked since 07.00 that morning beneath an ash tree in the extensive parking area at the rear of the garden centre a short way along the road from Tollgate Garage. It was air-conditioned, and furnished for purpose with the requisite high-tech IT equipment. Seated on a foldaway chair, Trader was working at a pull-down table behind the two front seats. Even as he returned to his plans, his mobile rang again; his caller was Superintendent Chase, who still had the death of Ansari's suicide bomber on his mind.

'Watch that vehicle holding space for the Mercedes, Kingsmith,' he ordered. 'We've no way of knowing at what time Ansari will be informed of the death of his bomber. Could be it won't be until the bomb-maker realizes his man's not going to show up, but equally it could be that Ansari's had minders on his martyr, in which case he has already received the news.'

'And there's always the possibility that as soon as he gets it he may alter the timing, or even abort the entire op.'

'Not that last, like I said before; the demise of the would-be martyr is without question entirely fortuitous for us, but with his op so close to climax, its vehicles and personnel already at or nearing their assault positions, no mission commander would abort.'

'On the principle that it's better to get something out of an op than damn all.' Trader's voice was grim. 'Yes, I'm with you there. We'll count on them going ahead with what they've got left and make sure they end up with nothing.'

★ ★ ★

In the radio van, Trader looked at his watch. It showed 10.40 so, having completed his latest checks with each of his officers, he picked up his plan for the arrest on site of Ansari, Mallory, their support gunman and the driver of their Range Rover, and ran his eyes over it.

ACTION SITE: LIME AVENUE

Richard Carter's house halfway along avenue. Overnight, the Range Rover is parked outside Carter's house, in front of his garage.

Three assault guns are already stored inside his house for RR's crew members.

06.00 Carter loads weapons into RR.

08.30 C. parks RR on the avenue, close to his house and facing towards Tollgate Garage.

09.00 Our Toyota to hold space for the Clio parks outside C's house facing RR and close as possible to it.

10.20 Four Special Branch officers occupy C's house and arrest him and any others present.

11.20 Ansari arrives Hereford, parks 5 mins walk from C's house, goes straight on to it, enters and is arrested. He's held there until op is completed then he and Carter are taken to interrogation centre.

11.30 Ted CARLTON and Eve SMITH

(their mark's the third assault man in the RR and its driver) park their Clio facing RR as Toyota vacates position. They get out and part company temporarily, locating themselves nearby ready to meet again later 'accidentally' a short distance from the RR. On meeting they stand together chatting, then arrest the RR's driver and A's support gunman as they approach from the round-about at the city end of Lime Avenue.

'Blake on the line from Tollgate, sir.' Miller turned to him.

'Problems?'

'Negative. Progress report.'

'I'll take it. You check with all officers at that roundabout . . . '

They kept at it, Trader and Miller, only too aware that at any stage of the counterattack some chance occurrence might yet cause all their plans to fail . . .

★ ★ ★

Mallory had breakfasted well — two fried eggs, bacon and two slices of black pudding, that last a 'special' served to him alone, but then he expected no less since the proprietor of The Lion commercial hotel in Hereford was a long-time friend of his who had for many years provided safe bed-and-board to travellers engaged on IRA business. For the Stingray operation The Lion had prepared overnight accommodation for Mallory and his two auxilliaries, the driver of the Range Rover and the gunman supporting Ansari and himself in the imminent assault.

Finishing his second cup of coffee a few minutes before 09.30 Mallory picked up a daily newspaper at reception, went up to his first-floor room and sat down in the armchair by the window to read it. But he did not even open it. Dropping it to the floor he leaned back, clasped his hands behind his head and gave himself over to consideration of Stingray since, as he saw it, that morning's operation would for him be the gateway to a bright future with Ansari's chief, Shakiri: after Stingray he would have a personal 'in' with the Sheikh, who was a mover and shaker in the world of Islamist-driven international terrorism.

At 11.38 Mallory went downstairs into the street and set off at a steady pace for Lime Avenue: a well set-up bloke in his early forties, bareheaded to the sunshine, his hip-length denim jacket open over a white T-shirt and black chinos, black Reebok trainers almost new. The jacket swung easy over his lithe body; the handgun shoulder-holstered beneath it was, of course, loaded.

* ★ ★

12.15 hours: on the forecourt of Tollgate
Garage the driver of the white Ka alongside
the second pump was filling up with petrol.
Inside the shop, the driver of the green
Octavia drawn up in front of the Ka was
chivvying his teenage son to make up his
mind which canned drink he wanted so that
the bill could be paid and they could get back
on the road.

And on Lime Avenue all of Stingray's
vehicles except for the Mercedes were in the
places from which they would press home the
attack. By this time Ansari had contacted by
mobile the leader in each vehicle, and
received from him confirmation that his
position was secure and his assault personnel
ready for action. To each he had ended his
call with the same words:

'I remind you that this line of communication is now closed to you until after our
mission is completed. Repeat: this line of communication is closed to you from this moment
on. May God go with you all this day.'

★ ★ ★

At his crowded-in little work table Trader
smoothed out the large-scale map of Lime

Avenue and conned over the dispositions of the officers he had committed to the arrest of Mallory, the third gunman and the driver of the Range Rover, all of whom would — separately — be approaching the Rover shortly. Miller had just reported all those officers in position and ready to roll; now, head bent over the map, Trader used his forefinger to trace through the strategies of his counter attack, recalling the disposition of his forces as he did so.

1. Lime Avenue. Carriageway bordered by wide verge planted with lime trees, pavement between it and houses, which are set well back from the road. Ansari's Range Rover: parked roughly halfway along Avenue on west-bound side, facing away from city (drives off to assault position on Ave. at 12.15)
2. Roundabout at city-end of Avenue, three approach roads to it from city direction. Mallory plus gunman plus RR driver approach roundabout, turn left into Avenue; they are as yet unarmed (assault weapons in Range Rover).
3. We have:
a) Unmarked police vehicle (Vauxhall, 3 armed officers) stationed in central access road to roundabout. Its orders

are to give back-up to any/all officers in action as called on with or without radio reference to me if emergency situation develops.

b) Unmarked black people-carrier (Honda, one-way vision to all rear windows) parked 10 yards up Avenue from roundabout. 3 armed officers aboard plus driver.

Purpose: to transport hostiles to interrogation centre on their arrest or as ordered. (This vehicle designated for Mallory, the support gunman, and the driver of the Range Rover.)

c) ACTION

3 officers in place along Avenue, each to arrest his mark: SALTER to take Mallory.

CARLTON to take RR driver.

SMITH to take Ansari's third gunman

NOTE: Ansari and Carter already in custody inside C's house: they will be driven to interrogation centre immediately following successful arrests detailed above.

Trader pushed the map aside, planted both elbows on the table and sat chin in hand . . . I'd give a lot to be there when Sean Mallory is arrested, he thought, for there is a man I loathe with everything in me. In my life so far he's the only man I've met for whom I've felt real primitive gut-hatred.

18

Lime Avenue, Hereford. Friday 11 August

By 11.30 the city was lazy with summer warmth, and in the middle-income detached houses lining Lime Avenue the breadwinners had long since gone to work, while housewives had either gone out to do their shopping or stayed in the cool of their homes and gardens.

Ted Carlton and Eve Smith — he to target the driver of the Range Rover, she Ansari's third gunman — met on the pavement, as though by chance, beside the front gate of a house thirty yards or so along the road from the roundabout and ten short of Stingray's parked RR, and stopped to chat together. Both in their late twenties, they were a good-looking couple: Eve around 5'7" tall, clean-limbed and cool in a loose linen jacket over a leaf-green T-shirt and beige cotton trousers, her straight black hair tied back in a ponytail with a narrow scarf the same green as her T-shirt. Carlton was a head taller, blond and deeply tanned, athletic-looking in jeans and a black jacket open over a white shirt. Both carried their guns in shoulder holsters, well hidden beneath their jackets. They had become lovers four days earlier, but officialdom was as yet unaware of the fact.

Salter lay in wait for Mallory some ten yards closer to the roundabout than those two. In his mid-thirties, he was a bit of a loner and noted for a temper that ran on a very short fuse. Narrowly built and wiry, he was wearing a navy-blue jacket over pale-blue shirt and chinos and, like his fellow officers up the Avenue, was armed with a holstered gun. There was a certain bleakness about him, a moodiness in the grey eyes; he had not wanted this job — he should have been on leave, but that had been postponed at the last minute owing to 'shortage of manpower', and he resented it. Standing on the kerb at the edge of the grass verge of the Avenue, in the shade of one of the lime trees colonnading the road, he was playing the part of a man waiting to be picked up by a friend or workmate who was late: glancing at his watch, pushing a hand through his mouse-brown hair as he tapped an impatient foot on the kerb, peering down the carriageway towards the roundabout as though whoever he was waiting for would approach him from that direction — as indeed he would, given 'hostile' instead of 'friend'.

At 11.50 several subtle changes came over this peaceful scene. At the roundabout two men turned the corner into the avenue and walked on up it. Spotting them, Smith and Carlton moved as one into the middle of the pavement and continued talking together there, smiling, animated. And from his place closer to the roundabout Salter drifted across the verge to the edge of the pavement and stood head down, idly kicking turf. Risking a glance their way he sized up the two hostiles approaching him: much the same height as each other and clad in dark sweatshirts and jeans. They were walking side by side, one bareheaded, the other sporting a white baseball cap and, although there was less than a yard between them, they were not talking together, each seemed lost in his own thoughts. Stupid bastards, Salter thought, they weren't even clocking the situation around them; they'd be an easy take when they got up to Smith and Carlton. Then they were past him and, looking back towards the roundabout Salter swiftly made ready for action, honing mind, body and brain to their sharpest edge because any minute now his own mark would come round that same corner as the other two and, like them, start on up the avenue. Mallory, the big catch . . .

That was him, just turning into the avenue!

336

A well-built bloke, easy-moving. As he drew closer Salter recognized his face from the mug shots — knew him for sure, glanced up the road, saw the other two hostiles almost level with Smith and Carlton.

At that moment Mallory sussed him! Swinging along the pavement with every nerve and sense in him fiercely alive to everything around him, suddenly he intuited close danger and stopped dead, eyes raking the scene. Saw up ahead of him two strangers accosting his Stingray comrades, looked round at the man close to him on the verge, recognized him for what he was and *went for him*.

Up ahead of Salter, 'Hot, isn't it?' Carlton said, friendly casual, moving a little to one side as though to give passage to the two darkly-clad strangers approaching, while Eve Smith stayed where she was and favoured them with a dazzling smile.

'Sure, but I reckon it'll be *too* hot later — ' But the man wearing the white cap got no further with his careful response to the chat because the friendly blond stranger had yanked a handgun from inside his jacket, crowded in close and stuck the muzzle in his side. Out of the corner of his eye he saw the girl had his mate at gunpoint too so there was no hope there. *'Fucking bastard!'* he said low and hard, then spat in Carlton's face.

Controlling a basic urge to smash his fist into the snarling mouth, Carlton held the narrowed, hate-filled eyes and, slowly, wiped his face clean with his free hand. 'And a happy Christmas to you too,' he said to him then, his grin lit with the unholy glee of knowing oneself indisputably in the driving seat. Then he jabbed the gun in harder as he saw the unmarked police Honda pull up alongside them in the middle of the carriageway. 'Now, *get in the fucking car.*'

Mallory took Salter out fast, bulling into him as he was pulling out his gun. The two of them crashed to the ground together, Salter on his back, Mallory on top of him grabbing his gun arm as they went down and forcing it out sideways, then suddenly feeling it go limp as the cop's skull hit pavement. At once, he grabbed the gun from the unresisting hand and was up and running, shoving the weapon into his jacket pocket as he went. Sprinting back down the avenue, he turned the corner by the roundabout and slowed at once to a purposeful walk. Other than an instinctive compulsion to get clear of the danger area as fast as possible he had no purpose in mind — yet. There raged in his soul a great anger: a primitive and at present anarchic craving to wreak vengeance for his total defeat when on the cusp of triumph. Undirected at first, even as he worked his way through Hereford's quiet back streets to the city centre his anger began to range his world hungrily in search of prey. His rightful *prey*: one particular individual whom he could identify as the prime mover in his defeat — and then destroy. *Lex talionis*: Mallory had lived by it all his life; its practice was normal to him.

Eve Smith had got no lip from her mark — he was simply the driver, was in it for the money, she already had him handcuffed and heading for the Honda. Cuffing his man, Carlton followed her.

'Any sign of Salter, down the road?' he asked the driver of the Honda as he and Eve Smith got their prisoners and themselves into the car.

'Can't see, too many parked vehicles between him and us. Whatever, my orders and yours are to proceed according to plan whatever may happen elsewhere, so that's what we're going to do. The Vauxhall will pick up on Salter as soon as we're on our way, call in to Trader if necessary.'

★   ★   ★

When the emergency call came in from Lime Avenue Trader was taking a call from Watson,

339

the officer in charge of the preemptive strike against the Stingray assault at Tollgate.

'. . . all Stingray personnel on site arrested, all their vehicles taken over,' Watson reported.

'Good,' Trader said. 'So what's your ETA for — ' He broke off as, on the wall facing Miller, a red light began flashing and a discordant buzzing shrilled out from beside it. 'Hold the line,' he said to Watson, 'I'll be back.'

'It's down by the roundabout, sir. The Vauxhall.' Miller was monitoring the emergency call and now relayed information to Trader as it came to him. 'Mallory's escaped arrest, Salter's out of action, Mallory's on the run, left the scene the way he came in, via Park Road.'

'Our Ka stationed there — ?' Trader was at his side.

'Had already followed orders, returned to base as soon as they'd reported Mallory gone past them on his way to Lime Avenue. The Vauxhall's following up, has called in support, requests an all-officers-on-standby alert to seal off the area.' Miller looked up at Trader.

'Will do. I'll take over from you here. Salter? What happened there?'

'Mallory floored him. Ambulance on scene.'

Trader nodded, sliding into Miller's chair

as he edged out of it. 'You contact Rapid Reaction, set up all necessary communication channels.'

* * *

Passers-by who chanced to look at Mallory as he strolled into Hereford city centre around 12.50 that day would have had no reason to suspect he was a terrorist on the run, had set out that morning with the intention to gun down its citizens in cold blood. A tall, dark-haired bloke, he sat down on one of the wooden seats dotted around the square, bare-headed under the sun. As he did so the handgun in the right-hand pocket of his jacket bumped against his thigh and he grinned to himself, thinking it feels good to have the Brit cop's gun on me and with luck the bastard's cracked his skull. I'd have shot him dead but for the fact that the sound of the shot would've brought his mates running.

Abruptly, the grin went. Dropping his head he stared down at the pavement between his feet and let the black evil of the situation he was in take him over. *The Brits must have known!* They must've known every detail of the Stingray op — timing, place, movement of personnel, *every bloody thing!* Because apart from what had happened to him he'd seen his two comrades-in-arms up ahead of him in Lime Avenue about to be challenged.

'Is he OK, d'you think?' the blonde girl asked, bright gypsy skirt swirling round her bare tanned legs as she stopped in front of Mallory, pretty face upturned to the tall young man at her side. 'Maybe we should help him?'

'By the look of him he's stoned out of his head. Leave him be.' Suspecting that the dark-haired bloke on the seat was best left alone with whatever demons were so clearly eating him up, the young man took her hand and drew her on along the pavement. 'C'mon, we're late already.'

So someone must've sold Stingray out! As the thought flared across his mind Mallory comprehended in one lightning-strike paroxysm of perception the abysmal *humiliation* — the disgusting *shame* of his personal defeat. And from that moment on there was no thought in him for his Stingray comrades: his world narrowed down to himself and an all-consuming, urgent craving for revenge. Everything in him became concentrated on wreaking vengeance on whoever had brought about such a catastrophic shaming of Sean Mallory. The different mindset, the assumed persona of his twin brother James was gone from him as if it had never been and, sitting in the sunshine with his hands clenched into white-knuckled fists, Sean set his mind to working out how he might exact retribution.

First, he reasoned his way to the identity of his enemy. Ansari alone had had in his possession the comprehensive master plans for the Stingray strike and he had kept them in his own house, securely locked away (he'd said) in a drawer in his desk. *But* locks had keys to them, didn't they? So how safe had those plans really been? Ansari was regularly away from home on business all day, twice a week overnight, and for security's sake he surely wouldn't have carted them around with him. So, they'd have been accessible during those periods of time to anyone in the house — particularly *to his wife!* To *Melissa*, daughter to Cristin Daley by James — and Cristin was the bitch who'd lured James away from the beliefs and lifestyle which the Mallory twins had shared, preaching at him her terrorist-hating ethos, prising the twins apart. *Melissa*: the one person who not only had the moral motivation to wish to destroy Stingray, but also had been in a position to do so! Yes, *Melissa* had to be the one.

With the identity of his enemy established to his satisfaction, Sean Mallory now set his mind to plan his revenge. And as he did so he smiled to himself, because the killing

— which he must do *that day* because the hunt for him would already be up and running — would assuage not only his lust for vengeance but also that other older and more complex score, the one against Cristin Daley who had with her weasel-words shattered the splendid oneness of The Mallory Brothers.

Some ten minutes later, he got to his feet and rejoined the public world within which he would have to operate for the next few hours.

'Could you tell me the way to the railway station please, ma'am?' he asked a pleasant-faced matronly lady passing by.

Turning her benevolent blue-eyed gaze upon him — such a nice well-spoken and polite young man, he seemed — she directed him as requested and then went on her way.

And Sean Mallory went on *his* way, smiling under the sun.

19

'Trader out.' Relaxing for a moment, he wondered bleakly where Sean Mallory was by this time. The IRA man had been free for over four hours and there had been no leads to his whereabouts since the last sighting of him in Park Road, from a householder weeding his garden who had watched him go up the road and 'turn left into St Luke's Way'.

'Still nothing?' he asked Miller, seeing him sit back from the computer he had been using. He knew his question was likely to be pointless since the IT buff would have told him instantly if anything new had come up. He had spoken simply to have converse with a friendly voice: the calls he had been taking over these last few hours from various Intelligence and counter terrorist quarters had been anything but friendly in tone; not yet accusatory but unmistakably cold.

'Nothing.' Miller sounded tired and dispirited. 'Still, practically all the rest of SeaSnake's personnel are under arrest now so — '

'That doesn't cancel out the Tollgate mess, does it? And we've wanted a case against

Mallory for a long time; we've old scores to settle with him from his earlier days, Horse Guards in The Mall, Enniskillen . . . ' he fell silent, brooding on past horrors.

'And others like them; not least, two of our own men.'

Also, in a different way, Sean Mallory's twin brother, James. The thought insinuated itself into Trader's head; he had had no knowing hand in its formation, nevertheless for a moment it claimed his attention and, briefly, he debated whether or not to call Steve Court on his mobile and give him up-to-date news of the trashing of Ansari's Operation SeaSnake; its strikes at Torquay, Bournemouth and Bristol all dead in the water and their major players under arrest. But should he do so he would have to tell him also that the Tollgate counter-attack had failed in one important respect — Sean Mallory had avoided arrest and was still running free.

No way was he going to do that. 'Take me through the main points of the net we've spread for Mallory,' he snapped at Miller.

Miller took his boss's temper in his stride and did as asked. 'Alerts out to airports and helipads including private ones. Road blocks on — '

'Hell. Leave it, I know it all. Sorry, Miller.'

346

Pushing himself to his feet, Trader stood irresolute. In spite of knowing that all that could be done to apprehend Mallory was being done, he was assailed by fears that, somehow, Mallory would manage to get clear away.

'What will he do now?' he asked Miller, eyes narrowed as in his mind he tried to put himself in Mallory's place and intuit his intentions. 'Where will he go? I don't reckon he'll try to leave the country right now by sea or air because he'll know the hunt is up, we'll have got on to all that side of things instantly. So will he go to ground in a safe house — in London maybe to cut his travelling time?'

'He'll know we have to call off the top-priority search for him some time; it can't go on for ever,' Miller said, most of his attention on his display screen. 'Shortage of manpower, same as gave him his chance in the first place; that fucking mantra was what they gave you as the reason for turning down your request for *two* officers to deal with Mallory, and only allowed you one.'

Trader knew he was right, but took no comfort from the fact. Grim-faced, he considered again the possible answers to the question he had asked Miller. *Where would Mallory go next?* Knowing Stingray was poleaxed and himself hunted, surely he'd go to ground? And if he did, it was odds-on that for a while he'd be lost to them; the ex-IRA splinter groups had sleepers and safe houses scattered across the southern half of the country; he could contact any one of them by public phone — he wouldn't use his mobile — and be home and dry by this time.

★ ★ ★

During lunch, both Melissa and Steve were increasingly on edge, assuming that by now the counter attack against Stingray had run its course and, consequently, both Majed Ansari and Sean Mallory were under arrest. But each held back from talking about it, having at the back of the mind a nagging fear that, once started on, the subject would bedevil them for the rest of the day.

As they cleared the table and loaded the dishwasher, it was Melissa who finally broke this unspoken but intuitively accepted ban.

'Sean Mallory and Majed . . . they'll know it was me, won't they?' she said. 'But in a way — a pretty vicious way, I suppose — I'm glad they will. In fact, I'd like to go to them in gaol and say it to each of them. 'I put you there, and it's my earnest hope you'll stay there until you die.' That's a really horrible thing to admit to, isn't it?'

'It's known as 'getting your own back', I think.' Handing her the last used plate, Steve looked into her eyes as she took it from him and his heart went out to her because he saw in them the utter desolation created by the hatred consuming her. Melissa, Melissa, Daughter mine —

'I hate Sean even more than I do Majed.' She held her father's eyes. 'Never knew how to hate, before. Do now. So that's something learned, isn't it?' Turning away she started up the dishwasher but then faced him again. 'Steve, dear Steve, I need *to do* something; let's go out and set about some gardening, get our hands dirty, sweat a bit. I feel like I'm dying inside.'

He took her in his arms, folded her close for a moment as words died in her mouth and, silent, she clung to him.

'Come on, then, love,' he said, speaking quietly to the top of her head as she buried her face in his chest. 'Tell you what we'll do: we'll cut down that sycamore at the edge of the front shrubbery, a yard or two back from the lawn. You said this morning that it was getting too big and you'd like to see it gone, so let's you and I go do it.' He shook her gently; smiled into her eyes as she looked up at him. 'You want dirt and sweat — well OK, your wish is granted, both await you out there so come on . . . '

★   ★   ★

Sean Mallory was closing in on his target now, was drawing near to where she lived and, he assumed, was getting on with her life unaware that he had escaped and was gunning for her. At Hereford Station he had been lucky; he'd had to wait a mere fifteen minutes for a train bound for London to arrive and, as the booking-clerk had told him, it was a stopping one, so he would be able to detrain in the suburbs of the capital and continue his journey by bus.

He had always enjoyed travelling by bus: liked looking out over countryside or conurbanization, catching glimpses of villages and towns, of people you'd never ever see again, but who, for a moment, were yours to look at as they went about the business of their lives. For him that Friday afternoon, however, no outside world existed except in so far as its public services were of use to him. He was possessed by his need for — and the prospect of soon achieving — his revenge on the source of his defeat and resulting humiliation: *Melissa Ansari*. Only after he had put two bullets into the back of her head would he seek safety for himself.

Twice he had to change buses, his journey was not straightforward. However, by his good luck the route of the second bus he travelled on took him fairly close to Ansari's house. He had been to the Palestinian's home with him twice before and was on the lookout for landmarks as soon as he was in its area. He recognized a tall office block a short distance from it and alighted at the next stop. Standing on the pavement he looked around him for a moment — remembered seeing the pub further down the street before, orientated himself from that and set off at a fast walk for Ansari's house.

Both his earlier visits had been by car and timed to coincide with Melissa's visits to her mother, and now as he made his way towards the house he called to mind its layout in preparation for what he intended to do once inside. Entering through the front door I'm in the large, square hall. The door on my left leads into Ansari's study, that on my right into what he called the 'morning-room'. There's a staircase at the rear of the hall, facing the front entrance. To the left of it, a passage leading to dining-room, sitting-room and, beyond them, kitchen and utility area. She could be anywhere in the house.

Upstairs? Unlikely, but you never know. Also, of course, it's possible someone'll be with her, a friend or whatever; if so, I'll take out him, her or them as well. One thing I know for sure is that she'll be in the house: Ansari told me yesterday she isn't well and will be staying home all day.

He turned into Ansari's road. In a few minutes' time he would open her gate, walk down to the house and . . . well, he'd be the one with the gun — two guns in fact. Sure, Ansari kept a loaded automatic stashed in the top drawer of his desk in case of emergencies, and left the drawer unlocked for swift access, but she wouldn't be toting the thing around the house, would she? And she certainly wouldn't have time to get it, he'd make sure of that.

Smiling to himself, he slipped his hand into the pocket of his jacket and felt out the shape of the handgun in there, the cop's weapon from back in Lime Avenue. I'll use this on her, he thought, not my own shoulder-holstered one. And when I'm done with her I'll give it back to them: leave it beside her where she lies dead.

★ ★ ★

'Not bad, eh?' Stepping out on to the lawn Steve laid down the chain-saw and stood arms akimbo, surveying their handiwork: the felled sycamore, not yet a big tree, had come down along the edge of the shrubbery, and he had just finished sawing its branches clear of the trunk. 'Some of this is probably good enough to burn,' he went on, pushing his shirtsleeves back above his elbows. 'Any of your friends have open fires?'

'Natalie and Rob do, next door.' Straightening up from hauling the last sizeable branch clear of the trunk, Melissa pushed her hair behind her ears and gave him a grin. 'Got what I asked for, didn't I?' she said. 'My hands are filthy *and* bleeding a bit, and you know what, Steve? I want a shower — I *need* a shower for the public good.' Placing her sandalled feet carefully amongst tree-debris she stepped out from the shrubbery to stand beside him. 'I'm going in now. You coming too?'

'You go on ahead. I'll saw up some firewood for your neighhours. Won't be long; there's not a lot, it's too young.'

'They'll be thrilled, anyway,' she said, then started off towards the house. 'Bring all the tools in when you come, won't you?'

'And you make sure there's cold beer in the fridge!' he called after her; then for a moment stood watching her swing away across the grass: a tall, graceful girl in biscuit-coloured pedal-pushers and a sleeveless blue top — *his daughter*. After all these years she's mine again, he thought; what a strange and lovely thing.

Pushing his way back into the shrubbery he piled together secateurs, lopper, chain-saw and, last, the auger which he had thought might be useful but in the end hadn't been. Then he picked up the bow-saw and set about cutting up a couple of suitable branches for firewood.

Going in through the front door and remembering to leave it slightly ajar for Steve to follow her in, Melissa crossed the parquet flooring of the hall, went along the passage and into the kitchen to check beer supplies in the fridge. There were four cans of Foster's in there so that was Steve catered for but — shit! — she'd forgotten to refill the ice trays which were still upside down on the draining board. Going over to the sink she washed the dirt and blood — only a little blood, and she grinned to herself that she had fussed about it — off her hands, dried them, refilled the ice-trays, slid them into place and closed the fridge. Then, debating what to wear after showering, she went out into the passage and headed for the stairs in the hall. Heard movement in the direction of the front door and smiled, thinking, heck Steve can't have sawn much wood and a good thing too, he's done wonders out there and he can enjoy a beer while I wash and change.

'The Foster's is ice-cold; you have one,' she called to him, but then as she came out into the hall and looked towards the front door words died in her mouth and she froze with fear because there was a man standing just inside her front door and he wasn't Steve! His face was Steve's but he hadn't a white streak in his hair so it couldn't be him. *and there was a gun in his hand and it was pointed straight at her!* But his *face* was Steve's so if it wasn't him, it had to be —

'Hi there, Melissa,' he said quietly, mocking her.

'But . . . You're *Sean?*' A strangled whisper came from a throat dry with terror, and the hairs rose on the nape of her neck.

'That's me. Jamie's brother, Jamie's twin,' he said. Then his voice changed, turned hard and hating, vicious. 'Operation Stingray is shot to pieces and Ansari's in custody,' he went on, his eyes never leaving hers; he was avid for revenge and savouring its imminence but was in no hurry now, these next few seconds — minutes, even, no need to rush it — were time to be enjoyed to the full; the terror in her pleasured him. 'So, Melissa, you are now going to tell me how that came to pass *and* the name of your Brit contact. It could only have been through you; I know that for a certainty because Ansari's the only one who had in his possession all the plans, and I know he kept them in this house.'

'He never told me *anything* about his work!' Her eyes were riveted on the muzzle of the gun aimed at her heart. 'Majed never told me about what he was doing and I didn't ever ask, I just wanted us to —'

'Ansari's an arrogant bastard, and a fool to have been suckered by you. Well, he's the one who'll suffer for it — and you, of course. Me, I'm going to get what I want from you then —'

'But I don't *understand*! Look, I'll answer any questions I can; just tell me what's going on.' Somehow she got the words out because she'd realized that if she could keep him talking long enough there was a chance that Steve would come in from the garden. He'd come in and —

'Here's how things stand.' Sean Mallory gave her a thin smile. 'British Intelligence must've had prior knowledge of Stingray. Ansari kept the plans for it here, in his desk, and it is my belief you photographed them and passed them to the Brits. You're the only person who could possibly have accessed those files.' He took a step towards her, gestured minimally

356

with the gun. 'Now listen to me carefully because your life hangs on this,' he said to her — lying, for when he had got what he wanted from her he intended to give her the traitor's death, down on her knees and two bullets in the back of the head. 'Clearly, you must have handed photographs over to British Intelligence, and to do that, you must have had a contact. Give me his name, and I'll let you live: refuse me, and I'll shoot you dead right here.'

'But I *can't* give you any name! I *don't have* a contact! All you said — it's not right! Besides, why does it matter to you? What good is it to you now?'

'*It matters*. I shall make him pay. It may take me time, but he's a dead man, Melissa. It's the only way I can exact compensation. Get even. So if you want to go on living you'll have to tell me his name.'

But as he was speaking a slither of movement behind him flickered across the background of Melissa's field of vision — and changing focus she saw a man's right hand grip the edge of the front door and slowly, stealthily, ease it further open —

'I did have a contact, but he wasn't anyone important!' She sent words rushing out now because she knew she must win time for the man at the door — *Steve*, surely? It had to be him and she must keep words flowing out so that Sean's attention stayed concentrated on her and he didn't notice what was going on behind him. 'I just knew him as Mars, you see; he had to report to his boss and he didn't tell me who that was so . . . '

Steve had heard the front gate open as he stood looking over the tangled mess of felled sycamore branches in search of three or four big enough for firewood. At once on the alert he darted into cover behind a bush, peered through its leaves towards the paved path up to the house, recognized Sean at once and, seeing him walking along the path towards the front door, realized in one mind-blowing instant of horror and fear that there could be only one reason for his brother's presence there: he must've pinpointed Melissa as the only person who could have betrayed SeaSnake to British Intelligence. So, being Sean, he'd come gunning for her.

On the thought, adrenalin surged, mind raced. Sean must have a gun for sure. He himself was without one — Melissa had told him there was a loaded pistol in Ansari's desk but there'd be neither time nor chance to get hold of that so he must find a weapon of some kind here, *now*. Searching frantically among his tree-cutting tools, Steve found only one that might serve: the auger, an eighteen-inch-long cast-iron rod with a heavy knob one end and a threaded driving point at the other. Grabbing this up he looked round for Sean again, saw him push open the front door and sneak inside — then noticed the door was still slightly ajar and thanked God for that small mercy, it meant he'd be able to get inside the house without making a sound.

'I . . . so you see I *can't* tell you, I simply *don't know!*'

Almost, Sean shot her then. But didn't: now he'd thought of it, killing the MI5 officer who'd roped in Melissa to work for him would be an added bonus to collect some time later, and if he could get to this 'Mars' character she'd mentioned he'd be able to break him for sure, get from him the name of his boss.

'Give me Mars, then,' he ordered. 'Where he lives, how you contact him . . . '

Light-footed swift across the grass, Steve reached the front door. Heard voices inside but shut them out of his mind and, with the auger in his left hand, slid his right round the edge of the door, eased it further open until it stood just wide enough, then slipped through into the hall. Saw Sean standing three yards in front of him with his back to the door and Melissa on the far side of the room facing him. Sean was holding her at gunpoint — *but now she had seen the movement at the door!*

Don't give me away, girl! Don't let your eyes or body movement tell him I'm right behind him! Willing her not to give his presence away, Steve transferred the auger to his right hand, gripped the middle of its shaft and, with its knobbed end pointing forwards closed in on Sean with lion-stalking stealth, silently, moving one foot at a time.

'I've got a phone number for him, for contacting him.' Melissa kept her eyes focused on the gun in Sean's hand because that was what he would expect her to do, but nevertheless she sensed and half-saw the pattern of things changing behind him. Steve was stealing towards Sean step by soundless step, but he hadn't got a weapon, had he? *No way could he have one* — but wait! He was holding something in his right hand . . . it was that long sort of spike thing he'd taken with him when they went out to do the tree, an iron bar with a knob at one end and a spike at the other, 'Might come in handy', he'd said.

'Come on, now. Give me that phone number or — '

'I can't remember it. Look, it's in my diary, I can go and get it; it's upstairs in my bedroom.'

'We'll go together. And remember, one false move from you and — '

'*Freeze, Sean!*' Close behind him now Steve jabbed the knob of the auger into his back like the muzzle of a heavy handgun. '*If she dies, you die!*'

Sean's body froze, but the voice and his intuition told him who was digging the gun-muzzle into his back and for a split second, shocked to the core of his being, unbelieving but *having to believe*, his mind and spirit spun into freefall through cold empty space, beset by demons. Then fiercely exerting his will, he controlled them.

'Hi there, Jay,' he said quietly, at once deciding to play on the closeness of their shared past, reasoning that Jay simply wouldn't have it in him to shoot him dead, the blood-tie would prohibit it. 'Let's you and I work this out together, like we've always done. By the way, though, how'd you come by the gun?'

'I brought it with me. And Sean, don't think I won't use it. To me you died in Ballymena in 1994. To kill you now would be no big deal. But . . . I don't like killing, so maybe we can do this my way. Like so: in a moment I tell you to put your gun down on the floor and raise your hands above your head. Then Melissa will approach you from

361

the side, pick it up, back off, move well clear of you and train it on you. Then with her gun on you as well as mine, I will arrest you.'

'I don't see it that way.' Softly spoken, and Sean thinking to keep his brother talking — then suddenly shoot the girl, dive sideways as he fired and twist round fast to take Jay out as well. 'I'm not going to drop my gun, Jay. You try to make me, and I'll put a bullet into her and she'll be dead. *Your daughter will be dead.*' As he spoke he shifted his weight — smoothly, imperceptibly — on to the balls of his feet in readiness to make his move.

'No, I don't think you'll do that; you're not the man to commit suicide.' Keeping his eyes on Sean, Steve then spoke to his daughter. 'Lissa, forget about him,' he said. 'Forget him, forget the gun, and look at me.' He saw her will herself to do it, then her eyes slid away from the gun and met his own. Deliberately, he winked at her twice in warning of imminent action — hoping she'd get the message — and went on talking, needing Sean's brain to be fully occupied in listening to what was being said and, therefore, slower to respond to direct assault. 'Listen to me, Lissa, and do what I tell you. I have Sean at gunpoint. In a moment I shall order him to place his gun down — '

On the word *down* Steve reversed the

auger in his right hand, drove it point-first into Sean's side. Swinging his left arm up as he struck he hooked it around Sean's upper body, hugged him to his own chest and used his weight to send the two of them crashing sideways to the floor — giving a last violent heave as they fell to make sure he landed with Sean lying on his back beneath him.

Sean fired a nanosecond after the auger struck home but as he went down realized his bullet had gone wide, that the girl was standing shock-frozen staring — then he hit parquet flooring, screamed with pain as the impact drove the auger deeper into his body and lost his grip on the gun as his right hand slammed knuckles-down on the polished wood. Saw the weapon lying no more than a yard to his right, reached for it — but Steve grabbed his wrist, pinned it down.

'Get hold of his gun!' he shouted. '*Lissa, get his gun!*'

Galvanized, she dashed forward, picked up the gun, backed away a couple of steps and — using both hands — trained it on Sean's head.

'Put both arms out to the side well away from your body then lie absolutely still, Sean Mallory, or I'll blow your head off!' she cried loud and clear. 'Do it! *Do it now!*'

Steve felt his brother's body stiffen beneath his own, then with one convulsive jerk Sean flung his left arm out sideways, did likewise with his right as the grip on it was released, then lay rigid, still as stone.

Nevertheless Steve watched him like a hawk. 'Easy now, Lissa,' he said quietly, not looking at her but sensing her on the edge of terror. 'I'm going to stand up so I can get on with what's necessary here. I'll move slowly, and I shall not obstruct your line of fire. Keep your gun on him, don't take your eyes off him for a second and shoot him if he makes a move against either of us, but put your bullet in his shoulder not his head, we want him alive . . . Are you ready to do all that?'

'Ready.' Her voice was cold as ice and a quick glance at her showed him the gun rock steady in her hand.

Working himself clear of Sean limb by limb, Steve got to his feet. For a moment then he stood gazing down at his seemingly semi-conscious twin as he lay spread-eagled with one side of his head against the floor, his eyes closed. And there came in him a soul-racking sense of aloneness because to him, now, it was no more than 'a male individual' he saw — a wounded man with the point of an auger sticking into his side and a pool of blood beneath it, a *stranger* . . . .No, worse than that, much worse: he saw and felt there only a terrorist brought down in conflict.

'End of the road, Sean.' He murmured the words, they were for himself alone, but he observed that although the stranger's eyes stayed closed, the mouth twisted a little as though perhaps to smile. Thinking nothing of it, he turned away and went to close the front door.

Behind him, Sean's eyes opened a fraction. In fact he was fully conscious and there was a new directive driving him now, one which had subsumed the pain of his wound and his weakness from it. Melissa was forgotten, all other things were forgotten; he was one of the Mallory twins, the integer composed of Sean and James, and saw his brother as traitor to that absolute, sacrosanct, brotherhood. And traitors should die: in Sean's world, that was First Law.

Through slitted eyelids he saw the girl turn her head away a little and start edging towards the hall table beneath the mirror, the muzzle of the gun in her hand drooping a fraction lower as she did so. Slid his eyes towards Jay and saw him at the door now, his back still to the room — so at once, and careful not to make the slightest sound, he levered the upper half of his body clear of the floor, rested his weight on his left forearm

365

and slipped his right hand in under his jacket, reaching for his holstered gun, the one neither of his two enemies present knew he had with him, his own. Lips tightening as pain seared his guts, he felt his straining fingertips touch the holster as he saw Jay put his hand on the doorknob — so closed his fingers round the butt of the gun and, easing it free of holster and jacket, turned the muzzle sideways towards his brother's back —

'*Steve! Get down!*' Melissa screamed. Hear-sensing Sean's movement she'd turned to him, seen the threat — and as she shouted the warning she swung up her gun and fired once. Her bullet ploughed deep across the back of Sean's hand then sent his weapon flying across the hall.

'*Lissa don't shoot again!*' Steve yelled. He'd hurled himself sideways at her shout, rolled with the impact and was scrambling to his feet. 'It's OK! Don't shoot again; he's out of this now; put the gun down; *put it down!*'

Hunched over his smashed and bloody hand, Sean had collapsed on the floor, was lying still in silent, tight-lipped agony, blood pouring down over his shattered hand.

'Dear God.' Melissa's whispered words rasped across the silence, wrenched up out of the shock and horror laying her waste inside.

Going to her, Steve took the gun from her,

put it down on the hall table then turned to comfort her, but found her already in command of herself once more, the horror swiftly confronted and driven back into the dark from which it had emerged. It might return to haunt her, he suspected, but for the moment she had it beat and that was enough for now.

'You'll phone Matt?' she asked quietly.

He nodded. 'That first, then call an ambulance. Sean can wait; he'll be OK for a bit — '

'I'll check on him, then do the ambulance stuff from this phone here. Better if you talk to Matt on the phone in the sitting-room.' Melissa was turning away as she spoke, but he laid a hand on her arm and swung her back to face him.

'Leave the bastard lie,' he said harshly. 'Let him sweat it out.'

'No. I'll keep an eye on him while I make my call. I know he's a bastard, but he's losing a lot of blood and the way he is now he's not much of a threat, is he? If he tries anything again, he'll be sorry, I promise you that. OK?'

Steve smiled at her, 'OK. And — thanks. Thanks for my life; you were quick there.' Quietly, he called that last to her as she moved off towards Sean. She made no answer, but he intuited she had heard him from the sudden pleased lift of her head.

20

Hillsdown, 10.30 that evening

Alone in Melissa's sitting-room, Steve carried
his whisky-on-the-rocks across to the armchair by the window overlooking the garden
and sat down. Forced himself to relax then,
and realizing he would find no peace of mind
until and unless he had taken the measure of
everything that had happened in Melissa's
house during the last three or four hours, he
set himself systematically to recall every one
of those pivotal incidents.

Melissa and he cutting down the sycamore.
She going indoors to shower. He staying
outside working . . . then hearing the front
gate being opened — and seeing *Sean* come
in, go up the path and into the house!
Himself grabbing the auger then and going
after him fast —

Thump-thump-thump! The knocking on
the front door shocked Steve back into his
present. At this time of night who could it be
out there but the enemy? But almost at once
he laughed that out of court — all SeaSnake
personnel were in custody, Sean among them

now. Pushing himself to his feet he went out into the hall, telling himself it must be either the police or some friend of Melissa's. After all, the night was still young if you yourself were young.

Nevertheless he took precautions because doubtless Sean too had friends.

'Who is it?' he called through the locked and bolted door.

'It's Cristin. Melissa told me you'd be coming down — '

He opened the door at once. And she looked so gorgeously, sanity-restoringly normal that he said nothing, simply stood gazing at her, her older face unmistakable, the soul of it sure and true, as it had been when he'd loved her all those years ago. And for a full minute they stared at each other in silence — but during it their eyes spoke truths between them, and the truths built bridges across twelve years of their other lives.

Then, 'It's a lovely thing, to know you're still Jamie,' she said to him. 'To know that the 'James Mallory' Sean made of you isn't the real one.' She gave him a brief smile. 'Matt — that's Trader to you — has told me the whole story. I'm glad you've made yourself such a good life. It can't have been easy.'

'I had . . . a friend.'

'Only one?' But she was smiling.

'One — one like him, that is — was enough. And you, Cristin? You're happy?'

'Life's good. Will soon be even better, though.'

'In what way?'

She quirked an eyebrow at him. 'Am I to tell you that standing on the doorstep of my daughter's home? Shame on you — '

'Christ!' His hand was on her arm, urging her inside. 'I'm sorry, forgive me. I was lost . . . twelve years is a long time.'

Following him into the sitting-room she sat down in the armchair he drew up to face his own. Said yes, she'd love to join him in a drink. Asked him where Melissa was and, on being told her daughter had announced herself dead beat and gone to bed half an hour ago, accepted the tall gin-sling she'd said she'd like, put it down beside her and looked across at him.

'Why were you so shit-scared to open the door?' she asked quietly.

'Was afraid it might be some fellow-terrorist of Sean's come looking for my blood,' he said, then seeing her look of puzzled incredulity, realized she didn't know. 'Sean was here,' he said bluntly. 'He came looking for Melissa.'

'What the hell are you talking about?' She was on her feet, the fear and terror in her blazing down at him. 'Sean's in custody, the Stingray strike — '

'He escaped, at Trader's operation at Tollgate Garage.'

A few seconds longer she stared at him in disbelief — then she believed, because it was Jamie telling her.

'I didn't know,' she said harshly. 'So give me all of it, Jamie. And don't . . . don't dress it up at all for my sake; tell me the truth; if it's bloody tell me so. Begin with how he escaped custody, please, and tell me the whole thing right through to why Melissa is now asleep upstairs.'

Without reserve — and indeed with a kind of relief — Steve did as she'd asked. Turning away from him, she listened staring out of the window: afterglow was flaring the western sky out there, making smoothly shifting, night-coming patterns of light and shadow on lawn and flowerbeds. But she was not seeing any of that. For although he told it starkly, his hard little words giving her the bare bones of all that had happened at Hillsdown that evening, in the eye of her mind she was seeing that action, and the sheer horror of it swarmed over her and into her. If Sean Mallory had had his way, she thought, both Melissa and Jamie would have died, this evening. When she knocked at the door there would have been no answer from inside this house she was standing in: only silence in there; and death, Melissa and Jamie both slain by Sean's hand.

'I wish she had shot him dead.' She said it as Steve fell silent; there was no expression in her voice and her back was still to him. 'She'd have got away with it, wouldn't she? She hadn't *planned* to kill him; she was just a girl facing a killer, with a gun in her hand that she didn't know much about except how to pull the trigger to make it go off.'

For a moment Steve let a silence lie between them, then he said, 'On my account, she hated him enough to do it with malice aforethought. But I think she's glad she didn't. *Now*, she's glad.'

'Where *is* Sean, then?' Suddenly, she turned back to him. 'What — ?'

'Come and sit down again, Cristin, please do that.' She looked cold, he thought, cold deep down inside herself. 'Sean's in hospital under police guard. The auger missed all his vital organs, didn't go in deep enough to cause life-threatening damage. His hand . . . that will take time, and will never be quite right. And he lost a lot of blood.'

'Why hasn't Matt called me? Surely he could've — '

'No he could not!' Swiftly, mercilessly,

Steve thrust reality at her. 'Cristin, use your brain. You know perfectly well he couldn't do that. There's still a nationwide terrorist alert in force and he's in the thick of it, personal affairs have to be put on hold.'

'Dear God. What a bitch I am sometimes. And stupid too.' Stricken, ashamed, she dropped her head. And when after a moment she looked up again, Steve intuited a new peace in her, a quite beautiful kind of serenity. Then he saw her lips curve slightly in a secret smile that told him she had pushed the recent terrible happenings of that day to the back of her mind, where, for a while at least, they did indeed belong.

She's back with me in 'now' time again, he thought; and asked evenly, 'why did you come down here tonight?'

She hesitated for a moment, but when she did answer he was sure it was the truth she was giving him.

'I came because I had something I wanted to tell Melissa — to tell you both — *in person*. E-mail and mobile, they're too . . . too distancing,' she said, but then fell silent.

However, the dream-smile was still on her lips so, 'It's important, then, this thing you have to tell us?' he asked, getting to his feet.

'Life-alteringly, for me.' She moved closer

to him and looked up at him. 'I'm going to marry Matt,' she said.

'You should've done that long ago.'

'No.'

'Why not? The two of you have been lovers for years, he told me.'

'Marriage is sharing *everything*, your whole *self*, your life and the living of it, not just bed — oh shit! I know that's blindingly obvious, but — '

'Why now? After all these years, *why now?*' But even as he spoke he realized what her answer would be and went on urgently, willing her to understand and forgive — if it mattered to her that much after so long? 'Cristin, dear Cristin. I didn't know about myself at that time! Didn't understand where I stood emotionally, politically . . . Then by the time I *did* know, I was married.'

'And loved her.'

'And loved her, yes . . . I'm sorry, Cristin. For not facing up to realities back then. So sorry.'

She smiled up at him and, reaching out, brushed her hand across his cheek.

'What, sorry you cheated death that night in '94, and went on to make a new life for yourself under another name? Well, don't be, Jamie Mallory! I did much the same, though not so dramatically as you . . . For a long while I just couldn't get my head round the thing of you-and-Sean, you-and-me, Trader, *and* those twelve years,' she went on, stepping back a little. 'But then this morning, early on, when Matt called me and told me about you coming down here, and as much as security allowed about MI5s operations today, I suddenly realized — no, I knew for sure and for ever — that I was free of the you-and-me I'd been hanging on to for so many years. And being free of it, I knew I wanted to marry Matt.' She looked down. 'It felt wonderful,' she said.

He could not see her face but he knew she was smiling to herself. 'Have you told him yet?' he asked.

Tossing back her head she laughed up at him. 'What, tell him *that* when like you said he's all wrapped up in — '

'Sorry. Stupid question.' Turning away he fetched her drink, gave it into her hand then picked up his own.

'I'd like us to drink to you and Trader,' he said, 'then you go and tell Melissa.'

'Yes to the first, no to the second. Let the girl sleep for now. For her tomorrow will come soon enough, and it'll be very hard.'

'At least she'll have you and Trader — '

'And you. She'll need you too, Jamie. She'll need all three of us . . . '